ABOUT ELIZABETH HOLLAND

Elizabeth Holland is a writer of romance novels. She enjoys the escapism of picking up a book and losing herself in a new world. Elizabeth is a keen advocate for mental health and often speaks out about her own struggles. She writes to escape her own thoughts. When Elizabeth isn't writing, she's usually outside walking the dog. Her favourite walks are when it's cold and rainy, so she can work on her next plot.

The Cornish Vintage Tea Shop

THANK YOU

A big thank you to Chris Towndrow
(Chrissie Harrison),
Deborah Klée, and Rebecca Chase, all of whom
helped to shape this book. They're all wonderful
authors, and I'd really recommend their books.

Copyright © 2025 Elizabeth Holland

All rights reserved

The characters and events portrayed in this book are fictitious. Any similarity to real persons, living or dead, is coincidental and not intended by the author.

No part of this book may be reproduced, or stored in a retrieval system, or transmitted in any form or by any means, electronic, mechanical, photocopying, recording, or otherwise, without express written permission of the publisher.

CHAPTER ONE

Florence bustled her way into the overcrowded train carriage, making herself as small as possible. Hailstones bounced off the windows, and the muggy August air filled the carriage. Fat droplets of water dripped from her hair and onto her shoulders, soaking through her light coat and silk blouse. It was an unpleasant, but not uncommon, feeling. Her expression mirrored the same withdrawn look that everyone else on the carriage was sporting. With some manoeuvring, Florence tucked herself away in a corner by the door, turned up the volume on her earphones to drown out the hum of conversation, and watched as the London suburbs whizzed past. Florence's grandmother, Iris, had always told her that happiness was the most important part of life, yet there was very little to be witnessed on the seven-fifteen to London Victoria.

When the train came to a halt at the terminal, commuters piled off, and Flo allowed herself to be swept up in the hubbub of the crowd. If she thought about it, she'd feel claustrophobic, so she focused on her music and descended into London's underground. The air was stifling; the crowds hadn't abated, and each step was taken on autopilot.

It was with great relief that she stepped out of Holborn station. The smell of exhaust fumes filled her nostrils, and as she took out her earphones, she could hear the steady thrum of the standstill traffic. Across the road, a coffee shop served her a burnt-tasting latte mixed with overly sweet caramel syrup, which she paid a small fortune for. If Grandma Iris were still alive, she'd have lectured Florence on supporting big coffee chains. They stole customers from the independent shops, and the coffee was never as good. Flo had yet to find a coffee that tasted like the ones her grandmother used to make. However, independent coffee shops were few and far between in central London, and so this burnt, bitter liquid would have to do.

"Morning," the bored receptionist greeted Flo as she crossed the reception area. Every surface was reflective, and the lifts had a tablet to operate them.

Flo's heels clicked across the tiled floor as she smiled at the woman. There was little point in learning the woman's name. She'd have moved on by next week. Flo bypassed the lifts and took the stairs up to her third-floor office.

"I thought you had today booked off?" Carmen, her desk neighbour and work friend, asked.

"Bella cancelled it," Flo said through gritted teeth

as she shrugged off her wet coat and switched on her computer.

"Again?"

Flo nodded.

A Post-it note was stuck to a stack of documents. With a sigh, Flo peeled it off and saw that Bella needed the documents proofreading in the next hour. Flo sank into the worn chair. With a wedge of tissues, she dried the wet patches on her shoulders where the rain had soaked through her coat. The chair creaked beneath, and Flo winced. Bella had promised her a replacement since she'd started at the company a few years ago.

"Don't forget those documents," a trainee called as she wafted past.

Carmen clicked her tongue. "Why do you let them talk to you like that?"

"There's a chain of hierarchy." Flo shrugged. "Bella is the top dog, and then her trainees are little minions. As her paralegal, I rank at the bottom. I'm the legal equivalent of fish food."

"You have the same qualifications as they do," Carmen pointed out.

"I know." When Flo accepted the paralegal role at Baker and Harlow, she had grand plans of applying to their trainee program. For the first couple of years, she was rejected, then her grandmother passed away, and all plans were put on hold. As each day passed, she became increasingly aware that this career path no longer made her happy. Her life was stagnant, but she didn't have the energy to do anything about it.

The day dragged as heavy rain pelted the windows. It was a gloomy day in London, which reflected Flo's mood. At twenty-six, Flo thought she would have life figured out. However, she couldn't be further from it.

Usually, Flo would stay late to work, but today she left at five on the dot. She joined the crowds as they descended on the station. Her heels splashed in the puddles, and water flicked up the back of her trousers. Once off the stuffy underground, she boarded a Southern train to Surrey. As she left the city and hurtled into the countryside, Flo flicked through pictures on her phone, lingering on one of her favourites. It was of her and her grandmother outside Iris's cafe, The Lavender Tea Shop.

"I miss you," Flo whispered and brushed a finger over the picture before she swiped at the stray tear sliding down her cheek.

Flo checked the time. There was still a while until the train arrived at her destination. She scrolled through her phonebook, her finger hovering over the name 'Victoria'. Gnawing on her lip, Flo pressed the button to call.

After a few rings, someone answered. "Hello?" they said, their voice a high-pitched, sing-song tone. "Who is this?"

Flo pinched the bridge of her nose. This had been a terrible idea. "It's Flo." Her voice shook.

There was a moment of silence on the other

end of the phone before Victoria spoke. "What do you want, Flo?" Her tone had shifted to one of frustration.

"It's a year today," Flo muttered, squeezing her eyes shut. The last thing she needed was for her unshed tears to spill down her cheeks on public transport.

"Is it?" came Victoria's cold response. "I thought it was last month."

Anger swirled in the pit of Flo's stomach. "No, this month," she said through gritted teeth.

"It's just another date, Florence."

"A date that means something to me!"

"Florence, it's been a year. You need to move on. It's not healthy to still be grieving."

Flo scoffed. "What would you know about grief or losing a loved one, Mum?"

Before Victoria could respond, Flo hung up. It had been a terrible idea to call, but occasionally Flo craved the love of a family member, and today she'd given in to that feeling, only for it to have caused her further pain. She chewed on her lip and turned her attention to the passing scenery, wishing Iris were there to give her a big hug.

Flo was used to a quick commute, so the journey to Surrey felt as though it lasted a lifetime.

"Aunty Florrie," a small, shrill voice called from the platform. Flo beamed as she spotted her best friend's daughter waving. Poppy's other hand was firmly clasped by her mother, Daisy.

"Hello, Poppy." Flo scooped the girl into her arms, smothering her in kisses.

"Has my daughter replaced me as your best friend?" Daisy huffed, a smile lighting up her face.

"It's so good to see you, Dais," Flo said, shifting Poppy to her hip to give Daisy a one-armed hug.

"You too, Florrie." They'd been friends since school, and even though their lives had gone in different directions, they'd remained close.

Flo swallowed back the lump in her throat at the familiar nickname.

"Mummy's cooked lasagne," Poppy said, realising the attention had shifted away from her.

Flo clapped her hands. "My favourite! Shall we go home and eat?"

Daisy had always been a wonderful cook. She'd started working alongside Flo at The Lavender Tea Shop when she turned sixteen. While Flo liked to bake cakes and be out front greeting customers, Daisy stayed in the back preparing sandwiches and jacket potatoes while dreaming up new flavours for the following week's soup. Everyone had always commented on what a good pair they made. Flo was the sensible, practical one, while Daisy was the creative and impulsive one. Although Flo loved her best friend very much, she sometimes felt envious of her laissez-faire approach to life. At ten years old, Flo had her A-level choices picked out, which were perfectly chosen to support her application to her dream university. She'd never made an impulsive decision in her life.

The three of them squeezed into Daisy's tiny car. Her parents had bought it for her shortly after passing her test. If the car could speak, it would recount many late-night drives and heart-to-hearts about stupid boys.

"I've been thinking of you all day," Daisy said, reaching over to squeeze Flo's hand.

Flo cleared her throat. "Thank you," she mumbled.

"I can't believe it's a year since we lost Iris."

"I know." Flo turned to look out the window, and a wave of emotions hit her as they drove past The Lavender Tea Shop. It looked nothing like it had in Iris's time, but it still sent a pang of pain through Flo's heart.

Daisy's flat smelled of home-cooked food, and Flo felt her muscles relax. She couldn't remember the last time she'd eaten a home-cooked meal or felt at home somewhere.

"I'll pour us some wine. Poppy's already eaten, but I told her she could have some garlic bread with us. Sorry, her dad was supposed to have her, but he cancelled, again."

"You know I love seeing both of you. How are things with him?"

"Don't ask." Daisy's sunny exterior slipped, and the heavy feeling of guilt settled in Flo's stomach. She hadn't supported her friend enough.

Daisy handed her a glass of merlot, and they joined Poppy in the living room while the garlic bread cooked.

"How's work?" asked Daisy as the dulcet tones of children's television hummed in the background.

"The same. Still no sign of a training contract, and I continue to be everyone's lackey."

"Can't you apply somewhere else? You've been there for long enough that nobody would question you wanting a new challenge."

"I should look," Flo said. She should have looked years ago, but somehow she'd fallen into the monotony of her everyday routine and couldn't muster the strength to leave it behind and search for something new. Then, when she'd lost Iris, all hope for the future had been extinguished with her grandmother's lively soul.

"This isn't the Florrie I know," Daisy commented, concern etched across her face.

"I haven't been that Florrie for a while now," Flo admitted.

"Aunty Florrie, which Spice Girl is your favourite?" asked Poppy, climbing onto Flo's lap and almost sloshing wine across her white silk blouse.

"Is your mummy teaching you about the Spice Girls?" The sadness lifted, and Flo couldn't help the giggle that escaped.

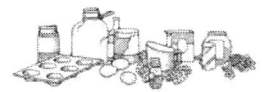

"She's got a lot of energy," Flo commented as Daisy returned from her third attempt at putting Poppy to bed.

"I know." Daisy huffed out a breath.

"How are you, Dais?" Flo refilled her glass.

"No, don't try to turn the attention onto me. I want to know about you. How are you really, Florrie?"

Flo took a deep breath, contemplating how much to tell her best friend. "I'm struggling," she finally admitted. "My job feels as though it's hit a dead end. I'm still living in that awful house share, and even though I've saved a small fortune, I'll never be able to afford a place in London. My life plans have been derailed, and I don't know what to do. It all seems so utterly pointless now." Flo hiccuped as she gulped her wine.

"You don't have to stay in London, Flo. You could go anywhere." Was that a hint of wistfulness in Daisy's voice?

"I can't move back here. As much as I would love to be around the corner from you, the memories would be too painful."

Daisy nodded. "I've got a box of grown-up chocolates in the cupboard. Hold on." Daisy went to fetch them, and Flo pulled out her phone, still considering Daisy's earlier suggestion of leaving London.

With alcohol dulling her sensible side, she chewed on her nail and considered where in the world she would go if she could go anywhere. It didn't take long before she landed on a place. The little village in Cornwall where Iris would take her every year. They'd close the cafe for two weeks in August, pack up the car, and leave. It would be swelteringly hot as they travelled in Iris's old car with its worn leather seats, which always burnt Flo's legs. They'd wind down the windows and let the hot, sticky air fill the car, pretending it was cooling them down. Iris would let Flo choose the music for the journey, so her favourite Spice Girls CD was always blaring out as they sang along. Their two weeks in Cornwall were filled with long walks as they rambled over the Cornish countryside, bracing swims in the bright blue sea, and huge slices of Victoria sponge cake from the cafe around the corner from their holiday let. Iris had always had a soft spot for the Cornish village, which she visited during her childhood. She'd been friends with some of the locals, not that Flo had cared. Whenever Iris began talking to someone, Flo would slink off with a book and find some shade. Flo tapped away on her phone, looking up the village. She gasped at the first search engine find. The cafe they visited was up for sale. Not only was it up for sale, but Flo could afford it.

"What's wrong? Your eyes have gone wild," Daisy said as she held a box of alcoholic chocolates.

"Look at this." Flo almost threw the phone at Daisy as she took the box. She plucked out a dark chocolate and rum truffle and popped it into her mouth, savouring the bitter taste against the tangy alcohol.

"You should buy it," Daisy said, her words slurred.

"I couldn't."

"You can afford it, right?"

Flo nodded, eating another rum chocolate.

"Call them." Daisy threw the phone back and Flo caught it, squealing as she realised Daisy had hit call.

"There's no answer," Flo said as the ringing ended and an automated voice announced she'd reached the voicemail.

"Leave a message," Daisy instructed, throwing another chocolate onto Flo's lap. This one had a whisky cream middle.

"Hi, this is, um." Flo furrowed her brow. What was her name? "Florence Alden. I'd like to make an offer on the Lavender Cottage Cafe."

CHAPTER TWO

Flo pressed her cheek against the cold train window. The motion of the passing landscape made her nauseous, so she closed her eyes. Her head was pounding, and her mouth felt dry. If only she could turn back the clock and stop Daisy from opening the second bottle of wine. Poppy's early morning wake-up call hadn't helped. She'd burst into the living room where Flo was sleeping on the sofa bed. In a flurry of excitement and high-pitched squeals, the little girl had turned on her favourite cartoon at full volume and had bounced all over Flo. Daisy was feeling just as delicate and had taken a little while to come to her rescue.

Over breakfast, Flo gingerly sipped a black coffee as a pale-faced Daisy made Poppy porridge and fresh fruit. As much as Flo loved her best friend's daughter, she left before Poppy subjected her to a second round of morning cartoons. Now, on the train heading back to her house share, the silence was deafening. It had been nice to spend the anniversary of Iris's death with Daisy, but it had simply filled the void for a few hours.

From the depths of her handbag, Flo's phone rang. She delved inside, casting aside rogue tissues, an old lipstick, a leaflet for the local takeaway, and pulled her phone out before it stopped ringing. It was an unknown number, but Flo was used to Bella calling her at weekends, so she answered. Her boss would often call from various luxury spas across the country, needing something emailed to her or requiring Flo to urgently proofread a document.

"Hello?" she croaked, her voice thick with the telltale signs of an evening filled with wine and too much talking.

"Am I speaking to Ms Alden?" a man asked.

Flo's brow knitted. She didn't recognise the voice. "Yes. Who is this?"

"This is Neil from the Cornish Agency."

The Cornish Agency? It rang a very distant bell, but Flo couldn't put her finger on where from.

Neil continued. "I received your voicemail when I got into the office this morning. Ms Alden, this is the first time I've had someone put in an offer for a property by voicemail at nine pm."

Flo's skin grew clammy, and her stomach flipped.

"Anyway, I contacted the sellers this morning. Since the property has been vacant for a few years, they appreciate it will need some love to bring it back to life and have accepted your offer. Congratulations."

Flo gulped. She racked her brains but couldn't remember making the call. How much had she offered? The vista sped past the windows, only adding to the dizziness swirling around Flo's head. Noises were amplified, and she could hear the whooshing of her heartbeat in her ears. With a deep breath, Flo calmed herself to tune back into the conversation. She'd missed whatever Neil had said.

"Sorry, I'm on a train and the signal's a little patchy." Flo crossed her fingers to make herself feel better about the lie. Her signal was fine.

"I'll make this quick. Nothing can be done over the weekend. If you give me your email address, I'll send over our details, and you can ping me your solicitor's information. Then, Monday morning, we can get the ball rolling."

Flo nodded and reeled off her email address. She was in shock. Neil promised to send the information by the end of the day, and they said their goodbyes. Once the call ended, Flo stared at her phone. What on earth had she done? Her stomach roiled as the train bounced over the tracks, and her brain rattled in her skull. The phone slid out of Flo's clammy hands, landing on her lap, but she continued to stare. Did she want the ball to start rolling on Monday?

Once off the train, Flo popped into the local supermarket. It was one of those tiny ones that only had a small selection, but they had everything she needed. With her bright orange plastic bag in hand,

Flo went home.

The house was silent, and the familiar musty scent filled the air. Although Flo shared the house with three other people, she hardly saw them and knew very little about them. In fact, she wasn't at all sure she would recognise them in the street. Flo climbed the creaky stairs to her bedroom, where she unpacked her shopping into the small fridge. There was a communal kitchen, but Flo liked to keep her things separate. She'd been brought up with her grandmother's high hygiene standards, which didn't include growing penicillin in a communal fridge.

Still feeling peaky, Flo headed into her ensuite and had a quick shower. Once clean, she pulled on her towelling dressing gown and delved under the bed for a suitcase. Inside the battered navy case, Flo pulled out her grandmother's old recipe book. It was covered in smudges of cocoa powder and grease marks from cubes of wayward butter. Baking was the only thing that calmed her brain, and she needed the clarity that came with it. Flo thumbed the worn pages. Each recipe held a happy memory of her baking with her grandmother. Truth be told, Flo didn't need the book. She knew the recipes by heart, but having it open on the counter was like having her grandmother beside her. Iris had written little notes in the margins, recommending various substitutions and warnings about timings.

Flo put the recipe book on the table and glanced around her room. Everything she owned was squeezed into this dark, damp space. It was cluttered with furniture she'd taken from her grandmother's home. Iris's will had left the cafe to Flo and half of the house, the other half going to Flo's mother, even though they hadn't heard from her for years. During the sale of her childhood home, Flo hadn't spoken to her mother; they'd only communicated through solicitors. Her mother hadn't cared what happened to the contents of the house, so Flo took what she wanted and sold the rest. That was why she now had her grandmother's old sofa pushed up against the furthest wall, side tables scattered around, and piles of books in corners. Beneath Flo's bed were suitcases filled with photographs, memories, and handwritten notes. The recipe book was the only thing she'd retrieved so far. The loss of her grandmother felt too raw to delve any deeper into the memories. Increasingly, the room felt claustrophobic, and Flo was aware that it was a snapshot into her past. Nothing had moved forward in the last year.

As Flo had lost herself in her thoughts, her hangover had ebbed away. She ventured downstairs with the book under her arm and the ingredients filling her hands. As expected, the kitchen was filthy, so Flo went to her stash of cleaning supplies beneath the sink. Unsurprisingly, nobody had touched them since she last used them. Every surface had to be scrubbed before she could begin baking. Despite not eating proper meals at the house, her housemates still made a mess. There were splotches of soup and dropped pasta shells littering the worktops. Flo had cleaned up after tidier toddlers at her grandmother's cafe.

After a lot of scrubbing, the countertops were clean, the dried soups and sauces had been wiped from the backsplash, and the floor no longer held the remnants of a week's worth of late-night snacks. Flo opened the back door, which led onto the small patch of concrete they called a garden. At a push, it was a courtyard. The humid August air swept in, and Flo rolled her shoulders, ready to bake. She'd French plaited her chestnut hair while it was still wet, and had thrown on an old tracksuit with her lavender apron over it.

Flo took out her purple mixing bowl and creamed the softened butter and caster sugar together. Her muscles ached, but she kept beating the mixture until it was a pale, fluffy consistency. As she added the eggs, flour, and baking powder to the mix, her mind wandered back to the Victoria sponge they used to serve at The Lavender Tea Shop. Every day, Iris would make a fresh one to sit under the domed cake stand. It took pride of place in their chilled counter. The golden sponges were big and soft, filled with thick whipped cream and homemade strawberry jam. During the school holidays, when Flo went to work with Iris, she would always be given the job of sprinkling the icing sugar on top. Nobody could glance at the cake without ordering a slice, and more often than not, they'd be back the following day.

The oven beeped to signal it was at the desired temperature. Flo split the mixture between two greased cake tins and slid them into the oven for twenty minutes. She switched the kettle on to make a coffee and set about cleaning up after herself while it boiled. As she did, she allowed her mind to wander over the conversation on the train. Her offer had been accepted. Over the last hour, some of last night's memories had returned, and Flo could remember the asking price. Even without her making an offer, it had fallen within her budget. Between her savings and her inheritance, she could easily cover the costs and renovate the little cafe. Flo made the coffee and pulled up the cafe's listing. She was thrilled to discover the sale included a small flat above. She drummed her fingers on the mug. There was nothing to keep her in London. She went to work, came home, and slept, only to repeat it the next day. Flo was unhappy and knew she couldn't keep on like this, but was moving to Cornwall the answer? Could she give up the career she had spent years working and studying for? Had she already given up her career? The timer for the oven went off.

A knife came out of the cake clean, indicating it was cooked, so Flo pulled the hot tins out and put them to the side to cool. They'd risen beautifully, and the top had a lovely golden colour to it. Iris would have been proud. While the cakes cooled, Flo whipped the cream. She didn't have an electric whisk, so she had to do it by hand. Her aching muscles protested. It had been so long since she'd used them to do something other than type on a keyboard. Just when Flo was about to give in and admit defeat, the runny cream began to form soft peaks and whipped into a cloud-like consistency. She spread it on one of the sponges, on top of the sticky jam, and then sandwiched the cakes together. With a sprinkling of icing sugar, it looked identical to the ones Iris made.

Flo cut a slice and took it outside with a fresh cup of coffee. There were a few rusted picnic chairs, and Flo tentatively sat on one. She sipped her coffee before putting it on the floor since there was no outside table. Her fork sank into the sponge, and she took a bite. It was delicious. The cake was moist and sweet, which was balanced by the tangy jam. She let out a soft groan and tipped her face up to the sun as she ate. On the breeze, she could almost hear her grandmother's voice congratulating her on another successful cake.

"Well done, my dear," she would say. It had always been Iris's dream to pass the cafe on to Flo. She'd put on a brave face when ten-year-old Flo had announced her plans to go to law school, but she had never tried to sway her decision. Iris had always been proud of her granddaughter, no matter what direction she took in life. From that moment forward, Iris had been her biggest champion.

The slice of cake disappeared in minutes, and Flo savoured her coffee as she stared at the train tracks beyond their concrete courtyard. She yearned for the countryside and the sound of the crashing sea.

As if London were mocking her, a train whizzed by, causing everything to shake. Flo let out a long sigh. It was time she took control of her life again and did what made her happy. She pulled up her emails. At the top of the list was one from Neil, with the subject reading 'The Lavender Cottage Cafe'. Flo sipped her coffee and almost choked when she saw the agreed price. She'd offered considerably less than the asking price. Flo scanned the details to see what was included in the sale. Although the ovens hadn't been used for a few years, the listing promised they were still in working order and the owner had taken good care of them. In later years, Flo had been more involved in the business side of The Lavender Tea Shop as Iris had struggled to keep on top of the books. From her experience, she knew everything included in the sale was a bargain. With shaking hands, Flo dialled Daisy's number.

She answered on the second ring. "Hello, you. Are you feeling as awful as I am? Poppy has been bouncing off the walls, but somehow I've kept her sitting in front of the—"

"Dais," Flo interrupted. "I'm moving to Cornwall."

CHAPTER THREE

A loud creak echoed through the sparse bedroom as Flo unlatched the window. It was a crisp September morning. A flurry of paint flakes blew off the window ledge and floated onto the frosty street below. The window hadn't been opened since Flo moved in, since the street below was usually noisy into the early hours of the morning.

The sun rose in the distance above London's skyscrapers. It was a magical time of day when it felt like anything was possible. The cool air blew in, and Flo turned her back to it to survey her room. Boxes were stacked in one corner for the removal men to collect. Last night, she'd dismantled her furniture, so it was ready to go. That had been a fun couple of hours, but a few plasters and many expletives later, it was done. Flo's phone beeped from her handbag with a text from Daisy to say she was on her way and would be there in an hour. With time passing slowly, Flo padded downstairs to make a coffee.

She'd already had two in her room, so she hoped the change of scenery might speed time up. There wasn't a sound from the other inhabitants. They were all curled up in bed, oblivious to the fact that a new day had already begun.

Flo wandered through the communal rooms with her coffee as she waited for Daisy to arrive. These walls held so many memories. When she moved in, Flo was filled with excitement for life and couldn't wait to see what was ahead of her. Those feelings soon changed to grief and devastation as Iris became unwell and passed away. This house had seen her go from her highest to lowest, and leaving felt like she was shedding a weight from her shoulders.

Daisy texted to say she was outside.

"This place is worse than I remembered," Daisy said as she looked around the damp hallway. She'd offered to bring Poppy to visit many times, but Flo had always put her off, not liking the idea of little Poppy in this environment. Instead, they'd sometimes met in central London, or Flo had gone home to visit.

"I suppose I grew blind to it."

"Easily done. I think I overtook the removal van on my way, so they should be here shortly. Shall we make a start loading my car, then we can get off as soon as possible?"

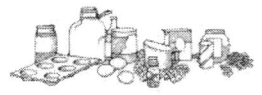

"There's no space left," Daisy complained as Flo tried to wedge another suitcase onto her backseat.

Flo had to admit, it was too much of a squeeze for Daisy's already over-laden car. "I'll throw it on the back of the van and then tell them we're finished."

Daisy climbed into the driving seat while Flo gave the removals some last-minute directions. She only had a room full of possessions, but it was too much to cram into Daisy's old car, and neither of them felt confident driving a van down to Cornwall. Flo hadn't even driven a car for many years.

"You're going to have to buy a car soon," Daisy reminded her as she climbed into the passenger seat. Flo plucked the bag of sweets Daisy had bought for the journey from the dashboard.

"I know." Flo sighed. There was so much she still had to do. "Am I doing the right thing?" she asked, clutching the bag of sweets as Daisy drove out of the estate Flo had called home for the last few years.

"Florrie, I can't tell you if you're doing the right thing. All I can say is that you're a shell of the vibrant woman you once were. You've lost your spark, and I don't think this concrete jungle is helping. The countryside and Cornish sea air will be good for you. Running the cafe won't be easy, but you were involved enough in Iris's that you won't be thrown in the deep end. There's always a sofa bed at mine if it all goes wrong and you want to move back."

"Thanks, Dais."

"Maybe you'll meet a handsome Cornish man, be

swept off your feet, and never think of us again."

Flo chuckled, but there was no humour in it. "I don't do relationships, you know that."

"I know. Sorry, I overstepped."

"You could never overstep. Anyway, tell me about Poppy. Isn't this the first time she's stayed overnight at her dad's?" Flo said, keen to move the conversation along.

"Yeah, I'm terrified. To be honest, I'm glad you asked me to help because it's the perfect distraction."

"He seems to be making more of an effort," Flo commented, popping another sweet in her mouth.

"We'll see."

Flo nodded. "I'm going to miss you," she said.

"Me too, but we'll visit for holidays." Daisy put her hand out for a sweet.

"You're both welcome anytime. I'm going to get a sofa bed for when you come to stay."

"I'll check my diary and we'll get a date in before I leave."

"I'd like that."

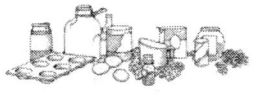

The drive was long, but as each hour ticked by, Flo's excitement built. She was almost home. It was strange to think of the cafe as her new home. She hadn't visited in almost fifteen years and didn't know what it even looked like these days. Estate agent pictures were renowned for hiding the truth.

The last few weeks had been so busy at work that Flo hadn't been able to visit. Instead, she had paid for the most expensive survey and crossed her fingers. She hoped the sun sparkling above was an omen of the new start she was embarking on.

They were in Cornwall and were a few miles from the village. Lush green fields stretched for miles on either side as canopies of trees arched across the road. The leaves were turning from green to gorgeous shades of deep reds, bright oranges, and golden browns. It was as Flo's gaze wandered across the scenery that she spotted something.

"Oh my, what's that?" she gasped, staring at a heap of fluff by the side of the road.

"I don't know," huffed Daisy. She was finding the country lanes difficult to navigate. Her fists were white where she clutched the wheel, and her seat was as far forward as the car would allow.

"Stop!" Flo screeched as she saw the little legs sticking out. "It's a sheep."

"There is no room in this car for a sheep!" Daisy slowed the car but didn't stop.

"We're not putting it in the car. I remember reading somewhere that if sheep are lying on their back, they need help. They can't right themselves."

"There's nowhere to pull over. I'm sure the farmer will be along soon."

"Daisy. Stop. The. Car," Flo said in the most serious voice she could muster.

The car jerked to a stop, and Daisy switched it off with a huff. "What now?"

"We flip the sheep onto its legs," Flo said, climbing out of the car. Daisy followed while grumbling under her breath.

They stood on either side of the bleating sheep. Daisy put her hands on her hips and glared. "Now what?"

"I don't know, Dais. I've never done this before." Flo leaned over the sheep, which was visibly in pain. Emotions were fraught, as neither of them wanted to cause the animal any further distress. Cautiously, Flo knelt, careful to avoid the sheep's flailing legs as it kicked out. "Her foot is caught in the wire fencing," she said, wincing at the sight of the bloody entanglement.

"What do I do?"

"Speak to her." Flo hissed as the wire fencing pricked her finger.

"About what?"

"Anything!"

Daisy sang a lullaby as Flo unwound the fencing.

A loud booming voice made Flo jump, and she tumbled back into a large, muddy puddle.

"What are you doing to my sheep?" the voice called.

Flo blinked as the cold water seeped through her thin leggings. Her hands had sunk into the thick mud, and she fought to pull them free. Meanwhile, Daisy was doubled over laughing.

The owner of the booming voice held out a hand, but Flo refused to take it. She fought against the slippery mud and hauled herself into a standing position. Mud caked her entire lower half, and damp clothes clung to her body. Flo fought the shiver that threatened to tear through her. She turned to the man who was untangling the sheep and watched as he inspected the sheep's foot, his fingers gentle as he whispered soft words to the animal.

"We were trying to help," Flo muttered and wiped her muddy hands on the grass verge.

"You could have done some serious damage to the animal." He stood, towering above her, with a scowl plastered across his face. His brown eyes were ablaze with anger, but Flo's gaze strayed to the rest of his face. He was good-looking, in a rugged-farmer kind of way. Brown hair was hidden beneath a cap, and a short beard covered his face. He wore jeans and Wellington boots with a big wax jacket. He was definitely a farmer. A faint blush rose on Flo's cheeks as she realised how long she'd been staring at him. Daisy's laughter had faded, and she was silently watching the interaction from the other side of the sheep.

Flo shook herself and felt the stubbornness inside her awaken. How dare he accuse her of harming one of his animals? Flo had spent many hours of her life ensuring insects and creepy crawlies of all shapes and sizes made it out of the cafe alive before any overly excited little feet could squish them.

"I was trying to help the animal," she argued, glaring at him and refusing to break eye contact. He may have been almost a foot taller, but she refused to let him intimidate her.

"You're all the same, you tourists. Interfering busybodies." He glared back at her.

"I saw an animal in pain, and I tried to help it. I didn't realise that was illegal in Cornwall. I'm sorry, I'll do nothing next time," she sarcastically spat at him. "Now, if you don't mind, we have a journey to continue."

"You're covered in mud," he said, his voice strained as he unsuccessfully held back a laugh.

"And whose fault is that?"

He shifted his weight from one foot to the other. "Would you like me to drive you to the next village? There's a small clothes shop. Your friend can meet you there in the car."

Although Flo's trainers squelched as she walked, and she felt awful getting into Daisy's car in this state, there was no way she was going anywhere with this rude stranger.

"No, thank you." With that, she headed back to the car, not giving Daisy a chance to protest. Flo spread her coat over the passenger seat. "I'm sorry, Dais," she whispered as they got in.

"It's okay. Poppy's been just as muddy sometimes. We'll clean it once we've unpacked your things." Daisy's car took a few goes to start, and the surly farmer watched them the whole time.

As they drove off, Flo watched him in the mirror. His gaze didn't leave them.

CHAPTER FOUR

The mud didn't have time to dry before they pulled up outside Flo's new home. Memories flooded back as she looked at the stone building. Beyond the iron gate, with a faded sign that read 'Cafe', was a cobbled path leading to the doorway. The building itself looked like a stone cottage from the road. The little wooden door still had the same open/closed sign hanging on it. There were sash windows on either side, with barren window boxes below them. Come summer, she'd fill them with blooming flowers. Yellowing net curtains stopped you from seeing inside. Flo made a mental note to take them down as soon as possible. The sun deserved to shine into the cafe. It looked quaint, if a little shabby around the edges.

Neil, the estate agent, stood along the path, waiting to give her the keys. Flo's hands shook as she closed the car door and greeted him.

"Flo, lovely to meet you in person," Neil said as

she approached. She watched as his brow furrowed at her appearance. Neil was a jolly-looking man, almost the same height as her, which wasn't very tall at five foot three. He had a small balding patch in the middle of his grey hair, and his face lit up with a friendly smile. They had spoken several times on the phone, and he had always been pleasant.

"Hi, Neil," Flo said and shook his outstretched hand. She introduced him to Daisy.

"It's so quaint," Daisy said.

"Would you like a tour, or can you find things for yourself?" asked Neil. He looked eager to leave.

"We'll be fine. Thank you so much for all of your help."

They said their goodbyes, and Neil handed Flo the keys. There was one old-fashioned key and a modern one on a plain silver keyring. The keys felt heavy in Flo's hand.

"Shall we look?" Daisy nudged her. "Or should I hose you down first?"

Flo let out a nervous chuckle. "I forgot I was covered in mud. Come on, let's go inside so I can shower and find a change of clothes." Flo sucked in a deep breath. The air was crisp and fresh, and she closed her eyes and slowly drew in another.

They walked along the cobbled path to the cafe's door. Flo took out the old-fashioned key and slid it into the lock. With a deep groan, the door edged open. The air was stale, so they left the door ajar. A thick layer of dust coated everything, but the cafe still had all the original furniture. Flo lifted one of the lacy tablecloths, which had yellowed over the years with grime and dirt, but beneath, the table looked in good condition. With a good scrub, it would be usable. Flo wandered through to the kitchen and sighed with relief. The appliances must have been fairly new before the cafe shut. With a lot of cleaning, the cafe would be on its way to reopening.

"How do you feel?" asked Daisy.

Flo leaned against the wooden counter. Discoloured bunting hung above, but you could make out the faded illustrations of flowers. Flo's eyes caught on the little triangle of fabric with a sprig of lavender on it.

"I feel good," she whispered, knowing it was a sign from Iris.

"On that note, shall we look at your living quarters?" Daisy eyed the door at the back of the kitchen.

They went up the small flight of stairs to the flat. It was very different from the cafe. At the top, they found themselves in a minute hallway, which led to the open-plan living and kitchen area. The stone structure of the building was exposed throughout, and the wooden floor matched the beams that ran along the ceiling. Everywhere needed a deep clean, and Flo's muscles already ached at the thought. There was a beautiful stone fireplace in the middle of the room. Once it was clean, it would be the perfect setting for a roaring fire. It was also her only source of heat, since there were no obvious radiators.

"It's sparse," Daisy commented.

Flo nodded and went to the opposite side, where a small kitchen was hidden away in the corner. It was covered in a thick grime and was dated. After the relief of the cafe downstairs, Flo felt her emotions turned on their head.

"Perhaps the bedroom and bathroom will be better," Daisy said, her tone reassuring. She ushered Flo through a closed door.

The bedroom had the same exposed brickwork and beams, but the full-length window stole Flo's attention. Bright sunshine flooded into the room. She'd have to install some blinds, but it was the least of her worries. She wandered over to look at the view. Fields stretched out ahead with tiny dots of fluffy sheep. Below was a small garden, which looked as though it might have once been a kitchen garden.

"According to the listing on the agent's website, the bedroom boasts views of the neighbouring Evans farm," Daisy informed Flo. She slipped the brochure under her arm and tapped away on her phone. "It looks like the Evans family owns most of the land in the area. They live in a big house at the top of the village."

"They have beautiful fields," Flo said, finally turning her back on the view.

"Perhaps don't use that as an opening line when you meet them."

"What do you think?" It was Flo's turn to ask.

"It's all cosmetics, right? The survey came back fine?"

Flo nodded.

"Then I think with a good clean and a lick of paint, this will be a lovely little home. Maybe a little chilly in the winter."

"Shall we fetch that box of cleaning products you bought me? We should get started before the removal van arrives."

"What about the mud on you?" asked Daisy.

Flo glanced down. "I guess I should try out the shower."

There was no hot water. After a freezing wash over the bathroom sink, Flo changed into a pair of old jogging bottoms she'd stuffed into a holdall in the back of Daisy's car. Together, they scrubbed every inch of the cottage. With no hot water, they boiled the new kettle Flo had thought to pack. They opened all the windows, and the cottage soon smelled of the crisp day mixed with an armful of cleaning chemicals. It looked liveable by the time they were finished. The removal van arrived, and with a lot of trouble, they got the furniture through the cafe and up the small flight of stairs. Daisy made endless cups of tea while Flo directed everyone.

Once the removal firm left, the two women collapsed onto the sofa. It was cold now that they'd stopped running around.

"Do you know how to make a fire?" asked Flo.

"No. Why would I know?"

"You're a mum. Aren't you supposed to know these things?"

Daisy snorted. "I'm as clueless as you, Florrie. The only difference is I have to pretend I'm not when Poppy's around."

"Do you think we can find a how-to video on YouTube?"

After many failed attempts, they gathered some logs from the wood store and scrunched up some of the packing paper Flo had used. The fire was dismal, but it emitted a small amount of heat.

"Do you want to go out for dinner?" Flo offered.

"Not really, but if you want to get acquainted with the locals, then I'll go with you."

"I'd rather not. I'll wait until I can get some hot water, and then at least I can shower before I meet everyone. We should sort dinner before we fall asleep. I wonder what takeaways they have." Flo took out her phone and groaned as she realised there was no signal.

"It doesn't matter if you have signal. There are no takeaway delivery services out here, Flo. You're in the sticks."

"Pot noodles it is."

Flo didn't own a television, so they plugged in her laptop and watched a film as they ate. It was an old one that Flo had downloaded years ago and never got around to watching. The sorry excuse for a fire spluttered out in the background.

"What are you thinking?" asked Daisy.

Flo stared out the window at the darkness beyond. She could make out the shadowy outline of a willow tree in her new front garden. Her mind was far away, remembering the grumpy farmer from earlier that day. A blush crept up her neck, and she pushed away the thoughts before the telltale rosy hue could reach her face.

"You're blushing! Are you thinking about the hot farmer from earlier?" Daisy's tired eyes sparkled as she pulled herself into a sitting position.

"Who?" Flo did her best to wipe any expression from her face.

"The hot farmer who got you all flustered." Daisy wiggled her eyebrows.

"He did not!"

"He did. You fell head over heels."

Flo sniffed. "I fell because he was being a rude idiot."

"You liked him." Daisy leaned towards her.

"I'll admit I thought he was good-looking, but I don't do relationships, do I?"

"This is a new chapter for you, Florrie. Why shouldn't the new you do relationships?"

Flo bit back a wave of emotions. Her voice was small as she spoke. "Because whether I'm in London or Cornwall, rejection still feels the same."

Daisy's face fell, and she wrapped her arms around her best friend. "I'm sorry. I didn't mean to push."

"I know."

CHAPTER FIVE

Daisy set off early the following day, eager to get home to her daughter. They'd settled on a date for her return visit with Poppy, and Flo hoped to have the cafe up and running by then. The flat felt empty without her best friend. Needing a distraction, she made a cup of black coffee since they'd run out of milk while plying the removal firm with endless cups of sugar-laden tea. Opting to take the mug back to bed, Flo watched as the odd fluffy cloud blew across the stretch of blue sky. The sound of sheep bleating penetrated the thin pane of glass, along with the cold. With winter approaching, Flo needed to order some heaters. She couldn't wait to lie in bed and watch the seasons change.

"I should get up," she groaned. There was still so much to do before she could think about opening the cafe, and there was only a finite amount of time before she needed the income. Swinging her legs off the edge of the bed, Flo squealed as she spotted a figure outside her window. Well, not quite outside her window, he was in the field next to her garden. Flo squinted to see what he was doing. He was filling the troughs for the animals. She could make out the familiar features. It was the grumpy farmer they'd bumped into yesterday. He might have terrible manners, but he was rather nice to look at and only improved the view. As he walked out of sight, Flo dragged herself from the warm bed and went to have a cold wash in the bathroom.

Wrapped in a towel, Flo grabbed a pair of tatty jogging bottoms and a jumper from the open suitcase on her floor. The wardrobe in her house share had belonged to the property, so for now, she was living out of a case.

A knock on the cafe's door sent Flo's thoughts scattering. What if it was the farmer? She halted, wondering why her thoughts had gone straight to him. Flo shook her head and tiptoed to the living room window to catch a glimpse of who it was. Her shoulders sagged. It wasn't the farmer, but instead, an older woman. She ran downstairs to greet her visitor.

"Morning, can I help you?" Flo asked as she opened the door and took in the woman's appearance. She looked to be in her sixties. Her greying hair was elegantly tied back, and she wore jeans, a wax jacket, and green wellies.

"You must be Flo. I'm Claire Evans. I live at the top of the village." She held out a hand, and Flo shook it. The name rang a bell.

"Would you like to come in?" Flo offered, although she glanced behind and instantly regretted the offer.

"No, thank you. I just wanted to pop by and welcome you to the village. I've bought you a little welcome pack." Claire handed over a wicker basket filled to the brim with goodies. Flo's stomach rumbled at the sight. She hadn't eaten since last night's pot noodle.

"Thank you."

"There's some of our produce inside. Perhaps when you have a moment, you'd like to come up to the house? We would love to be the suppliers for the cafe."

Flo nodded, and realisation dawned on her. The Evans family owned the farm surrounding the village. That meant the woman on her doorstep was related to the grumpy farmer.

"That would be great," Flo said.

"Drop in when you have a moment. There'll always be one of us around to have a chat. Have a lovely day." Claire waved before jogging down the path and jumping into a four-wheel drive. Flo barely had the chance to call out goodbye before she drove away.

Flo had planned to head straight out to do some shopping, but now that she had this basket of goodies, she decided to eat.

There were scones, crackers, biscuits, cheeses, milk, butter, and clotted cream. Thankfully, the old fridge had worked when they'd switched it on last night, so Flo unpacked the food and switched the kettle on. She made a quick breakfast of a buttered scone and a cup of tea, mentally adding jam to her shopping list so she could enjoy a proper Cornish cream tea that evening.

Once she'd inhaled every crumb, Flo set out to see what she could pick up in the village. It was Thursday morning, so she hoped places would be open. The sun was shining, but it was cold, so Flo threw a scarf around her neck. It had been her grandmother's, and her perfume still faintly lingered on it. The walk into the village only took a few minutes. There were four shops in the village square: a florist, a convenience shop, a hardware shop, and a small clothes boutique. Dotted around the side streets were a handful of smaller places which appealed to tourists, selling little trinkets for them to take home. It was out of season, but in the summer months, the village would be thrumming with visitors who flocked there to enjoy the beautiful surroundings and the nearby beaches. Flo headed for the convenience shop. It was a beautiful mint green, with a white awning out front, covering a selection of fresh fruit and vegetables, which all glimmered in the morning sunlight. The little bell above the door rang out as Flo walked in.

"Good morning," called a voice from the back.

"Morning," Flo greeted the woman behind the counter. She was around Flo's age, perhaps a year or two older, with beautiful red hair flowing down her back, and freckles across her delicate features.

"Oh, are you the newbie?"

"Is that what they're calling me?"

"No, it's only me." The woman laughed, and Flo's shoulders relaxed. "I'm Emma," she introduced herself. "What's the cafe like now? I used to work there in my teens."

Something about Emma pulled at memories buried deep in Flo's mind. "I'm Florence, but everyone calls me Flo. I think I remember you?" The memories were slowly creeping up. "We met when I was here on holiday. It must have been almost fifteen years ago. Your mum worked at the cafe and you would sneak us scones, and we'd sit in the churchyard and eat them while my grandmother chatted away to the cafe's owner." Flo recalled a particularly hot day when they had taken a picnic and spent the day lounging around by the stream, eating cucumber sandwiches, followed by orange-flavoured scones. Their hands had been sticky, and they'd paddled in the stream. They had laughed endlessly as the cold water lapped at their legs and they jumped up and down, trying to warm up.

"I remember you!" Emma squealed. "What a small world. So, what brings you back?"

Flo gave Emma the short version of why she'd left London and bought a cafe in Cornwall.

"This is so exciting. I worked at the cafe in my teens until it closed down. Do you want some help cleaning? I'm off work tomorrow and have no plans."

"Are you sure you wouldn't mind cleaning on

your day off?"

"Of course not. There's not much to do out of season, so you'd be doing me a favour. I'd only spend my day binge-watching something on television."

"That sounds like a good day off to me," Flo joked.

"It is, but not every day off."

They arranged for Emma to come over at ten the following morning, and then Flo filled a basket with one of each cleaning product in the shop. She got a few bits for dinner over the next few days, mostly pasta and sauces.

"You don't happen to have the number of a local plumber, do you? I've got no hot water, and it's freezing." Flo lifted the heavy basket onto the counter.

"Arthur is our resident plumber, but he had a fall last week and is in hospital. Tom is quite handy. You could drop him a message and see if he can help. Give me your number and I'll send you his."

"Thanks, Emma." Flo left with her bags of shopping and mentally reminded herself to look at cars.

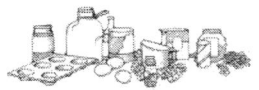

Flo lined up the cleaning products on the cafe's counter beside her laptop, which was open on a new document, ready for her to make a list of things that needed doing and buying. She added 'talk to the Evans family', followed by 'buy new tablecloths'. Flo had removed the yellowing lacy ones and decided there was no salvaging them. They were too far gone. Her plan today was to dispose of anything that couldn't be cleaned, leaving it a blank surface for her and Emma to tackle tomorrow. Before she got stuck in, Flo sent a message to Tom.

With music playing from her laptop, Flo filled a bin bag with old napkins, menus (putting one to the side to help her create a new one), and general rubbish. She opened all the windows and had a quick whizz around with an old hoover she found in the cleaning cupboard. As she sipped her mug of instant coffee, she stared longingly at the coffee machine and wondered whether it was in working order. It would be a big expense if it weren't, and Flo was putting off finding out.

It wasn't until Daisy called to let her know she was home safely that Flo checked her phone and saw she had a reply from the handyman. He'd offered to pop around that evening after work. Flo quickly fired back a response, thanking him. She couldn't wait for a warm shower.

Outside, the light was fading, and there was little more Flo could do in the cafe without beginning the deep clean, so she disappeared back upstairs with her laptop. With another pathetic fire spluttering in the hearth, Flo went online to order some essentials like heaters and a washing machine. She'd discarded her muddy clothes from yesterday in the bath and didn't know what to do with them. Flo made another cup of tea and a plate of crackers and cheese from the basket Claire had dropped around. The butter was beautifully creamy, and the cheeses melted in her mouth with a wonderful tang. She lit a few scrunched up balls of newspaper in the hearth and began searching for cars in the local area. She had no idea what she was looking for, but she needed transport. Her eyes felt heavy as she scrolled, all the information merging into a blur on the screen. Would it be so bad to pick a car based on its price tag and colour?

CHAPTER SIX

Flo jolted awake at the sound of a fist on her front door. She glanced around the dark room, trying to piece together where she was and what was going on. The fire had gone out, and it was cold. Her laptop had slipped onto the sofa beside her when she'd nodded off. There was another knock at the door.

"Coming," Flo called as she stood and stretched, her muscles aching in protest. As she descended the stairs, Flo remembered that the handyman had promised to stop by after work.

Flo's stomach plummeted as she opened the door.

"Oh, it's you." The grumpy farmer's brow furrowed. "Little Miss London."

"What are you doing here?" Flo narrowed her eyes as she took in his appearance. Her gaze lingered on him for a moment too long. She crossed her arms, waiting for an answer.

"I heard you have a boiler that needs fixing?" His voice was gruff, and his body language suggested he'd rather be anywhere than on her doorstep.

Flo huffed. "*You're* the handyman?"

"Tom Evans at your service." There was a slight upturn of his lips, but his demeanour remained surly.

His name reminded Flo that she wanted his family to supply the cafe, so she swallowed back her sarcastic retort. "Nice to meet you, Tom. I'm Flo." She held out her hand for him to shake. "Do you think we could, um, start again?" she suggested.

"Sure thing, London. Do you want to show me your boiler?" he suggested and picked up the toolbox at his feet.

"Mhmm." Flo glanced around. Where on earth was her boiler?

"It'll be oil since the village isn't on mains," Tom said as if that would help.

"Okay?" Flo drew out the word.

"Most of them are outside. Let's walk around the perimeter."

Flo joined him, and a shiver ran through her. She wasn't sure if it was from the chilly evening air or from being beside him. He kept glancing towards her, and Flo could see him sizing her up.

"How are you enjoying village life?" he asked. "Must be quite a change for you."

It was taking all of Flo's energy to stop her teeth from chattering. "It's good." She kept her answer short.

"Here it is." He knelt to look at the boiler.

"I only arrived yesterday. So far, everyone seems

lovely. Well, all but one person." She glared.

"Can you hold this for me?" He gave her a torch and showed her where to shine it. "We're generally a lovely bunch, aside from when outsiders try to harm our animals."

"I was not trying to harm your sheep! I was trying to help it. Besides, I'm not an outsider. I live here now."

"We'll see how long you last, London." He stood and wiped his hands on his tight-fitting jeans. Flo's gaze strayed to his legs and muscular thighs, which now had streaks of dirt on them. "You're out of oil."

"Oil?" Flo frowned.

"That thing that makes your boiler work." He raised his brow as he spoke slowly. "It's the equivalent of putting petrol in a car."

"I don't have a car." She shrugged.

"Are you purposefully missing the point?"

"Spell it out for me, please." Flo shook herself and focused on what he was saying.

"Your boiler needs oil to run. I'm assuming you haven't ordered any?"

Flo shook her head.

"I've got a small amount at the farm that should last you a day or two. I'll fetch it and then give you the number for the company we use."

"Why are you helping me?" asked Flo.

"That's what we do around here, London." He didn't wait for a response. Instead, he strolled down the path and jumped into his car. It was another four-wheel drive, but this one had 'Evans Estate' printed on the side. Flo stared after him, still clutching the torch. The wind whipped across the field, and Flo scarpered inside to wait for Tom. She switched the lights on in the cafe and sat at a table. As time ticked by, she started to make plans for the place.

The tables would look pretty with fresh lace tablecloths and pots of seasonal flowers. Flo made a mental note to pop into the local florist. Underneath the grime, the stone floor should be salvageable. It might be cold in the winter months, but unlike the flat, there were storage heaters downstairs. Flo could only hope the heat would rise and warm her home. There was potential with the cafe, but it needed love and hard work. A weariness had settled over Flo, and she was grateful Emma was helping tomorrow. When she'd decided to move to Cornwall, she'd focused on the everyday life of running a cafe but hadn't considered the work involved in opening the business.

Headlights outside drew Flo's thoughts away from her ever-growing list of things to do. She ran upstairs and put on a coat before joining Tom.

"Can I help?" she asked.

"Unlock that gate so I can reverse the tank up." He pointed to an old wooden gate that led to her driveway.

Flo jogged over to the gate and pulled on the lever to undo it, but it had rusted shut. She braced her leg on the bottom panel and yanked as hard as she could, but still, it didn't move. Flo took off her coat and tried again. "It's stuck," she called over the howling wind.

"Wiggle it."

It worked. With a loud creak, the gate swung open.

Flo watched from afar as Tom backed the tank into her driveway and deposited the oil. Why hadn't Neil warned her about the boiler needing oil? Perhaps he had. Those final weeks in London had been chaotic.

"All done," announced Tom as he coiled the pipe and threw it into the tractor.

"Thank you. What do I owe you for the oil?" Flo took her phone from her pocket, ready to transfer the money.

"Nothing. Call it a moving-in gift. Give it an hour before you turn the boiler on to let the oil settle."

Flo transferred her phone from one hand to the other and glanced dubiously at the boiler. "How do I switch it on?"

Tom ran a hand through his hair, pushing it in all directions. It looked like he'd just rolled out of bed. "Why don't I come back in an hour? I can check if the oil solved your problem."

"Oh, err." Flo was grateful for the lack of streetlights to save herself from the embarrassment of Tom seeing her flustered expression as well as hearing it. "I couldn't ask you to come back." She would have to find the patch of signal in her bedroom and Google how to turn it on or wait until Emma arrived tomorrow.

"It's no trouble. I'm popping into the village in a bit to pick my mother up from her monthly knitting club at the pub. I can pop in on my way."

"Knitting club? At the pub?" It wasn't something Flo had ever stumbled across in London.

Tom chuckled at her puzzled expression. "It's an excuse for her to meet her friends for a few drinks. Not that she needs an excuse. They all turn up with their balls of wool and needles, but very little knitting is ever done."

Flo nodded. "Makes complete sense."

"I'll see you soon, London."

While Flo waited for Tom's return, she made dinner. It was a simple meal of pasta and sauce, but the cheese from Claire's hamper made the bland meal taste delicious. Flo ate by the window, watching as the odd car drove past, wondering whether it was Tom returning. Each time, she held her breath until the car had turned the corner. There was something about him that got under her skin. He'd already judged her and deemed her incapable of making a life here, but little did he know, Flo was stubborn and she was determined to prove him wrong.

In the end, Tom didn't arrive until Flo was washing up. There was a beep from downstairs, and she threw on a coat to meet him. In the passenger seat, with the window rolled down, was Claire. Flo waved, and she returned the gesture. Flo followed Tom to the boiler and watched as he turned it on.

"How long will it take to warm up?" asked

Flo, partly because the silence between them was growing awkward but also because she was hankering for a bath before she fell into bed.

"Should only take ten to fifteen minutes." Tom wiped his hands on his jeans. "Come say hello to my mum while we wait. She's looking forward to having a chat with you about what we can supply for the cafe." He gestured for her to walk ahead.

"I've been trying some of the things your mum dropped around and they're all delicious. Once I've got myself settled and have a rough opening date, I'll pop around for a chat."

Claire smiled as they approached. "Flo, how lovely to see you. I would get out, but I'm a little unsteady on my feet."

Flo chuckled. "No worries, Claire. I'm sorry for delaying you getting home."

Claire swatted away the apology. "How's the place looking?"

"I'm making slow progress."

Tom leaned against the car, his arms crossed. "What's next on your list?" he asked.

Flo shrugged. "There's so much. Emma is coming around tomorrow to help me clean, and then I can step back and see what needs to be replaced. I also need to buy a car."

Claire leaned out of the window. "Do you know much about buying a car?" she asked.

"No." Flo shook her head. "I've never owned one. When I lived at home, I used my grandmother's, and then I moved to London and didn't need one."

Claire looked thoughtful for a moment before she clapped her hands, making Flo and Tom jump. "Why doesn't Tom take you this weekend? He knows enough to help."

"Oh, he doesn't have to do that," spluttered Flo. She was racking her brains to come up with an excuse as she glanced at Tom's scowl.

"How else are you going to get a car?" he asked, his scowl deepening.

"Um, I hadn't thought about it," she admitted.

"Unless you've got any other plans, we'll go on Saturday. You only need something to help you get around, right?"

Flo nodded, confused as to how her weekend plans had taken such a turn.

"I'll pick you up at ten."

Flo nodded and grumbled her gratitude.

"Wonderful," Claire said, smiling.

There was a moment of silence before Tom suggested that enough time had passed and they should be able to check on the boiler. Flo said goodbye to Claire and showed Tom inside. She debated showing him through to the cafe's kitchen, but she wasn't even sure the water was switched on in there. Instead, she gestured for him to go upstairs.

"Do you think you'll have the cafe open soon?" he asked, making small talk as they climbed the stairs.

"I hope so. I can only live on my savings for so long."

Tom strolled over to the kitchen and switched on the tap. He held his finger under the running water as he waited for it to warm up. "Shouldn't take long."

Flo nodded and looked away before she stared for too long. "You don't have to take me car shopping at the weekend," she said. "I know your mum pushed you into it."

"It's fine. I don't mind. That's warm. I'll check the bathroom before I leave."

Flo pointed to the doorway but didn't follow. She wandered over to the fireplace, where the embers of her attempts at a fire lay.

"You've officially got hot water again," announced Tom.

"Thank you." Flo turned from the fireplace to find him standing beside her.

Tom scratched the back of his neck, and he glanced around the room. "Would you like me to make a fire?"

Flo chewed the inside of her cheek. He'd already done so much for her, but the flat was cold and she had no idea what she was doing. "Yes, please."

She tried to watch as Tom built up the logs and screwed up an old newspaper before setting it alight, but she couldn't see properly. Although she could have asked him for help, she felt she'd already made enough of a fool of herself that evening without admitting to not being able to make a decent fire. The flame took hold almost immediately, and warmth filled the room.

"Right, I'll be off." He rubbed a hand across his stubble. "You have my number, so give me a shout if you need anything."

"Thank you for all your help. I'll see you on Saturday, but if you find yourself with other plans, don't worry about it."

"Bye, London." Tom shot her a rare smile before he disappeared downstairs. Flo felt her cheeks flush. It was the first time she'd seen him smile. It had lit up his entire face, and his eyes had shone. Flo shook herself and went to run a bath. Despite the avocado green bathroom suite, the bath didn't look too bad. Flo dug out a bottle of bubble bath from her toiletries bag. She'd received it as part of a Christmas gift from some girls in her office, but since she'd only had a shower at the house share, she'd saved it for a night away. As the bath filled, the lavender scent infused the air, and Flo pushed away thoughts of Tom's inviting eyes and his charming smile.

CHAPTER SEVEN

On Friday morning, Flo enjoyed the luxury of washing her face with warm water. With an old pair of joggers and a tatty t-shirt on, she called the oil company to order a delivery. She didn't want to risk running out of hot water again. Once that job was done, she scrubbed a table in the cafe and laid out the remaining scones and clotted cream alongside a pot of tea. Flo had kept one of her grandmother's teapots from the cafe. They were all beautiful, floral, vintage ones that they'd picked up from second hand shops or boot sales. During the spring and summer, they would wake early on a Sunday morning to go scavenging around the local boot sales before opening the cafe for the breakfast rush. Flo's favourite teapot had been white with pale purple irises faintly hand-painted on it. When she'd seen it at the boot sale, she'd spent the last of her pocket money on it, despite Iris telling her not to. It had hairline cracks across it, meaning it couldn't actually be used, but it could still be displayed. Flo had been thrilled at the connection with the flowers and her grandmother and hadn't thought twice about purchasing it. They'd amassed great collections of vintage teapots, cups, and saucers. Unfortunately, when the cafe was sold, Flo had been forced to sell the china with it, since she had nowhere to store it. She regretted it now, but she promised herself she'd create a new collection that Iris would be proud of.

The table was all set for Emma's arrival.

"Morning," called Emma from the open doorway, which Flo had left open to allow the smell of cleaning chemicals to disperse.

"Come in. I thought we'd start with some breakfast."

"Oh, lovely." Emma dropped a bag of cleaning products and a mop by the door. "We'll get more done if we have double the supplies."

"Excellent thinking. Thank you so much for this." Flo held up the teapot, and Emma nodded, so she poured two cups.

"I'm looking forward to seeing this place open again." Emma broke a scone in half and slathered it with jam and cream.

"So am I. I wish I could click my fingers and it all be clean and ready."

"We'll get there. You won't recognise the place by the end of today."

"What do you think of the butter and cream?" asked Flo as she bit into her scone.

"It's delicious. It's from the Evans farm, right? They supply the convenience store, and we sell out almost immediately."

Flo nodded. "Claire wants to supply the cafe."

"I'm going to be in here every day for scones," Emma said, reaching for another. "Have you met all of the Evans family?"

Flo gulped her hot tea to put off the inevitable conversation. "Claire popped around yesterday morning, and Tom came to look at my boiler last night."

"Isn't he dreamy?" Emma sighed.

"He's a bit full of himself." Flo rolled her eyes. She told Emma about the unfortunate encounter she had with the surly farmer on her way into the village. Emma sprayed crumbs everywhere as she doubled over laughing.

"Sorry," she wheezed. "We're rather nervous of outsiders. Lots of people buy second homes in Cornwall, and it's causing havoc for us locals. Underneath the grumpy exterior, Tom has a heart of gold. We were at school together."

"Have you ever…?" Flo let the question trail off.

Emma raised her eyebrows. "No. He's all yours."

"He's taking me to look at cars tomorrow." Flo realised her mistake as soon as the words left her mouth.

"You've got a date with Tom Evans!" teased Emma.

"It's not a date," argued Flo. "He was very reluctant to offer, but Claire sort of pushed him into it."

"I can't believe you've been here a couple of days and already got yourself an Evans man. Women spend weeks throwing themselves at him, and he barely glances their way."

"He's just taking me to look at cars," mumbled Flo. She did her best to ignore the flutter of excitement in the pit of her stomach.

As they finished breakfast, Flo steered the conversation onto safer topics and asked Emma about the locals and who she might expect to see popping into the cafe regularly.

They scrubbed every surface until it shone in the autumnal sunlight. A handful of locals had wandered past and called in a hello. Flo reassured them it wouldn't be long until the cafe was open. She was beginning to feel positive about the future and hopeful that she would have the support of the village.

Flo's arms ached, and she needed a break from scrubbing. "I'm feeling brave. Let's see if this thing switches on." Flo crossed her fingers as she walked to the coffee machine.

"Good luck," Emma called. She was scrubbing the inside of the counter where fresh food would be displayed. Thankfully, the doors had been kept shut while the cafe was empty, so it was nowhere near as grimy as other surfaces.

Flo took a deep breath. Her hands shook as she flicked the switch.

"Oh no," she groaned as nothing happened. Flo felt like the rug had been pulled from beneath her. She'd been pinning all her hopes on the machine working.

"Is it on at the plug?" called Emma.

Flo followed the wire to the plug point, which wasn't switched on. Her stomach was doing somersaults as she flicked it on at the wall. A gentle hum filled her ears, and Flo let out a whoosh of air. "It's on!" she shouted and jumped up and down.

"What a relief. You should get it serviced, though," Emma said, joining her in the kitchen.

"I've already emailed someone. I'm waiting for them to get back to me."

"I cannot wait to get a decent coffee. At the moment, it's a half-hour drive to the nearest coffee shop." Emma stared longingly at the hissing machine.

"I'll get it running as soon as possible, and you can have as many free coffees as you can drink after all your help today."

Emma tried to argue, but Flo wouldn't take no for an answer. "Would you ever be interested in working at the cafe again?" asked Flo. She'd need help during the busy months, and who better than someone who had worked there before?

"I'd love to." Emma's face lit up.

"I'll have to see if the cafe turns over enough profit, but if it's a success, I'd love you to pick up some shifts."

They stopped for a quick lunch of cheese and

crackers. Flo was even able to use the cafe's kitchen to prepare them. They then spent the afternoon cleaning some more. Flo tackled the pantry, which was overflowing with out-of-date food. She held packets at arm's length as she dropped them into black bin bags. Meanwhile, Emma scrubbed both the inside and outside of the windows. They'd torn down the yellow lace nets and thrown them straight in the bin.

"Do you have a name?" asked Emma as they put down their cloths.

"I was thinking *The Cornish Vintage Tea Shop*." Flo had been mulling it over all afternoon. She was eager to create a nostalgic atmosphere, and the name seemed to suit that.

"It's perfect." Emma beamed. "I'll spread the news."

"Thank you so much for everything today."

Emma convinced Flo to meet her at the pub for Sunday dinner, and they said their goodbyes.

"Have fun on your date tomorrow," Emma called as she left.

Flo didn't respond. The sun was setting, so she closed the door and windows and turned to look at her little cafe, or rather, tea shop, since she was now settled on the name. The pine tables and chairs were scrubbed clean and stacked up on the left side of the room. They'd spent a couple of hours cleaning the stone floor, but it had been worth the achy knees. The grey flagstone floor was an original feature of the cottage, and with some rugs, it would be perfect. Although the counter was clean, it would benefit from a lick of paint and perhaps the new name painted across it. Flo would ask around to see if there was a local artist who might be able to do it. Soon, it would be heaving with cakes and sweet treats. Flo wandered through to the kitchen to check everything was switched off. The appliances seemed to work, and the ovens were clean after lots of scrubbing. They'd switched them on, and they'd warmed up the whole cottage. Flo rolled her aching shoulders and turned off the lights before going upstairs.

Some warmth had risen, but there was still a chill in the air. Flo set about trying to recreate the fire Tom had made, but she was met with little success. She gave up and had a hot shower instead, hoping the oil would last until her delivery. Dressed in the fleece pyjamas Daisy had bought her for Christmas last year, Flo made pasta for dinner again. It was awfully quiet as she ate. Flo was used to the buzz of London outside her window. Despite it being Friday night, there was no sign of life in the village, but she didn't feel as lonely as she had in London.

"I miss you, Gran," she whispered as she put her empty bowl in the sink, promising herself she'd do the washing up before bed. Flo eyed the pile of tatty suitcases in the corner. She hadn't been sure what to do with them, so she instructed the removal firm to stack them behind the sofa. Flo bit her lip as she moved the top case into the middle of the room. Kneeling beside it, she opened it. The rusty lock was fiddly, but with some force, it eventually opened. Inside were books, journals, and notes that once belonged to Iris. Flo hadn't been able to part with the memories. Instead, she'd packed them into suitcases, and they'd remained hidden beneath her bed until the move. Now she was starting fresh, and it seemed a good time to work out how the relics from her past could be integrated into her future.

Flo pulled out a torn piece of paper. It was a note from Iris telling her she'd left to open the cafe and to pop by when she was up. As a young child, Flo had always gotten up early on weekends to go with Iris to the cafe. However, as she reached her teens, she would often sleep in and join her grandmother later in the day. That particular Saturday morning, fifteen-year-old Flo had been out the previous evening to the cinema with Daisy. Iris had left her to sleep. Flo remembered getting up late, throwing on some jeans and a t-shirt and making the short walk to the cafe. Iris had beamed as she stepped through the door and sat her at a table with a cup of tea and a bacon sandwich. Once the lunchtime rush came around, Flo was behind the counter helping.

Each of these scraps of paper held a memory, and Flo couldn't bear to part with them. She scooped them into a pile and put them to one side, making a mental note to buy a box to keep them in. Now that she owned a flat, she could put up some bookshelves and display these keepsakes. Flo hadn't opened this suitcase before. Shortly after her grandmother's death, Flo had packed away everything sentimental before the sale of the house went through. She had considered offering some photographs to her mother, but she'd probably throw them away, like she did with everything else in her life. So, Flo took everything for herself, determined to keep Iris's memory alive. Beneath the letters, Flo took out a tatty red book. It was a diary. The date on it suggested Iris would have been twenty at the time. With the throw from the back of the sofa wrapped around her, she curled up and opened the book, ready to immerse herself in her grandmother's memories. The diary fell open to a date in August.

11th August 1963,

I'm finally on the train. If I'm honest, I'm a little nervous, and Mum almost didn't let me go. The train robbery that happened a few days ago is all over the newspapers. I'm scared, but I don't want it to ruin this.

Dad insisted on dropping me at the station this morning with my bags and told me he'd be there to collect me in two weeks. Two whole weeks in Cornwall alone. We usually go to Cornwall on holiday each summer, but this year, Dad can't get the time off work. I was so upset that Mum wrote to her friend, who told her the local cafe was looking for seasonal staff and suggested I apply. Last Christmas, I waitressed at our local cafe, so I have experience. I only had to send a letter, and the woman offered me the job. The cafe's an adorable little place with lace tablecloths and Victoria sponge cakes. It's all worked out better than I could have hoped.

I can't wait. Two weeks in Cornwall. I'm going to paddle in the sea, walk down the little streets of St Ives, and eat chips on the seafront. Two whole weeks of being by myself in the most wonderful place! My friends are all green with envy, but I've promised to send them postcards.

Anyway, I've got the entire train journey to think about S. We wrote to each other last week and he's promised to pick me up at the station and drive me to the B&B where I'm staying. Mum thinks I'm writing to one of the girls from the farm. She'd be angry if she knew the truth. I don't know how it's all fallen together like this. My parents didn't suspect a thing! If I'd been on holiday with them, then we would have had to keep our dates a secret, but now it'll be so much easier.

I think the next stop is mine.

Speak soon.

Flo's heart raced as she glanced up from the page. She wondered whether this was the cafe her grandmother spoke of. When they holidayed here, Iris had never mentioned working at the cafe, but she always knew her grandmother had visited the area growing up. Flo also wondered who S was. Her grandfather's name was Eddie. He'd been a Londoner through and through and had been very happy with her grandmother until his untimely death at thirty. Iris had grieved her late husband and had never moved on. Whenever Flo had broached the subject, Iris always promised she was happy alone. Wanting to know more, Flo flicked to the next page.

13th August 1963,

I've missed a day. I never miss a day, but life has been so beautifully busy. The train journey to Cornwall went smoothly. Everyone treated me like an adult. I suppose sometimes I forget that I'm twenty. The platform was busy, but somebody helped me carry my suitcase off the train, and then I spotted S in the crowd waiting for me. My cheeks still hurt from smiling so much. It was his eyes I noticed first, those big brown eyes, which feel like they're staring into my soul. He had a bunch of sunflowers for me and said he'd grown them and cut them down this morning just for me. Isn't he romantic?

We stopped off on the way and had tea and scones at a little cafe by the side of the road. It was so busy, but S used his charm to find an empty table in the back courtyard. We had a pot of tea and smothered the scones in jam and cream. I took a bite and got it all around my mouth, but S leaned over with a napkin and wiped it for me. It was perfect.

Once we ate, he drove me to my B&B and said he'd be back later to take me out for dinner. I'll have to be careful in case Mum's friend sees me and writes to her.

The B&B is nice, if a little dated. My room has a single bed and a window that looks out onto the main road through the village. Not a single car went past while I unpacked and got ready for dinner. I changed into my bright orange mini-dress. The one Mum tutted at when I brought it home. She didn't see me sneak it into my suitcase.

Anyway, S loved it. He took me to the local pub for dinner, and everyone turned to look as we walked in. S introduced me to a few of his friends before we found a quiet corner. He treated me to dinner and wine. It was very grown-up. Then he took me home and kissed me. My lips still tingle.

S was busy today, but so was I. It was my first day in the cafe, and I loved it. There are lavender plants all around the outside. Inside, there are little pots of lavender on each table, and bunting with hand-stitched bunches of lavender is strung above the counter. It's all so quaint. Already, I've learned most of the regulars' names.

The owner, Mrs Jones, said I was a natural. She had me taking orders and making drinks. Everyone complimented me on my pretty black dress. Mrs J said she'll teach me how to bake a cake tomorrow. Of course, I've watched Mum bake lots, but I've never tried it myself. I'll let you know how it goes, and I'm seeing S tomorrow. He's promised to take me to the seaside.

I need to turn off my light before the landlady sees it underneath my door. Goodnight.

Flo's eyes were heavy as she finished the entry. She wanted to carry on, but the words were blurring on the page. It was so lovely to read her grandmother's diary. Iris had always been very out there with her fashion choices. The little village wouldn't have known what had hit it when Iris turned up in her bright orange mini-dress. Flo giggled at the thought. She closed the diary and put it on the sofa arm, ready to pick it up again tomorrow. More than anything, she wanted to know who the mystery S was. Had he been a summer fling, or was there more to it?

CHAPTER EIGHT

The sound of sheep bleating woke Flo. She needed to order curtains to dampen the noise and keep out the light. It was another cold morning, and Flo couldn't wait for her heaters to be delivered. Tom would be there in a few hours to take her car shopping. She put on her fluffy dressing gown and slipped her feet into her new fur-lined slippers. Unable to stomach another instant coffee, she fetched her cafetière from one of the packing boxes. The kitchen cupboards weren't big enough for all of her belongings, and so, for now, half of them were still in a box. Flo allowed the coffee to infuse as she made some toast and slathered it in butter. With her simple but delicious breakfast, Flo made herself comfortable on the sofa and picked up her grandmother's diary.

14th August 1963,

I made my first Victoria sponge cake! Mrs J gave me the recipe and helped me weigh all the ingredients. Then she left me to it. Mixing the ingredients was so satisfying. Mrs J told me to try the mixture before I poured it into the tins. It tasted so good. I'm not sure why people bother to bake the mixture. I don't know how I stopped myself from eating it all. It baked for half an hour and came out all risen and golden brown on top. Mrs J said it was one of the best first attempts she'd ever seen. Can you believe I blushed at the compliment? Anyway, we used homemade strawberry jam and whipped cream to sandwich the cakes together. Mrs J let me sprinkle the icing sugar over the top, and it went everywhere. She didn't get angry, though. She just laughed and told me to fetch a broom. We served it to our favourite customers, and Mrs J promised to teach me how to make a Swiss roll tomorrow. I'm going to write to Mum and tell her.

For my break, I had a slice of it with a pot of tea, and it was divine! So soft and light. I'm going to bake one every day once I'm home. But the thought of going home makes me feel sick. I don't want to leave S. He keeps telling me not to think about it because I'll ruin our time together, but it's the only thing I can think about.

Anyway, I must dash. S will be here in an hour, and I'm not at all ready. I still need to decide what to wear! Oh, shoot. I haven't told you what we're up to. I'll have to tell you later.

There was a smudge of ink and a gap between the

entries. Flo sipped her coffee. She'd never thought to ask Iris where her love of baking had come from, and Flo deeply regretted it. Was this how it had all started? She had a little while before she needed to get ready, so Flo read on.

14th August 1963, continued...

I love him. From the moment I saw S last summer, I knew I could fall in love with him. When I fell and twisted my ankle, he was in the next field and heard my cries. He was so caring as he felt for any broken bones and then carried me back to the village. The way he held me was so gentle, and his kind eyes met mine. I knew in that moment that I could fall in love with him, and now, a year later, I had. It slipped out as we walked back to his car tonight. My stomach flipped as the words left my mouth, and I instantly wished I could take them back, but before I could say anything, S squeezed my hands and told me he loved me too. I'm so happy I could sing. I won't, though. The landlady has already told us off for kissing on the doorstep. She said if it happens again, she'll telephone my parents. S said he'd park around the corner and kiss me in the car before walking me to the door. How sweet is he?

Anyway, I never did tell you what I was doing this evening. S picked me up at five and drove to the seaside. We went to St Ives and walked along the little streets. It was a balmy evening, so the beach was busy, but we didn't mind. S held my hand the whole time, and we shared a portion of fish and chips on a bench and spoke about the future. It was perfect, and I know lots of girls were looking at me with jealous eyes. They could tell S was only interested in me. S is busy with work at the moment, but he's promised to travel to London once summer's over. I'd have to tell my parents, but I wouldn't tell them that I knew him before this visit. They're very old-fashioned, and I don't think they'd like the idea of me alone in Cornwall going on dates.

It's almost midnight, but I'm going to sneak downstairs and use the phone to call Anne. She'll be green with envy. Speak soon.

Flo smiled as she closed the diary. It was so lovely to read about Iris's life and the fun she'd had. She'd been through so much with losing her husband at a young age, bringing up a child on her own, and then bringing up Flo. It was nice to see she had some time to live and be young. Although Flo wondered what had happened to S. Perhaps she'd find out in the diary. Things must have gone wrong before Iris returned to London for the summer. Maybe it had been a holiday romance that had fizzled out. Flo jumped as her phone buzzed with a text from Tom saying he'd be there in ten minutes. She looked down at her pyjamas and groaned.

It was so long since Flo had done anything other than work that she'd thrown out most of her casual clothes. With ten minutes until Tom collected her, she didn't have much time to fret over what to wear, so she pulled on a pair of smart black trousers and a plum-coloured cashmere jumper. She slipped on a pair of heeled boots and shoved her phone, keys, and purse into her expensive handbag. There was a beep from a car outside as Flo threw her hair up into a ponytail.

"Is it a bad time?" asked Tom as she walked out. He was leaning against the car in fitted jeans and a lumberjack-style shirt. His stubble had grown since she'd last seen him, and it looked good on him.

"No?" Flo's voice wavered as her heels slid on the cobbles and she fought to right herself before she fell.

"You look like you're dressed for a meeting with the bank." Tom raised his brow, and Flo let out a small huff.

"I'm just dressed in my clothes." She tried to shrug it off, but she slipped again with her next step.

"Can you test drive cars in those?" He looked pointedly at her stiletto boots with a pointed toe.

"I don't know. I've never gone car shopping before. Wait here. I'll get some trainers." Flo nipped back inside and put on the trainers she'd bought last year. On a whim, she'd signed up for a 5k. However, after two early morning runs, she'd realised it wasn't for her. The luminous pink trainers had been stashed at the back of her wardrobe and not touched again. She felt like an idiot in her office clothes and silly trainers, but she was out of options and Tom was waiting.

"Don't laugh," she said and narrowed her eyes as Tom pressed his lips into a straight line. It did nothing because his shoulders shook and his eyes danced with mirth.

"At least I won't lose you," he quipped, and she swatted at him, but he ducked out of her way. "Get in, London. Before you blind people with your shoes."

The car was another estate four-by-four, but this one wasn't caked in mud. Even the inside was clean. Flo set her handbag down in the footwell and put her seat belt on. "Where are we going?" she asked.

"I thought we'd head to St Ives. An old friend of mine owns a car dealership, and I know he'll give you a good deal." He effortlessly navigated the tiny lanes out of the village.

"Thank you." Flo's heart gave a little flutter at the thought of visiting St Ives with her grandmother's diary entry so fresh in her mind. She could imagine which bench Iris sat on and enjoyed dinner with S as they confessed their love.

Tom gripped the steering wheel and kept glancing at her, a scowl etched on his face.

"Spit it out, Tom," insisted Flo.

He frowned. "What are you doing here?"

"You're taking me car shopping."

Tom let out a frustrated sigh. "I mean, what are you doing here in Cornwall? You're obviously some fancy London corporate employee, so why are you here opening a cafe?"

Flo's skin prickled as she realised he was only helping her out of pity. He thought she didn't know the first thing about opening and running a business. She was the village charity case, and Tom had drawn the short straw since his mother had persuaded him to help. Flo didn't for a second think she was above accepting help, but knowing that Tom was doing it because he felt obliged made her hackles rise.

Flo scuffed her shoe on the footwell and fought the urge to throw a sarcastic comment back in Tom's face. "Yes, I had a corporate job, but I wouldn't call it fancy. My career had hit a dead end, and I realised it didn't make me happy anymore. Actually, it hadn't made me happy for a long time. There was nothing left for me in London."

"It's a big change."

"Perhaps. Growing up, my grandmother owned a cafe. I helped out in my spare time, so I know the industry like the back of my hand. I also know this area because we used to come here on holiday until I was around twelve, and then I begged Iris to go abroad."

Tom nodded and took a moment to consider her explanation. The scowl on his face had been replaced by a neutral expression. "Your grandmother must be very excited to visit you."

"She passed away a year ago," Flo said, inspecting her nails.

"I'm sorry." Tom's demeanour softened. He cleared his throat before he spoke again. "How's the cafe coming along?"

"It's getting there. I have a couple of engineers coming out in the week to look at the appliances. If they're all fine, then everything left to do is cosmetic."

"Won't be long until you open. I can't wait to pop in. It's been an age since I stopped at the cafe for cake. Mrs Jones's Victoria sponge was legendary around here."

Flo's ears pricked up. "Mrs Jones?"

"Yeah. She owned the cafe when I was growing up. Freshly baked cakes every day until the day she passed away. Then a few locals tried to run the place, but it was never very successful. Their hearts weren't in it like Mrs Jones's, and you could taste it. I've never had a Victoria sponge like it."

Flo suspected her Victoria sponge would taste very similar. "I'll bake you one soon."

"I'd love that. Thank you." He grinned. Something had shifted in Tom's demeanour, but Flo didn't know what, and she wasn't about to waste time examining it.

"I think my grandmother worked at the cafe for a couple of weeks in the sixties."

"You have connections to the village, then?" he asked, frowning.

"I guess you could say that."

"So, tell me what kind of car you're looking for?"

"Ideally, one with four wheels and an engine."

Tom sighed, and the scowl was back. "Beyond that?"

"I don't mind."

It only took half an hour to get to St Ives, and Tom spent most of the journey educating Flo on various makes and models of cars. Flo had tuned out and enjoyed the deep hum of his voice in the background as she watched the beautiful scenery pass by. The lush fields in the distance changed to the deep blue sea, and seagulls' squawks replaced the gentle rustle of leaves on the trees above. The salty tang of sea air filtered into the car, and Flo couldn't wait to get outside.

"Here we are." Tom swung the car into a small dealership, and Flo's eyes settled on a car. A small, mustard Fiat 500. It was like a modern version of Iris's old yellow Beetle, which they'd nicknamed Sunflower.

Flo walked over with Tom hot on her heels.

"Come on, London. You cannot be serious," he said, coming to a stop beside her.

"What's wrong with it?"

"What's right with it?"

Tom's friend appeared at that moment, so Flo took her chance to walk around the car and take it in while Tom was distracted.

"Flo, this is Jack. Jack, Flo," Tom introduced them.

"What kind of car are you looking for?" Jack asked.

"This one," Flo said.

"Flo, think about this for a moment. Don't you want something that can navigate the country lanes in the winter? Something big enough that you can fit your weekly shop in?" Tom pointed towards a big four-by-four. "Don't you want something like that?"

"Absolutely not. I've not driven in years and don't feel confident about the country lanes. Something small like this is perfect."

"Well, they'll certainly see you coming," Tom remarked.

"Shall we take it for a test drive?" suggested Jack. "Tom, grab a coffee and hold the fort while I'm gone."

Flo was relieved to discover the car was automatic. The roads around St Ives were busy, but she effortlessly navigated them. As she drove back to the dealership, she passed a second hand shop and made a note to drop in on her way home.

"What do you think?" asked Jack as they returned.

Tom was already outside waiting for them. "Well?" he asked.

"I'll take it." Flo beamed.

Tom groaned.

"Wonderful. It'll take me half an hour or so to get together the paperwork. Perhaps you'd like to go for a coffee and come back?" Jack suggested.

"There's a second hand shop around the corner. I may have a poke around. Thank you for all your help, Tom, but you can head home now."

"I'm not leaving you. I'll wait and follow you back in case anything happens. Besides, if you buy anything, you'll need my boot to put it in since yours is the size of a matchbox car."

"See you in half an hour," she called and strolled down the road.

Tom jogged to catch up.

"What are you doing?" she asked.

"Coming with you. Would you rather I didn't?"

Flo shook her head. "No, it's fine. I just didn't expect you to."

CHAPTER NINE

The shop was split over two levels and filled to the brim with a mixture of genuine antiques and utter tat. It was Flo's dream. She'd love to spend hours searching through the piles of bric-a-brac to find the hidden gems.

Tom groaned under his breath as he followed her through the front door. He had to duck to avoid hitting his head on the frame.

"What are you moaning about? This is perfection." Flo wandered over to a display of teapots. They were all so wonderful, she didn't know where to look first. She picked up a delicate one and turned it upside down. It was a Sadler teapot, but the price didn't reflect that. By the looks of it, there was someone's entire collection. The one she'd picked up was a pretty cream colour with delicate roses painted on it. They were exactly what she was looking for to begin her collection and stock the tea shop.

Tom narrowed his eyes. "Do you need a teapot?"

"I do, actually. Whoever priced these has no clue about teapots. Five pounds for a Sadler," she whispered.

Tom stared for a moment before he spoke. "How do you know this?" he asked with an incredulous shake of his head.

"Years of traipsing around boot sales."

"You're full of surprises, London. What's wrong with ordering some new ones from a wholesaler?"

Flo gasped. "Horrible, plain, white ones?"

He nodded.

"Absolutely not. A trip to a tea shop should be an experience. The pretty teapots and cute cups and saucers should be a part of it."

"How stupid of me," Tom muttered.

Flo shot him an appeasing smile, but her mind was elsewhere. She was considering how many tables there were in the tea shop and how many teapots she might need. A glance at the stock suggested there were nineteen, all with delicate floral designs. They were just what she needed.

"Can I help you?" an elderly woman walked over.

"I'm interested in your teapots. I don't suppose you would do a deal if I took all nineteen?" Flo crossed her fingers behind her back.

"Nineteen. What on earth do you want nineteen teapots for?" The woman gave her a stern look over her glasses, which were perched on the end of her nose.

"I'm opening a tea shop."

The woman's suspicious gaze dropped with that explanation. "We can do a deal. Do you need any teacups? We have a display through that archway. Why don't you have a look around, and we'll discuss any discounts when we know how much you're buying? I'll begin wrapping these for you." She took the teapot from Flo.

"Thank you," Flo called after her.

Tom trailed behind her up the stairs. "I thought you said they're worth a lot more than they're being sold for," he said.

"They are."

"Then why did you ask for a discount?"

"Because this is business, Tom." She shrugged and moved on to a display of teacups. An entire wall was filled with shelves of pretty cups and saucers. "This is going to get expensive."

"Perhaps you're not as green as I thought," mumbled Tom.

Flo couldn't decipher Tom's tone and didn't dwell on it as she cleared a spot on the floor to pile the items she wanted to buy. Tom stood back as Flo examined the contents of each shelf. Occasionally, she asked him to get something if it was out of her reach, but beyond that, they didn't speak. Flo chose a selection of floral teacups and matching saucers, a handful of pretty cake stands, some milk jugs, and a set of cake forks with delicate silver handles shaped into feathers.

Over numerous trips, Flo and Tom carried everything to the till, where the woman had just finished wrapping up the teapots. Tom offered to stay and help while Flo continued her browsing.

"Thank you," she mouthed and ran up the stairs despite her aching legs.

In the backroom were stacks of plates. Flo filled her arms with as many as she could handle. They were all pretty pastel colours, some with scalloped edges, others with flowers, and some with gold piping.

"Is that everything?" the woman asked, handing Flo a new roll of bubble wrap.

"Yes, although I'm sure I'll be back in a couple of weeks."

They wrapped the delicate purchases and stacked them in boxes that the woman had found in the storeroom.

"I'll go and get my car," Tom offered once they'd packed everything into four big boxes.

"Thank you." Flo gave him a sheepish grin. They wouldn't fit in her new car.

The woman gave Flo a generous discount, thanking her for buying so much stock that she could put some fresh things out to entice customers inside.

"I'm sure I'll be back to buy it soon," joked Flo.

"You're always welcome, dear. And I'll pop in for a slice of cake once you're open."

"It's on me."

Tom returned, saying he'd left the car outside the door to carry the boxes out.

"I'll give you a hand," the woman said.

"We've got it," Tom assured her.

They put the boxes in his large boot, and Flo gave him strict instructions to drive carefully.

He nodded. "You can follow me back. That way, you know that if my car fits, your toy car will also fit."

"Do you think my car's ready?"

"We should head back so you can sort out the insurance."

It didn't take long before all the finer details were addressed, and Flo's bank account was significantly lighter. Jack handed her the keys and promised to stop by the tea shop once it opened.

"You okay? I can come back and collect the car for you," offered Tom.

Flo blinked, unsure how to react. She wasn't used to someone thinking of her like that, and she didn't know how it made her feel, although she suspected the prickly feeling covering her body might be a bad thing. "I'll be fine," she brushed it off, keeping a bland expression on her face.

Tom nodded. "I'll give you a minute to get settled. Flash your lights when you're ready to go."

Flo said a final thank you to Jack and climbed into her new car. She ran her hand over the shiny steering wheel and took a deep breath of the clean car smell. She needed a name now. Flo flexed her fingers and pushed the button to turn the car on. She took a moment to settle her nerves while the car's engine hummed beneath her. With the radio on and familiar pop tunes playing from it, Flo flashed her lights and readied herself for the most nerve-racking journey of her life. Not because she hadn't driven in so long, or because she was driving on new roads, but because she wanted to prove to Tom she could do it.

The drive was fine. Tom drove slowly. So slowly that Flo had to fight the urge to overtake him. He was doing it for her benefit, and something about it aggravated the frustration bubbling away inside her. He'd already jumped out of his car and opened her driveway gate before she could think about it. Flo drew the line when he tried to signal her how to reverse the car into her driveway.

She opened her window. "I've got it," she shouted.

He held up his hands and backed away. Flo narrowed her eyes and concentrated very hard on reversing.

"Well done," Tom called as she got out of her parked car, which was at a very obvious wonky angle.

"Thanks." Flo's tone was icy.

"Do you want to put the kettle on, and I'll bring these in for you?" He tilted his head towards his car, referring to the boxes in his boot.

"I can get them." Flo squared her shoulders.

Tom chuckled. "Okay, Miss Independent. Why don't we both grab them?"

Flo couldn't think of a response that didn't sound petty, so she reluctantly agreed.

"How was the drive?" he asked, picking up two

boxes as if they weighed nothing.

"Fine," Flo huffed under the weight of the single box she'd picked up.

"Where do you want these?"

"Just leave them in a corner of the tea shop. I'll unpack them during the week and wash them up."

Tom lined them up against the far wall and fetched the other box as Flo stretched her back. She knew she was being unnecessarily prickly towards him, but she couldn't help it. His helpfulness had sparked something inside her. Flo was used to doing everything herself. She didn't allow anyone to see her vulnerable. From a young age, Flo learned that if you showed people your weaknesses, they would only hurt you. So now, she simply didn't allow anyone close enough to even see a hint of weakness.

"That's everything," Tom said. "I've got no plans for the afternoon. I can help you unbox and wash them up if you'd like?"

Flo's heart was torn. She liked the idea of spending more time with Tom and could imagine them at the kitchen sink. One of them washing while the other was drying. But the other part of her was determined to assert her independence. He'd already done so much for her today that she couldn't accept anything else.

"I'm fine, thank you. I'm sure you have better things to do with your afternoon off than look after the new girl." She crossed her arms and leaned her hip against a table.

"Maybe I like looking after the new girl," he

whispered and took a step towards her.

Emotions flooded Flo, but she couldn't decipher what they were. Something had shifted between them today. Tom's icy exterior had thawed, and for a moment, it felt as though his kindness came from somewhere other than pity. Then his mood would shift, and Flo's cautious nature would cause her to put her barriers back up.

"Do you want some help upstairs?"

"Upstairs?" She stumbled over the word.

A faint blush crossed Tom's cheeks. "I meant with a fire or something?"

More help. "No," she all but shouted. Flo was confused by the frustration that ran through her. It was mixed with something else, but she couldn't put her finger on what it was.

"I'll leave you be. Goodbye, London," he said.

CHAPTER TEN

As Flo waited for the cafetière to brew, she wondered what to do with her Sunday. She was meeting Emma at the pub for a roast dinner, but she had some time to spare before she needed to think about that. There was still so much to do in the tea shop, but Flo was eager to get out and explore her new surroundings, especially now she had a car. Not knowing where to start, Flo texted Emma, asking if she wanted to meet earlier for a spot of shopping. Emma's response came almost immediately. She couldn't, as she was working in the shop, but she suggested Flo take a trip to Ives-on-Sea to visit The Cornish Vintage Dress Shop. With nothing else to do and in need of some casual clothes, as Tom had so helpfully pointed out, Flo decided to take her new car out for a spin.

The drive to Ives-on-Sea was very different from yesterday's. Flo felt like a weight had been lifted from her shoulders as she controlled her route through the winding lanes and set her own pace. As she drove, Flo considered what to name her new car. It would be a shame not to factor in the car's colour. After a few disregarded options, she settled on Buttercup just as she turned the corner and saw the sea stretching out ahead. As beautiful as the green fields and golden trees were, nothing compared to the sight of the sea, even on this slightly overcast day. Flo parked at the bottom of the village and took a stroll up to the shops. Although the season was over, there were still tourists wandering around. Flo glanced longingly towards a cafe but decided to pop into the dress shop first, and then she could reward herself with a sweet treat. She'd never been much of a clothes shopper and had all too easily fallen into the trap of only wearing workwear.

"Good morning," the woman behind the till called.

"Morning." Flo smiled as she took in her appearance. The woman's vibrant, curly hair was piled atop her head. It was messy, but somehow it worked. Flo would never be able to pull off a look like that. She wore a maroon velvet dress with a corseted top and a full skirt.

"I'm Rosie." She gave a small wave. "Can I help you, or would you like to be left alone to browse?"

"Lovely to meet you, Rosie. I'm Flo, and to be honest, I'm not sure. I've been wearing smart workwear for so long that I'm not sure I have a style." Flo felt lost in the shop as she glanced to the left at a rail of vibrant sixties mini-dresses.

Iris would have loved them, but Flo lacked the confidence.

Rosie offered her a kind smile and stepped out from behind the till. "That's nothing we can't fix. My boyfriend was the same when we met, but I soon worked my magic on him." Rosie pulled out a tape measure. "Let me take your measurements, then I can pull some pieces for you to try on. Go through to the dressing room and put on one of the slips. Give me a shout when you're done."

Flo nodded and forced her legs to move. She had no idea what she'd agreed to, but it was too late now. The sight of the dressing room almost gave Flo heart palpitations. Bright pink, shimmering flamingo wallpaper was the first thing Flo noticed, followed by the matching pink carpet. Even the chandelier was pink. Flo gulped, but took a slip from a hanger and changed into it. Iris would have loved the shop and would have gone home and immediately redecorated the spare bedroom.

"Ready,' Flo called, and her voice shook.

"Don't look so worried." Rosie chuckled.

It took her mere seconds to take Flo's measurements and jot them down on a well-used notepad. "I'm assuming vintage isn't your usual style?" she asked and glanced towards Flo's folded clothes.

"Not recently. I enjoyed fashion in my teens and loved visiting thrift shops in London, but then I started university and adopted more of a sensible fashion." Flo tugged at the hem of the slip.

"Okay, that's fine. There's an outfit for everyone. What does your everyday look like?"

"I'm opening a tea shop," Flo said and met Rosie's eyes for the first time since she'd entered the dressing room. "A vintage tea shop."

Rosie gave her a knowing look. "How exciting. We'll need a group chat soon with all these vintage shops."

Flo wasn't sure if Rosie was joking, so didn't comment.

"Sit tight. I'll pull some outfits for you to try on. There's no pressure to buy anything."

Flo sat on the pink scalloped chair in the corner as she waited for Rosie to return. Her legs shook, and she fought to still them. It wasn't long before there was a knock on the door and Rosie returned with an armful of outfits.

"Try them all, even if you think they won't suit you. Sometimes, it's good to know what doesn't work. I'll be outside. Give me a shout if you want a second opinion on anything." Rosie hung the outfits on a rail and disappeared, leaving an overwhelmed Flo staring at all the options.

"Come on. Be brave and find yourself again," Flo muttered as she approached the rail. There was a bright green dress, which she was sure would look horrible, so she picked it up first and slipped it on.

The colour was awful on her, and Flo couldn't help the giggle that escaped her lips. It was an immediate no since she had no desire to glow in the dark, but the shape suited her.

"How's it going?" Rosie called through the closed door.

"The green is awful, but I like the shape." Flo did a little twirl in the mirror and felt giddy at the way the skirt flowed with her.

"Sorry, I wanted to test how adventurous you are with colour. The shape's good, though. It's a 1940s tea dress. I popped some more in. Try the mint green one next."

Flo glanced dubiously at the dress. The most adventurous colour she'd worn over the last ten years was burgundy. Well, excluding the pink trainers, but she'd only bought the colour so she could be seen during the dark and foggy morning commutes. Trusting Rosie's judgment, Flo put on the dress and gasped as she caught sight of her reflection. The pale green looked beautiful on her, and her chestnut hair shone. She unlocked the door to show Rosie.

"Oh, it's perfect. I can imagine you serving slices of cake and pouring pots of tea in that dress," Rosie said. "I popped a few designs in. Give them all a try now before you move on to something else. I suspect these will be a staple in your wardrobe, and they can be dressed up in winter with tights, boots, and a cardigan."

Flo nodded as though she were making a mental note. She quickly retreated to the dressing room and tried on all the other patterns and colours. She disregarded the yellow one as being out of her comfort zone, but moved the other five to her buy pile.

The to-buy pile had grown with pairs of high-waisted trousers and various blouses. They were all beautiful, and there were a few special ones that Flo could save for when she wasn't in the tea shop. Rosie had listened when Flo had said she was used to smart wear and had kept it in mind. There was one dress left to try on, and Flo had left it until last because it looked far too fancy. It was a short black 1950s dress with bows on the shoulders and a thin belt around the waist. The dress was stylish and sophisticated — the very opposite of Flo. There was a small petticoat to slip on underneath it. With a deep breath, Flo stepped into the dress. She closed her eyes before turning to the mirror. The feel of the dress was special. It fitted her perfectly, and the belt gave her a shape she hadn't seen in years. With the help of the petticoat, the skirt flared out at her waist and swished against her legs. Flo bit her lip and opened her eyes. A small squeak slipped from her lips. She hardly recognised the woman in the mirror.

"Are you okay?" Rosie called.

"I think so." Flo tiptoed over to the door, scared that any loud noise would shatter this moment. This was the woman she'd dreamed of being but had never been brave enough to embrace.

"Wow," the word slipped from Rosie's mouth. "That dress was made for you."

"I know. It's beautiful, but do I look like a fool in it? Am I trying to be someone I'm not?"

"Flo, you can be anyone you want to be."

"I'll take it," Flo said. The dress would probably sit in her wardrobe, and she'd occasionally gaze longingly at it, but at least she could sometimes slip it on and dream of the woman she wished she were brave enough to be.

By the time Flo left The Cornish Vintage Dress Shop, she had to walk back down to her car to drop off all her shopping bags. She'd left the shop feeling like a different woman. Rosie hadn't been joking about the group chat. *The Vintage Girls* was set up, and Flo was excited to meet her fellow business owners. Although Flo craved a coffee and a slice of cake, her aching feet couldn't face the walk back up the hill, so she headed home.

CHAPTER ELEVEN

The light was already fading by the time Flo got home. She didn't have long until she was due to meet Emma at the pub, so she jumped in the shower. The avocado suite was growing on her. Easing herself into a new style, Flo opted for a pair of waist-high black trousers and a black vest. To go with it, she picked the cropped forest green cardigan Rosie had thrown in at the last minute. Flo wiped the condensation from the bathroom mirror and attempted to throw her hair up in a messy bun. It didn't look the same as Rosie's, and she wanted to let it tumble down to hide her face again, but she left it.

It was a cold but clear evening, so Flo put on her smart black coat and a pair of heeled boots and walked to the pub. The Lavender Arms was beyond a small bridge that crossed a meandering stream. With a thatched roof and a chimney puffing out smoke, it looked like something from a fairytale. Emma had texted to say she was already there.

Inside was also picturesque, with wooden floors, tables and chairs with fur throws over the back of them, a huge roaring fire in the background, and a ceiling with hundreds of old tankards hanging from it. Emma waved from a table by the fire and held up a bottle of wine.

"I ordered red. Is that okay?" Emma asked, getting up to greet Flo.

"The last time I had a bottle of red, I put in an offer on the tea shop."

Emma raised her brow.

"It's a long story." Flo took off her coat. Their table was by the window, which looked out on the beer garden. It would be lovely in the summer. There was an apple tree in the middle and wooden picnic benches surrounding it. With the apple tree in blossom and wildflowers scattered across the grass, it would be the perfect place for an afternoon date on a hot July afternoon. Flo stopped her train of thought. A date?

As though Emma had read her mind, she leaned forward and whispered. "How was your date with Tom?"

"It wasn't a date," Flo hissed back, glancing around to check nobody could hear them.

"Well, now you have to tell me what happened to convince me it wasn't a date." Emma poured them both a glass of wine while Flo glared.

"He took me to a car dealership, helped me buy a car, and then trailed around a second hand shop with me and helped me when I purchased most of its contents." That was the short version.

"Very business-like."

"I'm revoking a slice of free cake every time you reference my non-date."

Emma held up her hands. "Okay, I'll stop."

"He's just being helpful out of pity. Underneath it, I think he's barely tolerating me. Shall we order?" Her stomach rumbled at the thought of food. She'd been so busy clothes shopping that she'd skipped lunch.

"Yes. We order at the bar."

"I'll get this. It's the least I can do to thank you for all your help cleaning."

The bar wasn't very busy, but with only one person serving, it took a few minutes to be served.

"Ah, you're the new girl," the man said, looking her over. "I'm Denzel, but everyone calls me Denny. Your one and only publican, well, besides my better half." Denny must have been in his late forties. He was a cheery-looking man with greying hair and a moustache.

"Lovely to meet you, Denny. I'm Florence, but everyone calls me Flo."

"We can't wait for you to reopen Mrs J's old place. It's been a long time since I've been able to walk down the road for a slice of cake."

Flo was taken aback by the warmth in Denny's tone. She'd been expecting some hostility from the locals. "Not long now," she said. "You grew up here?"

"Born and bred right on this very doorstep."

"I might have to pick your brains when you're not

so busy." Flo was aware of the queue that had formed along the bar.

"I'll look forward to it. What can I get you?"

Flo ordered and went back to the table. It was wonderfully warm inside, with the fire ablaze. A couple of men at the table beside it were feeding logs into the fire. Flo suppressed a groan as she realised who it was. Tom Evans was sitting across from her, and if she didn't look away soon, he'd spot her.

"Are you okay? You've gone pale." Emma peered at her. "You look like you've seen a ghost."

"Not a ghost. A farmer."

"Oh." Emma went to turn.

"Don't!" Flo shouted a little too loudly, and heads turned to them, including Tom's. He frowned as their gazes met, but he swiftly replaced the expression with a bland smile that didn't reach his eyes. He whispered something to his friend before he sauntered over.

"Hello, London," he greeted her. He grabbed a seat and pulled it up to their table.

"Why don't you join us?" Flo muttered under her breath.

"I saw your car was gone today. How are you getting on?" His eyes searched hers, and Flo felt her heart rate increase along with her frustration.

"Fine," she muttered. He obviously thought she wasn't capable of driving around here. Maybe it was because he still thought of her as an outsider.

"Good." Tom drummed his fingers on the table. "I like the outfit."

Flo blushed but pressed her lips into a firm line.

Emma looked between them. "Would you like to join us?" she asked.

Flo kicked her under the table, and Emma winced.

"Oh, err, thank you, but I'm here for my book club," said Tom, glancing back to his table, which was filling up with others. "It's a sci-fi book club. We meet every couple of months."

Flo nodded, allowing her eyes to flicker to his for a moment. He was staring, and as their gazes met, she felt a small fizz of attraction. It began in the pit of her stomach and spread across her body. Flo looked away. "What are you reading?" she asked.

Tom pulled a tatty paperback from his pocket.

"Oh, I love that one," Flo said, picturing her tired copy on a shelf at home.

Tom nodded. "I should, err, get back." He quickly returned to his table.

"What was that?" asked Emma.

"I don't know." Flo topped up her glass.

Emma fanned herself. "The tension between you is palpable."

"Don't be silly."

"I'm being completely serious. He likes you."

"Maybe I don't like him." Flo pressed her lips together and fought the urge to glance in Tom's direction.

"Your face says otherwise."

"Fine. I'm attracted to him, but we don't like each other. Besides, he's very overbearing."

"What do you mean?"

A waitress set two roast dinners down in front of them, and Flo waited until she was out of earshot to answer. "He keeps asking if I'm okay or if I need help with anything. I don't like it." She speared her fork through a carrot and nibbled on it. "These are amazing."

"Honey roasted. What do you mean, he keeps asking if you're okay?"

"Like yesterday, after I bought my car. He made me follow him home, and he went so slow because I'd mentioned I was nervous about the small lanes. He thinks I'm some weak little woman who can't do anything for herself, and he's throwing me breadcrumbs as he stands back and waits for me to fail."

Emma paused with her fork halfway to her mouth.

"Don't look at me like that, Emma." Flo pushed a potato around her plate. Despite her rumbling stomach and the delicious food in front of her, she'd lost her appetite. "One minute, he treats me like some evil outsider, then the next, he's overly thoughtful for an almost-stranger. I don't know whether the thoughtfulness is coming from a place of not believing I can succeed here, or maybe it is pity, but either way, I don't want it."

"It sounds like he was being thoughtful and wanted to make sure you were okay." Emma shrugged. "Do you know how rare that is in a man, Flo?"

"But it's too much and overbearing, and it doesn't

feel genuine."

Emma shook her head. "Who hurt you so much that a thoughtful man has you running? Tell me, because I'd like to string him up by—"

Flo couldn't bear it any longer, so she interrupted Emma's threats. "It wasn't a man. It was my mother. I don't need help from anyone, okay? I've spent my life looking after myself, and I will continue to do so. I don't need anyone. I'm perfectly capable of succeeding on my own." Tom's doubt had reignited a fire in Flo that she'd forgotten once existed.

Emma looked at her with such pity that Flo's stomach churned.

"I'm sorry, Emma, I don't mean to come across as ungrateful. I'm stubborn and determined to make the tea shop work. I appreciate the help you're giving me, but I don't want pity from anyone. My grandmother brought me up to be strong and independent. Nobody needs to make exceptions for me."

Emma nodded, but sadness still clouded her expression. "Of course. I'm sorry. Why don't you tell me about your plans for the tea shop? When are you hoping to open?"

CHAPTER TWELVE

The boxes were big and heavy, and the delivery driver had dumped them at the bottom of the path. Flo had called after them to ask for help, but they'd either not heard or ignored her. Somehow, she had to get these boxes to the front door, through the tea shop, and up a flight of stairs. She tried picking one up, but it didn't move, and sweat beaded on her forehead, despite the chilly autumn morning. Flo gasped for breath and leaned against her front gate, planning her next form of attack.

A chirpy voice infiltrated her thoughts. "Morning, London," Tom called out of his car window as he pulled to a stop.

Flo suppressed a groan. She'd tried not to rise to his nickname, but she was reaching the end of her tether. "Hello," she replied testily, still slightly out of breath.

"That looks fun," he teased.

"The stupid delivery driver dumped them here. I

paid for inside delivery."

"Do you want some help?" He'd already turned the car off.

Flo nibbled her bottom lip. As much as her pride didn't want to accept help, she needed it. This wasn't something she could do alone. "Please. I'm not keeping you from anything, am I?"

"No. I've already been out and fed the animals, gone home and showered, and I'm off to pick up some feed, but that can wait," he explained, and with little effort, lifted the box and started towards the cottage. Flo jogged to keep up.

"Can you put one in the living room and another in the bedroom?"

"I can in exchange for a coffee."

"It's only instant." Flo had run out of coffee for the cafetière. "I've got an engineer coming out this afternoon to service the machine."

"That's fine. I'll pop back later in the week for a proper one." He winked as she held the front door open. Flo's head spun from how friendly he was being. She couldn't detect an undercurrent to it either.

Flo was surprised to discover she was excited at the idea of Tom popping back later in the week. She chased away those thoughts by making drinks. Tom carried the heaters in, unboxed them, and plugged them in to make sure they were working. All without breaking a sweat.

"Thanks for helping." She handed him a mug.

"Glad I could help." He smiled, and Flo ignored

the way her heart juddered. "Can I do anything else while I'm here?"

Flo stopped herself before she could immediately turn down his offer. As independent as she was, she had to accept she couldn't do everything alone. "I have some curtains being delivered later, and I need someone to put them up for me. If I ask Emma for the number of the local handyman, is she going to give me yours again?"

Tom nodded. "I'm assuming you don't have any power tools or a stepladder?"

"No." She made a mental note to buy some.

"I'll pop in later." He drained his mug.

After seeing Tom off, Flo worked tirelessly organising the tea shop. A delivery of jars and containers came, and she washed them up as she waited for her food delivery. Once the supplies arrived, she packed them all away into the pantry. She had a painter and decorator coming around tomorrow to revamp the tea shop. The kitchen was fine, and once all the appliances were inspected, she could use the ovens. Within the next couple of weeks, she should be ready to open. If things went to plan, she would be in time for the October half-term, where the influx of tourists should boost her income. Flo felt an enormous weight on her shoulders when she thought of opening the tea shop. It had to be a success. There was no alternative. No backup plan.

It was dark outside as Flo said goodbye to the

engineer. All her appliances had been signed off, so the kitchen could finally be used. As Flo stared at the ovens, wondering if she should cook dinner in them, Tom strolled in.

"Sorry, it's been a nightmare day," he called.

"No worries," Flo said. "You don't have to help me tonight. It can wait."

"It's fine. Shall we start?" He picked up his toolbox and inclined his head towards her flat.

"Have you eaten?"

"No, I'll throw something in the oven when I get home." He followed her up the stairs and into the living room, where Flo had dumped the curtains and curtain rails.

"I have one of your pies. Emma put a couple aside for me at the shop. Do you want to share it?" Flo had wandered into the village at lunchtime during a brief gap between deliveries and appointments.

"That's my favourite. Mum makes the pastry. Shall I start a fire and then put these up? I'm assuming you've bought one for every window?"

"Ah. Well, that was the plan. Only I've miscounted how many windows I have."

"Easily done," he said, barely keeping the chuckle from his voice.

"It was confusing. Anyway, ignore the side window in the living room, and I'll order some more later in the week."

"Was this your grand plan to get me to come over again?" he teased.

Flo blushed at the suggestion. "I'll put the oven

on," she said, and scurried over to the kitchen. Despite busying herself, there wasn't enough distance between them to squash conversation.

"How's the coffee machine?" asked Tom as he lit the fire.

They spoke about their days, and Tom told Flo about a broken fence that had led to their cows escaping onto the road. All the while, he fitted the curtain rails in the living room and hung the curtains. As the pie cooked in the oven, Flo microwaved some pre-made mashed potatoes and mixed some gravy.

"I can cook," she reassured a dubious-looking Tom.

"If you say so." He'd finished in the living room and was having a break before he started in the bedroom.

"Do you cook?" she asked, wanting to know more about him. So far, Flo knew he was hostile to outsiders, but beneath it, he had a heart of gold and was willing to help anyone committed to the village.

"Of course. My parents taught us from a young age. They were keen to teach us how to use the produce from the farm. By the age of six, I could cook a shepherd's pie."

Flo smiled as she remembered cooking lessons with Iris. "Shepherd's pie was one of the first meals my grandmother taught me to cook," she said. "Although I think ours was technically cottage pie because I cried seeing the baby lambs."

"Ah." Tom nodded solemnly. "There won't be any

lamb sandwiches in the tea shop then?"

"No."

The sombre atmosphere broke as they laughed. "I'll have to cook for you sometime," said Tom.

Flo blushed. "That would be nice."

Silence fell as Flo pulled out plates. She was flustered and scrambled around in her mind to come up with a new topic. "I could do with putting in a new kitchen up here, but it would cost too much," she said and plated up the meal.

"With a lick of paint, and perhaps a new oven, it wouldn't be too bad."

"Perhaps. I'll add it to my very long list of things to do."

They took their dinners to the sofa, and Tom threw another log on the fire. Flo wanted to ask him to show her how to recreate his blazing fires, but he'd helped her so much already today that her ego wouldn't allow her to form the words.

"I know you've sort of mentioned it, but what brought you here, Flo?" asked Tom.

The question was out of the blue, and Flo blinked a few times as she processed it. "A lot of things, I guess. At the heart of it, I was unhappy in an office job, but I also realised there was nothing keeping me in London."

"That was brave." Tom was watching her with soft eyes, and Flo's stomach somersaulted.

"Well, I had some help from a bottle of red wine," she joked, trying to dislodge the butterflies in her stomach that his look had given her.

"I'm sorry for being so unfriendly when we met." Their gazes met, and Flo could see the sincerity in his words reflected in his expression. "We've had an endless stream of people turn up to the village and think they can open a business. Usually, they fail. As a community, we do our best to support them, but when it all goes wrong, we tend to get the blame. I'm afraid I tarred you with the same brush. I promise I have a heart of gold once you get to know me."

"I'm here to make it work, and if it fails, then I have nobody but myself to blame," Flo reassured him. "The coffee machine's working. You'll have to pop by tomorrow for a proper drink," Flo said as she took their empty plates to the kitchen.

"You do love to find an excuse to see me each day." Tom followed.

"No, that's not what I meant," she spluttered.

"I'm winding you up. I'd love a proper coffee. I'll drop by once I've finished my morning jobs."

"I look forward to it," the words slipped from Flo's mouth before she could stop them.

Once Tom left, Flo went to bed. Tom had left her bedroom heater on, so the room was toasty. She wrapped the duvet around herself and picked up her grandmother's diary to read another entry. It was late, and she had an early morning with the painter arriving, but she could spare a few minutes.

15th August 1963,

It's another hot and sticky day. The ovens have been

on all day, and I don't know how I haven't drowned in sweat. We opened all the windows, which created a small breeze, but it didn't do much. Also, the smell of the farm floats in with it! Mrs J says not to worry, as everyone local is used to it. Can you imagine being used to the smell of cow's muck? I can only imagine my mum's face if she had to sit and eat a slice of cake with the smell.

I baked another Victoria sponge today. This time, Mrs J left me to measure my ingredients. She left the recipe book out for me, and I've scribbled it down so I can bake it in the future for S. Perhaps when we have our own house. I can't wait. There are some cute cottages on the main road through the village. I'd be happy with one of those. Perhaps Mrs J would let me keep my job.

Anyway, the cake went as well as it did the first time. I think Mrs J was shocked, but she tried to hide it. She cut me a slice and put the rest out for sale. Every time I walked past the counter, I couldn't help but look at it. S came in and ordered it without even knowing I'd baked it! Said it was the best cake he's ever tasted and couldn't believe it when I told him I'd made it. He asked me to go to the pub again tonight, and I said yes.

This time I wore my yellow shorts and matching top. By now, everyone knows me, so we said hello and then found a quiet corner in the garden. We spent most of the evening making plans for the future, but I won't bore you with that. You'll find out soon enough. I'm so excited. I don't think I shall sleep for a whole week. This time in Cornwall has been more than I ever could have dreamed. I'm so excited to make this my home.

CHAPTER THIRTEEN

The painter arrived early, and Flo set about getting to grips with the coffee machine. It was similar to the one at her grandmother's old cafe, so she had some idea of what she was doing. Flo ran two shots of coffee through the machine and poured them away. The memories of weekends spent with Iris flooded back to her. A rich aroma of coffee filled the tea shop. Flo had carefully set out her vintage teacups below the machine, keeping a handful spare to display on the shelves with her teapots, cake stands, and bowls. Next to the machine was a selection of syrups, from everyday vanilla to the autumnal favourite pumpkin spice and, her personal favourite, a Christmas blend of cinnamon and ginger. Today, Flo opted for a soya caramel latte. The first sip was delicious. Once she was sure the coffee wouldn't poison anyone, she offered the painter one.

After much deliberation, Flo opted to paint the walls a boring shade of white. She wanted it to be a plain backdrop for her vintage china and scrumptious cakes. When she'd visited the second hand shop in St Ives, Flo had spotted a wall of framed vintage prints, so she was going to go back and choose some for her walls. Slowly, the tea shop was coming together.

Flo left the painter to it and disappeared into the kitchen. She'd promised Tom a Victoria sponge, so she ought to get baking. She also longed for the quietness that baking brought. Her mind was noisy after last night's conversation. The mention of cottage pie had unlocked a memory, which had resurfaced in Flo's dreams. She had been six years old, and her mother had been planning a visit. Iris had spent the week preparing, and on the day, she laid out a pretty dress for Flo to change into. Before that, they pulled on their aprons to prepare dinner. Flo was beyond her years in the kitchen. Without any instructions, she went straight to the fridge to pull out the ingredients, while Iris collected the pots and pans. They worked well together while discussing the things Flo wanted to tell her mother. She'd won a prize at school the previous week and couldn't wait to tell her.

As if it had happened yesterday, Flo saw herself standing in the hallway wearing her lilac dress at six o'clock, waiting for her mother to walk up the path and knock on the door.

"Why don't we sit down in the living room while we wait?" suggested Iris.

Flo shook her head, her feet not moving from the spot. She'd been a good girl all week in anticipation of her mother's visit. The children at school were taken on days out or bought new dollies when they were good, so Flo thought it might be her turn for a treat.

As the minutes turned into an hour, Flo refused to move. The dinner they'd spent so long preparing and cooking was burning, and the hem of Flo's dress was creased where she nervously played with it.

"She's not coming, is she?" her small voice echoed in the dark hallway.

Iris wrapped her in her arms. "I don't think so."

Even all these years later, the crushing sadness had enveloped Flo's heart as she woke from the dream. She wished so much she could go back and hug her younger self and tell her not to waste any more time on her mother. Perhaps she could have saved her from many more heartbreaks.

Shifting her focus to baking, Flo gathered the ingredients from her pantry and weighed and mixed. Flo could hear Iris's directions. *Don't over mix it. Add an extra sprinkle of sugar to be on the safe side. Have you greased your cake tins?* Over the years, Flo had made countless cakes, but her grandmother always had something to say. At the time, it had been frustrating, but now, Flo would give anything to hear that voice again. She'd left Iris's recipe book upstairs, not wanting it to get damaged during the decorating.

The ovens warmed the tea shop, and the gentle hum of the painter's radio filtered into the kitchen. Flo could almost imagine what it would be like when the place was open. There was a lot to do, like plan her menu and get the word out about her opening. At times, her to-do list felt overwhelming, but she knew the trick was to keep going. While the cakes cooled, Flo nipped upstairs to flick through her grandmother's recipe book and made a note of the cakes she wanted to serve. Victoria sponges and scones were a must, but Flo also liked the idea of a Battenberg, a lemon drizzle, and a weekly steamed pudding. As time went on, perhaps she could introduce weekly or monthly specials to entice the locals in.

Once the sponges had cooled, Flo whipped cream and sandwiched the cake together with a local strawberry jam. With a final dusting of icing sugar, she set the cake on a stand. It was white with pink hand-painted roses. Flo cut a slice for the painter and then put the rest on display in her refrigerated counter. It was The Cornish Vintage Tea Shop's first cake.

Tom popped in a little while later as Flo was rearranging plates behind the counter so she could easily grab them without fear of the rest toppling over. She'd painstakingly chosen ones that she didn't want to be on display.

"Afternoon," called Tom as he let himself in. He

said a quick hello to the painter and then joined Flo at the counter. "Sorry, I'm late. We had a bull emergency."

Flo raised her brows. "A bull emergency? I'll make coffee." The afternoon slump was hitting, and she could do with another caffeine hit.

"There was a weak fence and an angry bull. You can probably guess the rest." He dubiously eyed her display of pretty teacups.

"Funnily enough, I can't fill in the details, but I can guess it was a nerve-racking experience. Is this a common occurrence out here in the Cornish countryside? Should I put down some bull repellent?" She fetched a mug, assuming he wouldn't appreciate one of her delicate china cups and saucers.

"Are you teasing me?" The corners of his mouth lifted. "What's put you in such a good mood?"

"I baked a cake, and my tea shop is starting to feel like a tea shop."

"Wonderful. Are you busy this afternoon? Why don't you come back to the farm with me and have a chat with my mum? I know she's free."

Flo nodded. She wasn't the only one in a good mood.

"That sounds great. Do you want some lunch? I had some bread delivered this morning, and I could do with someone to taste test it with."

"I'm your man." He took his black coffee and inhaled the scent. "A proper coffee that I haven't made. This is a rare treat."

Flo made hers next in a pretty teacup. She'd had enough sugar that morning, so she also had a black Americano.

"Not bad, London. I thought you would be the kind to have a soya latte with some disgusting sugar syrup."

Flo rushed off to the pantry before he could spot the guilty look on her face. She made him a sandwich filled with meats from his farm and a local chutney she'd found in the convenience shop. The smell made Flo's stomach rumble, so she made one for herself.

"Your painter left. He said to say goodbye, and he'd be back tomorrow morning to do the final coat," Tom said. He'd removed the dust sheet from a table by the window and carried their coffees over.

"Thank you. It's looking lovely, isn't it?"

"It is. Won't be long until you have paying customers." Tom took his sandwich. "This is amazing," he groaned around his first mouthful.

"Everything is produced locally." Flo joined him at the table and bit into her late lunch. Tom was right, it did taste delicious.

They ate in silence, savouring the flavours.

"That was the best sandwich I've ever had," Tom declared, dusting crumbs off his fingers and onto the empty plate.

"It was very good. I made a cake. Would you like a slice?" offered Flo.

"I'd love a slice, but finish your sandwich first." He sat back in his chair, sipping his coffee.

Flo chewed her mouthful as she mulled over the question on the tip of her tongue. "Tom, are we friends?" she asked.

He laughed and sloshed coffee down himself. "Friends?"

"You know what I mean. You were so off with me when I first came to Cornwall."

Tom sighed. "I'm sorry for how I spoke to you when we first met, and how I treated you during those subsequent meetings. I'll admit, I was dubious at first. You turned up and tried to help a sheep, and ended up covered in mud." He paused. A ghost of a smile flickered across his face. "As I got to know you, I realised you're not as green as you came across. You're a hard worker with a love of good coffee. I guess you could say you won me over." He shrugged bashfully.

Flo's eyebrows arched. "I won you over?"

"I've spent my entire life growing the family business, London. Blood, sweat, and tears have gone into that farm from generations of my family, and there are businesses all over the village that are the same. Countless times, we have people coming here looking to start a new life. They have no idea what's in store or how to run a business, but they come with a large bank balance from the sale of a swanky pad in London, and they think that because their budget will stretch to a business, it will automatically be a success. I'm untrusting of new people, but you won me over quite quickly."

Flo nodded. She had nothing to compare Tom's

feelings to, but she could understand how it might feel to dedicate your life to something and see people waltzing in, thinking they could do the same just because they had money. "So, friends?"

His face lit up. "Yes, friends."

"Good. Let me fetch that cake."

As she cut the slices, she glanced at Tom. He was tapping away on his phone, so Flo took advantage and let her gaze wander over him. His skin was tanned from the hours he'd spent outside over the summer. His thick brown hair was sticking out in multiple directions, as if he'd run a towel through it and not looked at it again. He must have felt her gaze on him as he looked up and smiled as their eyes met. He had the most beautiful brown eyes she'd ever seen.

"How's the cake coming along?" he asked.

Flo returned to cutting the slices, her hand shaking around the cake knife. "Sorry, I zoned out. Do you ever do that thing where you stare at something but you're not really there? You're lost inside your head, just staring?" It was like an out-of-body experience, as Flo could see herself babbling away, but she couldn't engage her brain to stop.

"Just admit you were staring at my hair. It dried terribly while I was trying to wrestle the bull into a trailer."

"Yeah, it's awful. Looks like someone has raked their fingers through it." Flo groaned internally. He'd given her the perfect excuse, but she'd put her foot in it again.

Tom cleared his throat and drained his mug.

"Cake," Flo said, her voice a little too high.

"Did your grandmother teach you to bake?"

"Yeah. She brought me up alone, so I was always in the cafe. It's not easy keeping a child entertained while you're running a busy weekend lunch service, so she encouraged me to help. By the age of ten, I knew all the recipes off by heart, and could mix and cook anything."

"That's lovely. My mother's always been a good cook, but my dad's the baker. Every Sunday afternoon, after he finished the farm jobs, he'd bake a cake with me and my brother."

"I'm nervous about you tasting mine now." Flo picked up her cake fork.

"I'm sure it'll be lovely. The farm's expanded, so Dad hasn't had time to bake in years, and while Mum tries, they often come out flatter than a pancake." He chuckled, and the warmth in his eyes brought a sadness to Flo's heart. She'd have given anything as a child to grow up with a mother and father.

"Go on, try some," she encouraged.

Tom smiled his thanks and tucked straight in. "This is amazing," he said around the mouthful. "It tastes like Mrs J's used to."

"I think it's the same recipe. I've been reading my grandmother's diary, and Mrs J taught her how to bake a Victoria sponge, and I think my grandmother stole the recipe."

"Well, you've certainly done it justice."

"Thanks."

There was silence between them as they ate.

Once the plates were clean, Flo debated how to broach the topic of him driving her to the farm. Despite her attempts to embrace Tom's help, she still found it difficult.

"I can drive myself to the farm if you have things to do this afternoon," she said, stacking their plates.

"No, it's fine. I'll drive you, then we can whizz straight through the gates."

It did sound like it would make Flo's life easier, and she was determined to get used to accepting help. "Thank you. I'll bring the rest of this cake with us. The cream will go off, and there's only so much I can eat by myself."

Flo clutched the cake box tightly as Tom wound his way through the lanes to the top of the village. They drove up to imposing gates, which automatically swung open for them. The driveway was long, with fields on either side, each one housing different animals.

"The pigs are over there, and the chickens beyond that." Tom gave her a tour as they drove.

"It's lovely."

They pulled up outside the house, and Flo let out a soft gasp. It wasn't the lived-in farmhouse she'd been expecting. "You're not an average farmer, are you?"

"My family hasn't always farmed this land, but we have always owned it. Older generations preferred to live in the big house and rent the land. A few generations back, it changed, and my family farmed their own land."

Flo nodded as though it were completely normal. The house was a stately home and was substantial. Flo could have counted at least sixteen windows at the front. Ivy wound its way across the front, making way for a towering wooden doorway.

"Earth to Flo," Tom said. He'd stopped the car and walked around to her side in the time she'd been staring.

"Sorry." She shook her head and turned her attention back to him.

"Shall I take that for you?" he offered, signalling towards the cake tin.

"Do you promise not to eat it before you give it to your mother?"

"I was always taught not to make promises I can't keep."

Flo laughed and handed the cake tin to Tom as she climbed out of the car. "I can't believe this is your home," she said.

"I don't live here anymore. I've converted one of the outbuildings. My parents still live in part of the house, though. The rest is used as a B&B, and occasionally we host weddings. It takes a lot to produce an income to support a house like this," Tom explained as they strolled around the side. "We don't use the front door," he explained. "It's for guests."

Tom led her around to the back, where a stable door was open. Behind the house lay endless manicured lawns with a grand water feature and rose bushes surrounding it. They walked through the open door, through a boot room, and into a large kitchen with a table in the middle. The kitchen had original red brick flooring, which contrasted with the modern pale blue kitchen cupboards and dark wooden surfaces. The table in the middle of the room was made from dark oak, surrounded by benches, which looked like they would seat the entire village. A cream aga was billowing out heat as Claire bent down to put a casserole dish inside.

"I've brought a guest," Tom announced, getting his mother's attention.

Claire jumped and turned to face them. Despite leaning over a hot stove, her hair and makeup were still perfect. Flo brushed a speck of dust from her jumper. She couldn't remember if she'd even looked in a mirror today.

"Flo, how lovely to see you." Claire came over and enveloped her in a hug. The contact immediately brought tears to her eyes. It was such a motherly embrace, and it left her longing for Iris.

"Flo made a cake," Tom announced.

Claire stepped back and took the cake tin from her son. "How lovely. Would you both like a slice?"

"No, thank you, we've only ju—" Flo didn't have a chance to finish her sentence as Tom spoke over her.

"Yes, please," he said and shot her a cheeky grin.

"Are you sure, Flo?" Claire asked. "What about a cup of tea?"

"A cup of tea would be lovely, thank you."

Tom directed Flo to the table while Claire bustled around the vast kitchen.

"How are things coming along at the tea shop?" Claire asked as she set a pot of tea down.

"I'm hoping to be open in a couple of weeks, which is why I wanted to chat to you about supplies."

Tom ate his cake and sipped his tea while Flo and Claire discussed business. Occasionally, he chipped in with some figures or helped with logistics, but mostly left them to it. Flo agreed to an initial trial of their products and, depending on demand, she would tweak the order. Claire was lovely and wanted to work with Flo while she found her feet.

"I'm sure you'll be seeing lots of my boys as they pop in for cake," Claire said as they finished their business meeting.

"Tom already can't stay away."

Claire's eyes shone. "He always did have a sweet tooth. I have to go as I have a phone call in five minutes. Tom, why don't you give Flo a tour of the farm while she's here? What better way to learn about your produce than to see where it comes from?" She dropped a kiss on both of their cheeks and hurried away.

"Would you like a tour?" asked Tom.

"I'd love one."

CHAPTER FOURTEEN

"What would you like to see first?" asked Tom as they stepped outside into the courtyard. It was a pretty area with a bench against the wall, and hanging baskets filled with evergreens and ivy cascading down. In the corner were dog bowls filled with fresh water.

Flo thought for a moment. "I'd like to see your favourite place on the farm."

"Good choice. Come on." He led her to the car. "It's not far."

Tom drove past the house, down a small lane that was splattered with mud. On either side were tall hedges, the leaves just turning a crisp orange with the change of seasons. The road continued for a while, and Tom explained it was a private track, which bypassed many of their fields. Eventually, the road stopped at a wooden gate, and Tom jumped out to open it. Flo offered to help, but was relieved when he refused.

"It's not far," he reassured her. "Just across this field."

The field stretched out for miles ahead.

"It's worth it, I promise," he said.

Flo's breath caught.

"It's stunning," she whispered. They'd climbed to the highest point, and there was an undisturbed view of the landscape, right down to the sea. The sun was setting, and the sky was filled with soft oranges and pinks. Vibrant green grassy fields sloped towards the sea. The bright blue sky was reflected in the rippled water. To the right was a forest. It would look stunning in a few weeks once the leaves changed to burnt oranges and deep reds. Tom rolled down the windows, a soft breeze rustled through the car, and the gentle bleating of sheep carried in on it. The whole area oozed peacefulness, and for the first time in a while, Flo felt herself take a deep, uninterrupted breath.

"There's a stream that runs through the forest. It's magical inside. Growing up, my mum told us fairies lived there."

"I bet it didn't take much imagination. This is stunning."

"It is." He was looking at her.

Feeling flustered, Flo floundered for something to say. "Do you own everything the eye can see?" she teased.

Tom refused to meet her gaze.

"You do!" squeaked Flo.

He nodded.

"Is that why you like to come up here?"

"You're the only person I've ever brought here." His voice was low as he turned to her.

"I'm sorry for teasing you."

His cheeky smile returned. "I'd do the same."

"So, how much of this do you own?"

"All of it." He shrugged.

"Even the beach?"

"We own it, but haven't gated it off as a private beach. All the locals use it."

"I know where I'll be swimming in the summer."

"I'll pack a picnic," he said.

A warmth flooded Flo at the idea of going to the beach with Tom. In such a short time, he'd changed towards her, and Flo realised that he'd grown on her before she'd even noticed it. Now, as she sat beside him, it was dawning on her how much she liked him. As a friend and as a person. She was also attracted to him, and her heart raced each time he smiled, but she was determined to ignore it. Needing to distract her thoughts, Flo asked more questions. "Why is this your favourite spot? Obviously, the views are amazing, but I'm sure there are plenty of stunning views on the farm."

"It's the spot farthest away from any inhabited areas. I like to park up here, knowing that I'm the furthest I'll ever be from another person, and enjoy the quietness. Although I'm a farmer, I spend a lot of time in the office and talking to people. At the end of a long day, it's nice to disappear for a while."

Flo took in the view. There was no sign that anyone else shared this beautiful place with them. She let out a breath and felt a lightness in her bones. "I don't know if I've ever been this far from another person," she muttered. "In London, personal space is nonexistent."

"That sounds awful."

"It is. That's why I'm here."

"Come on. Let me give you the official tour."

Tom drove them back to the house, and they left the car to go on foot. He gave her a tour of all the animals. First, they visited the pigs, and Flo held back her squeals of joy when she spotted the piglets. She snapped a few pictures to send to Daisy so she could show Poppy.

"Let me know when your friend comes to visit with her little girl, and I can show them around," Tom said. He'd been watching her reactions the entire time.

"Would you? Poppy would love that. Daisy and I took her to London Zoo for her last birthday, and she adored all the animals."

"Of course. Come on, let me show you the cows. They're in the field, and then I'll take you to the dairy kitchen so you can see how we create some of our products."

The farm was impressive, and the way they treated their animals was admirable. Flo couldn't wait to bake with their ingredients. Tom took Flo through their industrial kitchens, where their milk was turned into cream and different cheeses. It was his mother's project, but the whole family was super excited, and Tom was helping his mother with the business side of it. He seemed to be juggling an infinite number of plates.

"There's a big market for artisanal cheeses," Flo commented as Tom cut her a slice of their latest cheese.

"I know. We're starting small with local businesses like your tea shop and the pub, and then we'll look at wider distribution." His expression was animated as he spoke about the future.

"I can't wait to serve this in the tea shop. The customers are going to love it." They shared a smile.

"If nothing else, I'm sure I'll keep you in business by popping in for a daily coffee and cake."

"I look forward to it."

"Evening," a woman called as she walked into the kitchen with a mop and bucket.

Tom introduced the woman as Eve and explained that she cleaned the kitchen for them at the end of every day. Flo said her hellos, and they left to avoid getting in her way.

"Thank you for this afternoon," Flo said as they returned to Tom's car. It was dark, and a chill was setting in.

"Are you having another of our pies for dinner?" asked Tom. He turned the heating up in the car.

Flo looked down at her nails. "I hadn't thought about dinner," she lied. Her fridge was filled with their pies. One for each night of the week.

"Why don't we go to the pub for something to eat?"

"I couldn't take up any more of your time," Flo said, although deep down she was surprised to realise she wanted to spend more time with Tom and wasn't ready to say goodnight yet.

"You're not taking up my time. Besides, we should celebrate since you've agreed to stock our produce."

Flo's stomach sank. This was a business meeting. Was the farm tour and showing her his favourite place on the farm a way to schmooze her? Flo felt like a fool. She thought Tom was being friendly by showing her around and trying to help, but the reality was that he was doing it so she would sign on the dotted line.

"I never say no to dinner," Flo said, plastering over her disappointment. Perhaps it wasn't Tom's fault that she'd jumped to conclusions. With a sickening feeling, Flo wondered if she was so desperate for male attention that she'd imagined Tom's help was anything more than business. She'd only had one boyfriend at nineteen and had quickly realised relationships weren't for her. Flo's deep-seated fears of abandonment had shown themselves, and instead of confronting them, she'd realised it was easier to push people away. Although she'd liked the boy, he hadn't fought for her when she'd pushed him away, and yet again, Flo was left with the familiar feeling of being abandoned, and she'd realised that to be happy, she would have to keep pushing people away.

The pub wasn't as busy as the last time Flo was there. Tom pointed her towards a table and went to order. Flo chose sausage and mash, which Tom had told her was an excellent choice, as both the sausages and the potatoes came from the farm. There was no escaping their enterprise in this village.

"Just a Coke for me, please," Flo called, not wanting to embarrass herself after a glass of wine. What if she slipped and told him she thought he fancied her? He'd probably laugh until the entire pub overheard. It was just business, and that suited her.

She sat in the chair beside the fire. It was a quieter crowd tonight, but the pub still felt cosy and welcoming. Flo could imagine wandering down on a cold winter's eve with a book in hand and finding a corner to wile away an hour or two. It would be a lovely way to ward off those lonely evenings.

"You've zoned out," Tom said, putting two glasses of Coke on the table.

"Sorry, it's been a long day, and the warmth of the fire is lulling me to sleep."

"If you'd rather go home and sleep, I can cancel our order."

Flo considered his offer for a brief moment but realised she would be disappointed to leave now and not spend the evening with Tom. "I'm fine, just a lot on my mind with opening the tea shop soon."

"I understand. Why don't we forget about business tonight? We're just two friends out for dinner."

Flo nodded.

"How did you spend your evenings in London?" asked Tom.

Flo watched as a droplet of water slid down the outside of her glass. She could lie and pretend she lived an exciting and full life in London. Instead, she sucked in a deep breath and met his eye. "I spent every night in my room. On my own."

Pity filled Tom's eyes, and Flo swallowed back a wave of nausea.

"I thought London was filled with fancy bars and extortionately priced cocktails?" he asked.

"It is, but I didn't want to be a part of it. I come from a small town in Surrey, and growing up, I thought I wanted more, but when more landed in my lap, I realised it was the opposite of what I wanted. On top of that, I lost my grandmother, and I was a shell of myself. I guess I shut myself away and spent all my time working." She shrugged to lessen the impact of her words, but Tom was no fool, and she could tell from the way he watched her that he knew the pain she had been through.

"Your grandmother sounds like an amazing woman."

"She was. I think she would have liked you. Iris would have a slice of cake ready before you even knew you were heading to her cafe."

"I hope you follow in her footsteps."

Their meals arrived, but neither of them ate.

"I want her to be proud of me," admitted Flo.

Tom reached across the table and took her hand.

"I'm sure she would be. Look how brave you've been, realising your life in London wasn't making you happy. You've packed up and followed your heart. The tea shop will be the beating heart of the village once it's open, and I've no doubt everyone will fall in love with you. You're going to be happy here, Flo." He squeezed her hand and let go to pick up his knife and fork.

Flo's fingers tingled where he'd held them, and she ached to feel his touch again. "Thank you," she sniffled and picked up her cutlery to keep her hands busy. "So, how do you spend your evenings?"

"I read a lot. After a day of being on my feet, it's nice to sit and lose myself in a book." A slight blush rose on Tom's cheeks.

"That sounds lovely. I've not read a book in ages. By the time I finished work, the last thing I wanted was to read more words on paper."

"I'll lend you some to see if you can get back into it."

"Thank you."

Dinner was lovely, and they kept the conversation light as they ate. They spoke about Tom's plans for growing herbs on the farm, and Flo ran some menu ideas past him. Tom suggested he taste-test anything Flo was considering. They ordered a dessert to share, and conversation flowed. Flo told Tom about Daisy and how they'd grown up together. It wouldn't be long until Daisy and Poppy visited, and Tom promised to send Flo some recommendations for child-friendly places to visit.

"I'll drive you home," Tom said as they stood and put their coats on.

"You don't have to. It'll only take me ten minutes to walk it."

"I'd rather drive you so I know you're home safe."

Tom opened the car door for Flo before he went around to the driver's side. The drive only took a few minutes, and Flo was too tired to keep the conversation going.

"Shall I drop in tomorrow for a coffee? Someone needs to keep your machine in working order until you open to the paying public." He grinned.

Flo didn't point out that she alone drank enough coffee to keep the machine going. "I'll see you tomorrow. Thank you for today." With an awkward wave, she climbed out of the car. Tom didn't drive away until she was through the door and had locked it behind her.

CHAPTER FIFTEEN

"I can't believe you're finally opening," squealed Daisy.

"I know." Flo nudged the phone with her elbow to stop it from slipping down the worktop. Her best friend beamed through the screen with her hair in a messy bun and her tired eyes shining. Daisy looked as though she'd rolled out of bed and immediately called Flo. The last two weeks had passed in a flash as the final touches to the tea shop had been made.

"I should let you get on. I'll speak to you soon. Love you, Florrie."

"Love you, Dais."

The phone cut off, and Flo rubbed together the butter and flour with her fingers as she suppressed a yawn. The sun wasn't even up, and she was baking in the tea shop's kitchen. She'd hardly slept last night, tossing and turning, worrying whether she had enough cakes for her opening day. Eventually, she'd dragged her weary bones out of bed and set about making more scones. Everybody liked scones, right? If she ran out of everything else, at least she could serve cream teas. Flo's mind quietened as she added the milk and brought the mixture together. She rolled the dough out on a floured surface and used a fluted cutter. With a brush of milk on the tops, Flo slid the tray into the oven to cook and set a timer. She looked at her grandmother's recipe book and saw the handwritten note reminding her to check the scones to make sure the tops didn't catch. Iris was very particular about her scones and took great pride in only serving the best. On a few occasions, Flo had left them in the oven for a minute or two too long, and Iris had refused to serve them. Instead, Flo had taken them home and put them in their freezer so she could get a scone whenever she fancied one. Flo had argued it had turned out quite well. With a final glance at her grandmother's handwriting, Flo closed the book and put it on the shelf above the counter so she could wipe down.

The timer went, and Flo took the perfectly risen golden scones from the oven and left them cooling as she ran upstairs to shower and get ready for her first day. Since it was a special day, Flo opted for a deep purple tea dress, which she'd purchased from The Cornish Vintage Dress Shop. She put on a pair of tights to keep warm and pulled on some flat boots, knowing her feet would ache by the end of the day. With her hair tied back and a small amount of makeup on, she looked in the mirror and smiled. This felt much more her than the stuffy business suits she'd worn.

Outside, the sun was rising, and Flo pulled her bedroom curtains to see Tom in the distance filling the trough. She recognised him from his cap. He'd been in every day over the last two weeks, each time staying for a coffee and trying a new item on the menu. Flo would miss their hour together each afternoon, but she couldn't delay opening any longer.

The tea shop was ready for customers. Tom had popped by one afternoon when Flo had been trying to hang the pictures she'd bought and had stayed to help. They were vintage prints of typically British cakes. There was a cherry Bakewell on one, a Battenberg on another, scones filled with jam and cream (she'd made sure they were the Cornish way before purchasing), butterfly cakes, and her favourite, a pink fondant fancy. They were all things Flo planned to sell, and the beautiful pastel prints added a much-needed splash of colour. Lavender bunting was strung across the counter as a homage to Iris's Lavender Tea Shop, and this tea shop's former life. A local artist, Zoe, had spent a few days carefully painting the shop's name across the front of the counter. It was beautiful with flowers twined around the letters. Flo had washed the floor so many times that it sparkled when sunlight hit it. A selection of her pretty vintage cake stands were set out on a new dresser in the far corner. Behind the counter, the shelves were filled with pretty teacups and saucers. Inside the chilled counter was a mouthwatering selection of cakes. Unsure what would sell the best, Flo had baked a large selection. There was a Victoria sponge filled with fresh cream and strawberries and with the perfect dusting of icing sugar, beside it was a lemon drizzle loaf with a sticky top, there was a small Battenberg, which Flo had cut to show the patchwork inside, then there was a fruitcake sitting proudly on a floral cake stand. A stack of scones was on the countertop under a domed cake stand. Behind the counter was a big blackboard listing the daily menu of sandwiches, jacket potatoes, and a soup of the day. The air was filled with a sugary scent, and Flo flicked on the coffee machine to make her first drink of the day. She wasn't sure how many people to expect. Despite dropping leaflets everywhere in a ten-mile radius, Flo didn't know how many people would turn up.

At seven o'clock, Tom knocked on the door.

"Morning," she said as she let him in.

"Happy opening day." He handed her a big bunch of flowers. "All your hard work has paid off." He glanced around.

"Thank you." She whisked them away and put them in a vase on the end of the counter.

"Are you nervous?"

"A little."

"You'll be fine. I already know your coffee and food taste amazing. Once word gets out, you'll have a queue down to the end of the road."

"Do you want a coffee?"

"You read my mind, and I insist on being your

first paying customer." He pulled out his wallet with a flourish.

"Thank you. As my first official paying customer, you can have a free scone with your coffee." Flo glanced at the clock and furrowed her brow.

"What's wrong?"

"The bread should have been delivered by now." Flo frothed the milk.

"Perhaps she's running late?"

At that moment, there was a tap on the door, and Tom sprang up to open it.

"I'm so sorry I'm late. The children's babysitter cancelled at the last minute, and it's put me behind," said Katie, the local baker.

"Oh, no! Don't worry about it. Why don't I make you a coffee to take with you?"

"I'd love that, thank you." In addition to running the local bakery, Katie was a single mother to a ten-year-old and an eight-year-old. She looked exhausted, but Flo recognised the happy glint in her eyes.

"How are the children?" Tom asked. Katie replied, and the pair chatted away as Flo made the coffee.

"Here, I've given you a reusable cup. If you bring it every morning, I'll make you a coffee on your rounds."

"You're a star. The bakery is shut on Sunday mornings, so I'll pop in and treat the kids to a slice of cake. See you tomorrow." Katie left with a big smile on her face.

"You're not going to be very profitable if you keep

giving away the stock," Tom pointed out.

"She's given me such a good discount on the bread that a daily coffee is nothing. Here's yours." Flo served him his coffee and scone at one of the tables. His eyes met hers, and Flo could feel herself in danger of getting lost in them until she was distracted by another customer at the door. It was Rosie from the dress shop.

"Morning," she called. "I hope I'm not too early, but I wanted to pop around before I open my shop. I've bought you a little present to say congratulations." Rosie handed over a neatly wrapped package with a big silk bow tied around it.

"You shouldn't have." Flo unwrapped the package to find three lacy aprons nestled in pale pink tissue paper. They were white with little cakes embroidered on the fronts, similar to the vintage prints Flo had chosen.

"They're beautiful. Thank you so much." Flo threw her arms around Rosie. They'd been talking a lot in the new group chat and had promised to plan a *Vintage Girls* Christmas lunch in a couple of months.

"I saw them at an auction last week and couldn't resist. It was an amazing lot. Anyway, I won't keep you. Can I have a coffee to go, and I'll have a couple of slices of lemon drizzle cake for myself and Matt?"

Rosie left as the clock struck eight, and Flo turned the closed sign on the door to open.

"I'd love to stay and support you, but I need to head back to the farm." Tom wiped the crumbs from his fingers. "I'll either pop by later or send you a message tonight to see how you got on."

"Sounds good."

With the tea shop empty again, Flo went into the kitchen to prepare the lunchtime soup. Claire had included some seasonal vegetables in her first order, so Flo embraced the season and set about making a pumpkin soup. Flo had hardly started chopping the vegetables when a customer arrived.

The next few hours were a whirlwind of customers. Flo found herself running back and forth from the counter to the kitchen to make sure she was ready for the lunchtime menu.

"Tomorrow, I'll do more prep for lunch before I open," she muttered as her feet throbbed and she prepared another cream tea.

By midday, the Victoria sponge had sold out and only one slice of Battenberg was left. Flo had been introduced to most of the locals and some people from further afield. Everyone was ecstatic to have the tea shop open and complimented her on how delicious the food was. Flo breathed a sigh of relief, and despite the weariness already setting in, she was ready for the lunchtime rush.

It was chaos, but in the best possible way. All the tables were filled, and people were asking for lunch orders to be taken away. Flo was barely keeping up with the demand. One mistake and everything would collapse. As she carried a jacket potato with cheese and beans over to a table, the door opened and Emma walked in.

"Wow." Emma stood still as she took in the scene. "Do you want a hand?"

"Would you mind?" Flo was not in a position to turn down help, and if she could afford to, she wanted to offer Emma some shifts.

"Of course not. I'll jump behind the till and run food. You get yourself back in the kitchen."

It took a while for the lunchtime rush to ease, but eventually just a handful of people remained, and Flo could finally catch her breath.

"Thank you so much for your help. Can I make you a late lunch to say thank you?" Flo offered.

"I'd love a sandwich and a coffee," Emma said, looking longingly towards the last few baguettes.

"Of course. Go take a seat, and I'll come over."

Flo prepared two sandwiches and two coffees and joined Emma at the table.

"You'll have to close before the school finishes. You don't have enough stock to feed the children and their parents."

Flo groaned. "I'll make more for tomorrow." Her original plan had been to open during half-term, but there was still a week of term-time left and she'd have to factor that into her baking plans.

"You'll find it gets quieter next week once people's nosiness subsides." Emma picked up her sandwich. "Although with food this good, it might not."

Flo had to admit it did taste good, even if she had made it.

"I hear you've been seeing a lot of Tom lately,"

Emma said between bites.

Flo spluttered as she swallowed her food too soon. "Who told you that?" she gasped and drained her coffee.

"This is a small village. Be prepared for everyone to know your business." Emma took another bite as she waited for Flo's reply.

"He's been helping me get settled and open the tea shop. I'd say he's just being friendly, but honestly, I think it's because I've agreed to stock the farm's produce. At the heart of it, Tom is an astute businessman. He knows if the tea shop does well, his business will do well." Although Flo did think they'd struck up a friendship.

"The pub stocks the farm's produce, but I don't see Tom popping around to Denny's every five minutes." Emma gave her a look as if to say, 'I know I'm right, so don't try to argue.'

"I'm not encouraging him." Flo sighed.

"Whoa. I didn't say you were. Anyway, Tom's a good man. You could do a lot worse. Trust me, I know all about the worst men in the village."

"That sounds like a conversation to unpack over a bottle of wine and dinner at the pub."

"Friday night?" suggested Emma.

"I don't know. It's my first full week, and I think the weekend will be busy." Flo chewed her lip. She wanted to see Emma, but knew better than to spread herself too thin on her first week open.

"Why don't you buy me dinner at the pub in exchange for my help on Saturday?"

"You'd do that?"

"Of course. Anything to keep me occupied and stop me texting my stupid ex."

"I want to hear all about the stupid ex on Friday."

"Deal." Emma held out a hand, and Flo shook it. They shared a grin before they finished their lunches.

"I should tidy some of this up and close before the after-school rush," Flo said, reluctantly rising from her chair.

"Do you want help?" offered Emma.

"No, you've done more than enough. Go and enjoy the rest of your day off, and I'll see you soon."

The last of the customers left, and Flo filled the dishwasher and switched it on. After the rush of customers, she had only a few scones left and a slice of fruitcake.

Once everywhere was cleaned and wiped down, she set about baking for the following day. Flo flicked on the radio and opened her grandmother's recipe book. She didn't need to read the measurements or check the oven temperatures, but simply having it open made it feel like Iris was with her. Flo kept listening for a knock on the door, but Tom never turned up. She baked Victoria sponges, lemon drizzle cakes, and made more scones. Flo made sure to bake extra of everything so she could restock the counter throughout the day. She also made some simple biscuits and used a pumpkin cookie cutter. The children would enjoy them after school, and hopefully, it was something that wouldn't sell out during the day.

By the time Flo flicked off the lights, every muscle in her body ached. She would be up tomorrow morning to do it all again, but despite the hard work, she was happy. A smile hadn't left her face as she'd measured ingredients, rolled out dough, and baked.

"I hope you'd be proud of me," Flo whispered into the darkness.

CHAPTER SIXTEEN

Flo's feet throbbed as she trudged upstairs to her flat. She wanted to collapse into bed and rest her aching body. Instead, she showered and popped a pie in the oven. After cooking all day in the tea shop, she couldn't face anything complicated tonight. Tomorrow, she'd plan ahead and save herself a jacket potato. A hot shower helped ease the tension in Flo's shoulders. She changed into her comfiest pyjamas and retrieved her dinner from the oven. The flat was warmer today with the heat from the tea shop rising, but she still switched on a heater. She needed to get to grips with the fire. As she ate, Flo pulled out her phone and checked it for the first time that day. There were a few messages from Daisy, wishing her good luck and a later one asking how it was going. Flo typed out a quick reply and promised to call her soon. Then she checked the *Vintage Girls* group chat to see lots of well wishes and a message from Rosie saying how good the lemon drizzle cake was. The last message was from Tom, and a swarm of butterflies flitted around her stomach as she pressed open.

Sorry I didn't make it back into the tea shop. Things got a bit hectic at the farm. I'll pop in tomorrow.

The butterflies dispersed at the simple message. Tom hadn't even put a kiss at the end. Flo sighed and put her phone down to finish her dinner. She wished she were eating something that didn't remind her of him. Over the last few weeks, Flo had thought a friendship had blossomed between them. Tom had grown to respect her and had been helping her get ready for the open day. Flo had learned to accept his help, and it had made her life much easier. Yet, a niggling worry had her wondering if he was using her to ensure the farm had another customer. Her phone beeped, but Flo ignored it. It was probably just Daisy replying. She finished her dinner while thinking through tomorrow's menu. The hot food had all been a success, so she wouldn't make any changes. Until autumn changed to winter, her current menu would be fine. Flo put her tray and empty plate on the floor and went to reply to Daisy, only the message wasn't from her. It was another text from Tom.

How was your first day? X

There was a kiss at the end of this message. The swarm of butterflies reassembled in Flo's stomach, and a smile crossed her face as she stared at the screen. From the moment she'd met him, he'd confused her, and he continued to.

Very busy! I sold out and had to close early. How was yours? X

Flo knew better than to stare at her phone, waiting for a reply, but she couldn't stop herself. There were a hundred and one things she could be doing. Her hair needed drying, there was a clothes wash to put on, or she could wash up her plate from dinner. Instead, she sat there, waiting for his response. Luckily, Tom's reply came almost immediately.

Far too long. I missed our lunch together X

Their routine for the last two weeks had been to sit down and eat together at lunchtime. Flo had enjoyed the company, and Tom had provided excellent feedback on her autumnal menu. She hadn't had time to miss him while she was working, but now she longed for their hour together. Flo chewed her bottom lip as she considered how to respond. During their time, Tom had imparted all of his knowledge about local business, and Flo had lapped it up. But they'd also spoken about themselves and got to know one another. Flo groaned as she considered how to reply. He'd said he missed their lunches together, not that he missed her. There was so much to think about. At least working in an office, there was a clear line between work and friends, but here, her relationship with Tom had blurred the line, and she didn't know where she stood.

I'll save you some lunch tomorrow. Just pop by when you have time X

Flo hit send before she could overthink it anymore. She hoped her message was enough, but not too much. To distract herself from waiting for his reply, she cleaned up after her dinner. Her hands ached from all the kneading and stirring, but she washed up the things. Once everything was tidy, she picked up her phone again to see that he had replied.

I look forward to it. What did you think of the book? x

Flo smiled. It had been a long time since she'd eagerly waited for a message from someone, and she'd forgotten the rush of happiness that accompanied a person's name popping up on a phone screen. Last week, Tom had dropped off a stack of paperbacks for her to read. He'd recommended she begin with his favourite. Over the last few days, when Flo could keep her eyes open, she'd read some. Instantly, she'd fallen into the made-up world within the pages and felt her worries ebb away.

I'm really enjoying it. Thanks again for letting me borrow them x

Flo held the phone and allowed her mind to wander as she waited for Tom's reply. She'd always been closed off to love, but that didn't stop her from going on a few dates and dating casually. She had a three-date rule, and then she would dump them to save anybody from catching feelings. For a time, it had filled an emptiness in her life until Iris had passed away, and Flo had lost all interest in connecting with others. Perhaps she could revisit the three-date rule with Tom. Flo shook her head. Why was she thinking about dating Tom? Her phone beeped, distracting her from that runaway train of thought.

Glad you're enjoying it. Off to bed now, night x

Flo swallowed at the thought of Tom going to bed. She wondered what he wore. Maybe he wore nothing. She shook her head. Clearly, she was delirious after the long day. She replied, wishing him goodnight, and took herself off to bed.

Over the last couple of weeks, she'd put some effort into furnishing her bedroom. A new wardrobe had arrived, and she'd paid extra for them to assemble it. She'd bought some fairy lights online and twisted them around the bed frame to cast a gentle glow. A new, fluffy rug lay by the side of her bed so she could get up in the morning and sink her feet into it. The room was beginning to feel more homely. On her bedside table, Flo had a vintage Tiffany lamp that once belonged to her grandmother, a framed picture of herself and Iris outside The Lavender Tea Shop, and beside it lay her grandmother's diary. Over the last couple of weeks, Flo had been too busy to read anymore. She'd found her evenings filled with poring over recipes, creating posters to announce the tea shop's opening, and when she wasn't doing all of that, she was reading the book Tom had lent her.

Tonight, however, Flo picked up her grandmother's diary and opened it to the next entry.

16th August 1963,

I have a secret, but I can't tell you! S made me promise not to tell. Does writing it down in my diary count? It's not as though anyone will read this. I don't know! I'll wait just in case. I sent a letter to my parents today. I should have told them over the phone, but I was too scared. They'll probably call once they receive it. I'm terrified of how they'll react. I should stop now, or else I'll tell you the secret. All I'll say is it was the most romantic afternoon of my life.

The cafe was busy again today. It's still really hot and sticky, so I've been going to the cafe an hour earlier to bake in the morning. When I got there, Mrs J sent me to the kitchen to start on the sponges for the day. She was in a particularly good mood and taught me how to make scones. I hope she'll let me continue working here. We were rushed off our feet all day. The village fair is tomorrow, so we've been baking extra in preparation. S has asked me to go with him, and I'm so excited. I've never been to a village fair before. It's not something we do in London. He said there would be animals, a dog show, and lots of cake. I can't wait!

S says I'll probably meet his family there, which I'm both nervous and excited about.

I hope they like me.

CHAPTER SEVENTEEN

Flo felt better prepared for the tea shop's second day of being open. Her dreams had been filled with memories of Iris, and she'd woken in a good mood. Katie had bustled in with the bread, and Flo made her a coffee to take away and slipped in a couple of biscuits for her children. Next, the postman arrived. There were the usual bills and flyers, but buried between them was an envelope. The writing looked like Daisy's. Flo slid the card out, and tears prickled her eyes as she saw the handmade card from Poppy. A barely legible 'good luck' was scrolled at the top with a drawing of Poppy, Daisy, and Flo beneath. Flo put the card next to the flowers Tom had given her so she could see it throughout the day. She texted Daisy to say thank you and promised to call Poppy once she closed that evening.

The first customer arrived before Flo had even

turned the sign on the door to 'open'. It was a local teacher, calling in for a cup of coffee to take to work with her.

"Do you sell whole cakes?" the teacher asked.

"I haven't thought of it, to be honest."

"When it's someone's birthday, we usually bring in a cake for the staff room. It's mine next week, and I'd love to bring one of yours in."

"I can do that. If you remind me the day before, I'll have it ready for you to collect." Flo handed over the takeaway coffee.

"Fantastic. See you tomorrow."

Flo jotted down a note to start advertising whole cakes available with a day's notice.

By lunchtime, all the tables were busy, and the hum of conversation filled the room. Although Flo was rushed off her feet, she was more prepared, so things went much smoother. Already, Flo recognised some of the faces from yesterday. Locals were back for another slice of cake, and tourists had popped by for lunch again. There was a sense of community building within these four walls, and Flo was excited for the future.

As the rush died down, Flo made a sandwich and ate it behind the counter as she surreptitiously watched her customers. In the corner was a table with a mother and daughter. The mother looked exhausted as she sipped her cappuccino. Her daughter looked to be around three and was similar to Flo at that age. With bright blue inquisitive eyes and curly hair. The girl sat on the chair with her legs swinging beneath her, eating the slice of chocolate cake she'd chosen. It was smeared across her face and fingers, but she was enjoying every moment. As Flo watched, the mother took a napkin and carefully wiped the daughter's hands. Flo felt an emptiness in her heart. She'd never shared a moment like that with her mother. Iris had cleaned her up countless times, held her when she cried, and celebrated with her when she had good news, but never her mother. For the first few years of Flo's life, her mother had sent a birthday and a Christmas card, but as she reached double figures, they became increasingly sporadic until they stopped for good. At ten years old, it was hard to understand that your mother didn't want to be in your life.

Flo jumped up and abandoned her memories as Tom's face came into view.

"Are you okay?" he asked.

Flo's mouth was dry as she mustered up a reply while pushing back the tide of emotions that the memories had brought with them. "Sorry, I was going through my to do list in my head." She gave him a weak smile, and from the furrow of his brow, it didn't look like he was convinced.

"Have you got time for some lunch?" he asked, tilting his head towards a free table by the counter.

"I've already eaten, but take a seat and I'll get you something." She ushered him towards the table.

Whilst stock levels weren't as low as yesterday, the lunchtime rush had still plundered Flo's supplies. She used the last of the bread to make

Tom a cheese and chutney sandwich. The chutney was a new one that Denny had dropped by that morning for Flo to try. If she enjoyed it, then she'd order more for the tea shop. It was a plum and port chutney, which would go beautifully with the mature cheddar from the farm. Flo was already considering what else the chutney would go with for a Christmas menu. With a handful of crisps and salad on the side, Flo carried the plate out and made them each a coffee. Customers were finishing their lunches and slowly leaving.

"How's your day been?" she asked, setting down a mug for Tom and a pretty china teacup for herself.

"Busy. My brother's off today, so I've been covering his duties, too."

Flo studied his face as he bit into the sandwich. His eyes were glassy, and he had dark circles beneath them. As usual, his hair stuck out in all directions, but somehow it was worse today. Despite it all, there was still a cheeky glint in his eyes as he looked at her.

"Don't work too hard," she said, brushing off the way her stomach flipped as their eyes met.

"Nor you."

Flo sighed. "It's a bit difficult not to with how busy we've been."

"I can help at the weekend."

Flo suppressed a smile. Tom was as eager as she was for the tea shop to succeed and wanted to help in any way he could. "Thank you, but Emma is coming in on Saturday to help." Flo was touched that he'd offered. Tom looked exhausted. The last thing he should be doing in his time off was working in the tea shop.

"Well, I'll pop by on Sunday," he declared.

"You don't have to, Tom. I'll be fine, and you have your work."

"We have some local boys at the weekend, which lessens our load. I'll pop in for breakfast, and if you keep me supplied with a steady flow of coffee, I'll sit by the window and only step in if you get super busy. Deal?" He held his hand out.

Flo chuckled, but nodded. "Deal." She reached over to shake his hand. Her hand tingled from his firm touch.

"And maybe throw in some cake if it does get busy," he added.

Flo rolled her eyes but continued to shake his hand, not wanting to lose his touch.

All too soon, he let go, and she busied herself by picking up her coffee. "What do you think of the chutney?" she asked, moving the conversation to a safe topic while she stowed away the feelings of attraction that had awakened from his touch.

"It's lovely." He chewed for a moment. "Quite Christmassy."

"Perfect. I'll put in an order for more."

"Have I inadvertently been used to trial a new item on the menu?" He quirked his brow.

"Yes, and I have an entire Christmas menu to plan, so expect more of it."

He sighed dramatically and rubbed a hand across his stubble. "If I must."

The tea shop was almost empty now, and Flo was itching to clear the dirty plates, but she didn't want to leave Tom.

He caught her looking around. "Do you want some help putting all this in the dishwasher?"

"None of it can go in the dishwasher. It's all too fragile." She shot him a guilty look, and he shook his head, but an amused expression played on his face.

"Come on then. You wash and I'll dry."

They gathered the dirty items and took them through to the kitchen. It was a small space, so Tom's hip bumped against hers as she washed. He took the role of drying very seriously before putting each piece away.

"Do you want to go out sometime?" he blurted out in one long stream.

The plate Flo was washing slipped from her hands and landed in the sink with a crack. She fished the pieces of china out of the soapy water and hissed as a shard sliced her finger.

"Are you okay?" Tom took the broken plate from her and set it aside to inspect her finger. "It's bleeding, but I don't think it's deep enough to need stitches. Where's your first aid box?"

He carefully cleaned the wound and wrapped a plaster around it.

"You didn't answer my question," he whispered, his gaze trained on her finger.

"We go out quite a lot," Flo's voice wobbled.

"I'd like to take you out on a date." He looked at her as he spoke, and Flo felt herself pulled into his hazel orbs. There was so much hope and emotion that she had to swallow back a lump in her throat.

A million different thoughts were flying around Flo's mind. She'd sworn off dating, but something about being with Tom felt so natural. It was as though he were the other half of her, but she didn't know whether she was looking for her missing half. She sucked in a deep breath. Unable to speak, Flo nodded her answer, and Tom's face lit up.

"There's a restaurant I'd like to take you to. Shall I book a table for Saturday night?"

"Perhaps not this weekend."

Tom's face fell before Flo could explain.

"I'm meeting Emma for dinner on Friday night, and I think this weekend will be busy in the tea shop. What about next weekend?"

"I'll book the table."

"Good," she said.

"I should go. I'm sorry about the plate."

"Accidents happen." Flo shrugged. "Will I see you tomorrow?" She unsuccessfully tried to temper the hopefulness in her voice.

"I'm away tomorrow and won't be back until Saturday afternoon. I'll try to pop by before you close."

"Are you off anywhere nice?"

"Depends if you consider a cattle auction to be nice."

"Ah. Well, good luck?"

He chuckled, and Flo felt a frisson of excitement that she'd made him laugh. "Thank you. I'll send you some pictures."

"Of the cattle, I hope," she teased, and he blushed.

"Only of the bulls. See you soon." He waved and sauntered out before Flo's blush had the chance to manifest itself.

On autopilot, Flo drained the sink, cleared out the remaining shards of china, and then carried on with her washing up. Her mind replayed the last half an hour, and realisation was dawning. She'd said yes to a date with Tom. Flo didn't date. They'd formed a lovely friendship, and she was about to ruin it all.

The afternoon dragged. It was Flo's first time open for the school-time rush, and while she appreciated the extra sales, her energy levels were low. At least the lull between rushes had given her time to do some prep for tomorrow. She'd thrown herself into the baking.

As soon as she closed for the day, she pulled out her phone and called Daisy, putting it on loudspeaker so she could clean and tidy while talking.

Poppy answered and excitedly told Flo all about her day. While they spoke, Flo cleaned the counter, wiped the tables, and swept the floor. By the time Poppy handed the phone to Daisy, the tea shop was sparkling clean and ready for a new set of customers tomorrow.

"Your daughter has inherited your ability to chat for hours on end," quipped Flo. She flicked off the lights and went through to the kitchen to finish tomorrow's baking. It was getting late and growing dark outside, but Flo had nothing to rush home for.

"She didn't draw a breath for a full five minutes."

Flo gathered the ingredients for a Victoria sponge. Yet again, she'd completely sold out, despite making extra. "I got asked out on a date today," confessed Flo. She focused on weighing the flour as Daisy's squeal echoed down the phone.

"By the hot farmer?"

Flo frowned. "How did you know?"

"There was chemistry between you, even if you were caked in mud."

Flo let out a noncommittal murmur.

"How do you feel about it?" Daisy's tone was serious, and the sounds of her moving about in the background had stopped.

"I don't know," admitted Flo. "A part of me is excited because I like him, and it's been ages since I've been on a date. But I could see a future with him, and it terrifies me. I was watching a mother and daughter in the tea shop today, and it got me thinking about my mum. It stirred up old feelings for me. The one person who was supposed to love me and care for me didn't. How on earth am I ever supposed to trust someone and think they'll stick around? I'm trying hard not to focus on it, but I'm scared."

"Oh, Flo. You've never settled into a relationship because of your fears. Please don't let your mum take away your chance to be happy and find love. You deserve someone good, and the right person won't abandon you. The hot farmer seems like a good place to start."

Flo beat the sugar and butter harder than necessary. "I know you're right. It's just hard for my emotions and fears to come to terms with it."

"You've got this. Enjoy your date, and we can have a debrief when I visit."

Flo nodded, even though Daisy couldn't see her. "It's not long now."

"The week after next. Poppy has Saturday night with her dad, so I thought we'd drive down on Monday, if that's okay?"

"That's perfect. The tea shop will be busy, but I'll put together some things for you and Poppy to do, and we'll still have our evenings together."

"We'll make the most of it. We can't wait to see you."

They chatted some more while Flo baked, but they kept to safer topics.

CHAPTER EIGHTEEN

By Friday night, Flo's feet throbbed and were covered in blisters. Last night, she had ordered a pair of memory foam trainers. The tea shop had been busy all week. Locals popped by for their morning coffee on the way to work, young mums met up for cake, and then the after-school crowd would descend and decimate Flo's stock. People came from further afield as word of the tea shop spread. If it continued, then Flo could afford to hire help. Things were looking positive, even if it was at the expense of Flo's feet.

Flo changed out of her flour-smattered clothes and into a long checkered skirt with a cream knit jumper tucked into it and a pair of tights and ankle boots. Rosie had styled the pieces for her, and Flo had to admit she had a good eye for fashion. The outfit looked lovely and was perfect for a cosy dinner. Flo was running late as she grabbed her coat and half walked, half jogged to the pub.

Emma was already there with a couple of drinks in front of her.

"Sorry, I'm late. I lost track of time baking," Flo said.

"I haven't been here long." Emma stood to hug her. "I got us both a gin and tonic, but with zero alcohol gin. Is that okay?"

"That's perfect. Thank you." Flo sipped her drink and sank into the chair, her muscles relaxing for the first time that day.

"How's your first week been?"

"Exhausting, but I'm adjusting. It's a big change to go from an office job to being on my feet all day."

"You poor thing, your feet must be shredded."

"I'm sure it will be worth it. Shall I order the food?" Flo pointed to the menu.

While Flo was at the bar, she caught Denny's eye and asked him to put in an order of chutney for her. She'd been surprised to learn that the chutney was Denny's husband's business. Despite her aching feet and tired eyes, Flo had spent her evenings this week thinking of her Christmas menu. It would have to be special to entice people out on those cold days when spare money was scarce. Planning the Christmas menu had also worked as a great distraction from her upcoming date.

"So, how are you?" Flo asked as she sat back down.

"Keeping busy. I split up with my boyfriend. He cheated on me, but we'd been together for five years. When I found out, I packed all my things and moved back in with my mum, but I don't know if I made the right decision." Emma wouldn't meet Flo's eyes. "I still love him," she whispered.

Flo reached across the table and squeezed Emma's arm. "I know it hurts right now, but you did the right thing. If he didn't appreciate or respect you after five years, he never will. I've only got to know you recently, but I already know you deserve a lot better. You're kind, caring, and funny. Someone out there is going to be very lucky to have you."

Emma nodded and swallowed before she spoke. "Most of the time, I know you're right, but then I have these weak moments. What if there's nobody else out there for me?"

"Then you're better off alone. You'd never trust him again. Imagine, every time he was five or ten minutes late, you'd be wondering where he was or who he was with."

Emma sighed. "I know you're right. I'm just struggling to be strong at the moment."

"Anytime you want to call him, call me. If you want to see him, come and visit me. I can keep you busy, and I'd love the company."

"Thank you, Flo. It means a lot." Emma's face lit up with a warm smile. "Anyway, enough about me. How's your love life?"

Flo groaned. "Surprisingly active after a long, and very dry period. I have a date next weekend."

Emma clapped her hands. "I can't believe Tom asked you out!"

"How do you know it's Tom?"

"It's obvious from the way you look at each other. Plus, he's always hanging around the tea shop." Emma had popped by during the week when Tom was having a late lunch with Flo. "You pretty much have daily lunch dates."

Flo scoffed. "I don't look at him any differently to how I look at you."

"You do not look at me like you want to rip my clothes off."

Flo choked on her drink. "I do not look at him like I want to rip his clothes off," she hissed across the table, conscious of the heads that had turned.

"Mhmm. So, where's he taking you? What are you wearing?"

Flo shrugged. "He said something about a restaurant."

"Find out where and I'll help you pick an outfit."

Flo nodded. "I don't know if I should cancel," she muttered, tilting her glass from one side to the other and watching the wedge of lime float around.

"Why would you cancel?"

"I don't date. Well, I do. I give men three dates, and then I end it."

"That's what London Flo did, but you're not in the city anymore. You've had a new start. Let this be the start of something new, too."

Flo nodded as she mulled over Emma's words. She had a point. Maybe now was the best time to try a new approach to dating. Emma tried to pry more details from Flo, but she had no luck. Flo either didn't know the answer or kept her replies brief. Eventually, Emma gave up and changed the conversation. They spoke about their plans for firework night. Flo didn't have any, but by the end of the conversation, she'd agreed to go to the village's firework display and promised to bring Daisy and Poppy along.

"I'll see you tomorrow," Emma said as she hugged Flo goodbye.

The walk home was dark since it was late enough that most people's lights were switched off and they were tucked up in bed. Flo was a confident woman, but in London, walking alone in the dark terrified her. Here, she felt safe, but she didn't dawdle and kept her pace brisk.

It was still warm in the tea shop, but upstairs, the heaters were needed. Flo glanced towards the empty fireplace and made another mental note to learn how to make a fire. She was sure it would be easy once she got to grips with it, but she hadn't found the time.

She changed into her pyjamas, wiped off her makeup, and decided to shower in the morning. Flo climbed into bed and picked up Iris's diary. As tired as she was, she couldn't go straight to sleep. Her mind was still buzzing from her conversation with Emma and her resolve to approach dating in a new light.

17th August 1963,

I adore this village, and I cannot wait to call it my

home. Mrs J gave me the day off, so S picked me up this morning. I wore my new white miniskirt, and S couldn't take his eyes off me. My cheeks were bright red by the time he walked me around to the passenger side of the car. He drove us up to the farm for the village fair.

We wound down the windows and followed the crowds. It was slow, but I didn't mind. Everyone kept looking at us and waving. All down the lanes, the hedgerows were blooming with flowers from pretty pastel pinks to buttery yellows. The sky was so blue, and there wasn't a single cloud to be seen. We could hear snippets of people's conversations and pearls of laughter as we drove beside them. The air was filled with excitement, and I couldn't wait to experience my first village fair.

Once parked, the first stall we went to was Mrs J's. The trestle table was stacked high with cakes and buns. I'd helped make most of them, so I knew how good they'd taste. We bought a couple for lunch and then walked around. There was a dog show we sat and watched. Hay bales were set out in a square, and S put his jacket down for me to sit on so I didn't scratch my legs. He's very thoughtful. The dogs were all so cute, and S asked me which breed I'd like. I pointed to a small fluffy dog called Snowflake, and S laughed. We stayed to watch a pig race, and then S went to help with the sheep. It was great fun, and a few of the local girls kept me company while S was busy.

Hold on, someone's calling my name. I'll be back in a minute to tell you all about the coconut shy and how S *won me a fish! He's keeping it for now, but it's our first pet.*

There's a car outside. I've just looked out my window and seen my parents. They must have received my letter. Wish me luck.

Flo was tempted to read on to the next entry, but her eyes were heavy, and she knew she'd regret it in the morning. She smiled as she set the diary down on the bedside table. Iris must have set some heads rolling with her miniature miniskirts in this remote Cornish village. Flo knew just the type since Iris had worn them well into her sixties and only stopped after a fall, saying she couldn't risk flashing people. There was something very special about knowing she was walking in Iris's footsteps here. It was a closeness to her grandmother that Flo had never expected to feel again. She wondered what had happened with Iris's parents, but she was too tired for her mind to mull it over for long. Flo had never met her great-grandparents, but her grandmother had always spoken fondly of them, so she couldn't imagine they had stopped her from seeing S. Something else must have happened.

CHAPTER NINETEEN

The weeks were passing at an alarming rate. It was already the day of Flo's date. Emma had come in that morning to help in the tea shop and had promised to stay to get Flo date-ready. Flo's new trainers had made a big difference to her feet this week. While they still ached, they weren't covered in blisters.

During the quiet moments, Flo baked as quickly as she could while Emma saw to customers. She wanted to finish early to give herself enough time to get ready. Already her stomach was a knot of nerves, and she'd considered cancelling countless times. Tom had been in and out of the tea shop all week, and there was never an awkward moment between them. Flo had to keep reminding herself that tonight would be no different. They would talk and enjoy some good food like any other day of the week. She took a deep breath to settle herself. Usually, baking eased her worries, but today it wasn't working.

Emma poked her head around the kitchen door. "Is Tom popping by for lunch?" she asked.

"I don't think so?" Flo's answer came out as a question. "Are we expecting him?"

"Not that I know of. There's only one bacon sandwich left, and I know it's his favourite. I would have put it to the side if he were stopping by."

Flo smiled as she remembered how excited he was when he discovered the new addition to the menu. "No, sell it to the next person who wants it. There's more bacon in the fridge, so I'll make him a fresh one if he pops in."

"No worries."

Emma left, and Flo went back to her baking, whisking the mixture a little too hard.

Tom didn't pop by for lunch, but he did text to say he was looking forward to seeing her later. The message distracted Flo, and she forgot about the scones in the oven, causing them to burn. She started from scratch and pushed all thoughts of Tom Evans from her mind.

The closing routine in the tea shop was much quicker with an extra pair of hands, but it still left Flo with just an hour to get ready.

"Get in the shower and I'll pick you an outfit," ordered Emma.

Flo showered as quickly as possible. Emma had switched on the radio and was singing along. The flat felt alive with company, and a niggling loneliness gnawed at Flo.

"You don't think the dress is a little too much?" Flo chewed on her lip. Emma had chosen the dress she'd bought from The Cornish Vintage Dress Shop. The one she thought she'd never have a reason to wear.

"It's stunning."

Flo took a deep breath. She would be brave in lots of different ways tonight.

Emma kept the conversation light and jovial as she dried and curled Flo's hair and did her makeup. Flo hardly recognised herself in the mirror. Her hair had grown over the last couple of months and was now below her shoulders, which Emma had styled in soft waves. Her makeup looked flawless, and the smoky eyeshadow made her blue eyes stand out.

The dress fitted as perfectly as it had in the shop, and Emma gasped as Flo stepped out of the bedroom to show her.

"It looks like it was made for you," Emma said, motioning for Flo to twirl. "It's stunning."

"You don't think it's too much?" Flo smoothed down the skirt and tweaked the bow on each shoulder.

"A dress that perfect can never be too much. You need a small pair of black heels. Do you have any?"

Flo went back into her bedroom and pulled out a box from underneath the bed. Inside were about twenty pairs of heels in various colours and heights.

"Are you a secret hoarder?" Emma asked.

"No. I used to wear them a lot for work."

"I know where to come when I need some heels."

There was a knock at the front door, and Flo felt her heart gallop in her chest. "He's here," she said.

"Come on then. Don't keep him waiting."

Emma held Flo steady as she slipped on her shoes, then passed her a clutch bag and her coat. "Be home before midnight," she teased and ran down the stairs.

Flo smoothed down the skirt one final time and went downstairs to meet Tom. Emma had let him in, and he stood in the doorway, waiting. He was dressed smartly in a white shirt, a black dinner jacket, and trousers. Flo was glad she'd chosen this dress.

His eyes widened at the sight of her, and his jaw slackened. He shook himself and met her gaze. "You look amazing," he said, his eyes alight.

"Thank you. So do you." She smiled, feeling like a giddy teenager on her first date. The sight of him had silenced her worries.

He held out his arm and walked her to the car. It was still warm, and Flo sank into the seat. The sun had set, and it was dark outside, but there was a cosiness in the warm car with Tom by her side. As they drove, Tom asked Flo about her favourite restaurants in London. She didn't have much to say since she hadn't been to many. There'd been a handful of work events or schmoozing clients, but she'd mostly blocked them from her memories.

"We're almost there," said Tom. They'd only been driving for half an hour, and they were heading in the direction of Port Isaac.

They rounded a corner, and Flo gasped at the sight. The harbour below looked ferocious in the dark October evening. Wind howled between the seawalls, and the waves crashed on the shore.

"We'll park here and walk down," said Tom, pulling into a parking space.

Tom helped Flo out of the car and held her hand as they walked into the heart of the village. He led her towards the Fisherman's Rest pub. It was beautiful, with ivy growing over the doorway and lit torches on either side.

"Are we going to be overdressed?" whispered Flo, peering through the windows to see what the patrons were wearing.

"Perhaps for the bar area, but I've booked the private room." He winked and held open the door for her.

They walked in, and Tom waved to the woman behind the bar.

"Evening, Elowen," called Tom.

Elowen waved them over. She was dressed smartly in a black blazer and a pair of fitted jeans. "There you are. I've set the room up for you. Head on through, and I'll be there in a moment to take your order."

Tom led Flo through a door into a smaller room. There was a fire roaring in the hearth and a table set for two in front of it. A pretty vase with a lobster painted on it was in the middle, with some bright chrysanthemums spilling over the top. Tom pulled out a chair and gestured for Flo to sit.

"I hope this is okay. You weren't expecting a fancy restaurant, were you?" asked Tom, doubt clouding his face.

"This is perfect," Flo reassured him.

"My family supplies the pub," confessed Tom. "The owner and chef, Finn, makes the most delicious food. I can't wait for you to try it. Actually, you might know Finn's fiancée. She runs The Cornish Vintage Furniture Shop."

Flo frowned as she thought back to the group chat. "Oh, this is Mabel's fiancé's pub." Although she'd spoken to Mabel through messages, they had yet to meet.

Tom nodded. "Mabel played a big part in the pub's reopening. All the furniture here is hers."

Flo looked around again and took in the weathered pine table, which fit so well with the surroundings. "It's lovely. So, tell me more about how the farm supplies the pub."

"We supply all the meat, lots of the vegetables, and even the herbs and seasonings. I thought you might enjoy tasting it."

"I can't wait." Flo's stomach rumbled. She couldn't remember the last time she'd eaten. "I wish I could take you to my grandmother's cafe. It wasn't quite as fancy as this, but the food was good, and the locals were like family."

"It sounds amazing, and although I'll never get to visit The Lavender Tea Shop, I think I can get a good idea of what it was like from what you're doing with your tea shop."

Elowen came to take their orders and talked Flo through the menu. She was leaning towards the lasagne, and Tom explained that even the pasta was made from the farm's eggs and flour. Everything had been thought of.

While they waited for their meals, Flo asked lots of questions about the farm and Tom's involvement. Tom told Flo all about his childhood growing up on the farm, feeding the baby lambs during lambing season, and playing hide and seek for hours in the fields.

"The farm almost fell out of our family before my dad inherited it. My grandfather—my mother's father—had no interest and left the place to his brother, who didn't have any children. By the time it fell into my dad's hands, it needed a lot of love, care, and financial investment."

"It must have been a lot of work."

Tom nodded. "It was. Dad was working for most of our childhoods, and all of my first memories were on the farm. When I hit my teens, I realised my parents weren't getting any younger, and I put my efforts into thinking of ways we could diversify to bring in more profit and to hire more farmhands. With Mum's help, we opened the B&B, started hosting weddings, and then we started producing our own food."

Flo was in awe of the man opposite her. He'd realised his family needed help, and he stepped up. "Do you ever feel like your life path was chosen for you?" she asked.

"In a way, but the additional businesses have allowed me to pursue some of my interests. I also run an initiative on the farm for children. We partnered with some local schools, and any children who are struggling are offered the chance to spend a few hours a week at the farm. It gives them an escape from whatever is going on in their lives, and we get some help." He shrugged.

"Tom, that's amazing." Flo shot him a warm smile, and a slight blush tinged his cheeks.

"I like to give back."

"I know what you mean. Despite working in a corporate environment, I still had some soul left. A lot of my evenings and weekends were taken up doing pro bono work. Especially after I lost my grandmother, it was a great way of keeping myself busy." In the early days after Iris's death, the pro bono work had been the only thing that got her out of bed on weekends.

"Cheers to being good citizens," said Tom as he held his glass for Flo to clink hers against.

The conversation moved on to lighter topics, and eventually, the food came. It was delicious. All the hard work that had been put into the ingredients and the chef's expertise shone through with every mouthful.

"What do your parents think of you moving here?" asked Tom. He'd chosen the steak and chips and had proudly told her how he'd planted the potatoes last season.

"My grandmother brought me up. I don't know

my father." Flo paused and pushed a piece of food around on her plate. "My mother had me young, and I was something of an inconvenience to her. When I was just a few weeks old, she left me with Iris. We didn't see her again until I was four. There's no mother-daughter bond between us."

"I'm sorry. I shouldn't have asked." Tom reached across the table and intertwined his fingers with hers. His touch lifted her mood, and she felt the deep sadness rooted within her ease a little.

"No, it's a perfectly normal question to ask. I think Iris would be very happy to know I was back in Cornwall. We spent many holidays here and loved every minute. I wish I'd been braver when she was alive." Flo sniffed. "Anyway, enough about me. Tell me more about your family."

They ordered dessert. Flo chose the cheesecake, and Tom went for the chocolate fudge cake. "It's my favourite," he said.

Flo made a mental note to bake one for the tea shop.

The cheesecake was amazing with a biscuit base that melted in the mouth, and a hint of cinnamon mixed into the buttery, sugary goodness. Then the top was fluffy and creamy.

"Can I try some?" Flo asked, pointing to Tom's cake.

He nodded and swatted her fork away. Instead, he got some on his fork and leaned across the table to feed her. They held each other's gaze as he slipped the fork past her lips. As the chocolatey goodness hit her taste buds, Flo closed her eyes and let out a soft hum.

"That's good," she said, licking her lips.

"The sponge isn't as good as yours," Tom said, still watching her mouth.

"How so?" Flo reached across with her fork to try some ice cream. Like everything else, it was delicious.

"Yours are much lighter." He shrugged as if it were common knowledge.

"Thank you." Flo felt a warm glow from his compliment. "Do you stock mini pots of ice cream?" Flo's mind had wandered to whether she could stock them in the tea shop over the summer.

"We have a few sample pots. Why?"

"I could stock them during the summer."

"That's a great idea. I'll run it past my mother and crunch the figures. Now, this is supposed to be a date. Can we stop talking about work?"

"Sorry. Before the tea shop, my work consumed my life, and instead of doing something about it, I've just allowed the tea shop to fill the gap. No more shop talk."

"Good. Shall we have coffee?"

They ordered coffee, and the conversation moved to Flo's memories of the village when she would visit on holiday with Iris.

"I must have seen you around," Tom said, furrowing his brow as though thinking hard enough would conjure up a forgotten memory.

Tom drove slowly on the way back as if he didn't want their time together to end. He pulled up outside and walked her to the door. Flo shivered as the cool evening air wrapped around her.

"I should let you get inside," Tom said, glancing behind her.

"Will you come in and light my fire?"

"Is that a euphemism?"

Flo spluttered, and a furious blush spread up her neck and across her cheeks. "No," she cried, hiding her face behind her hands. "I really would like you to light a fire. I've tried so many times, but it always goes wrong."

He chuckled. "Come on." With a hand on her lower back, he waited for her to unlock the door.

"I'm going to change into something more comfortable," Flo said as they reached the top of the stairs.

Tom didn't reply, so Flo turned to him. "What?" she asked.

"I'm getting very mixed signals here."

Flo realised what she'd said. "No, I really am changing into something more comfortable. Vintage dresses weren't made with comfort in mind. Sorry, I'll be back in a minute. Don't start without me. I want to make notes so I can light it by myself."

He nodded and left her to change. Flo put on a pair of navy silk pyjamas that Daisy had given her for her birthday.

"Better?" Tom asked as she joined him in the

living room.

"Much. I'm ready for my lesson now."

Tom carefully showed Flo how to stack the firelighters and kindling to allow the air to circulate. He handed her the matchbox and instructed her to set it alight. Flo followed his instructions and watched as he gently blew on the small flame to encourage it. Within seconds, the fire had grown.

"Now add a log," Tom instructed.

The fire caught, and the room already felt warmer. "I can't believe it was so easy." Flo shook her head and thought of all the cold evenings she'd suffered through.

"There I was thinking you were inviting me in for something more."

Flo laughed and turned. His face was so close to hers. Tom lifted a hand and cupped her face, his thumb trailing patterns across her cheek. Flo's eyes fluttered closed as her heartbeat whooshed in her ears. His soft lips touched hers, tentatively at first, but as Flo's fingers raked through his hair, Tom deepened the kiss.

It was over too soon. Flo's lips tingled as the world slowly came back into focus.

"That was nice," she whispered, offering Tom a shy smile.

"It was," he agreed and moved a stray strand of hair from her face. "I should go, but let me know if you have any more, um…fire-related problems." He winked.

"See you soon?"

"Of course." He pecked her on the lips before leaving. "Lock the door behind me," he called.

Flo followed him down and waved him off. She'd wanted to try her new fire-lighting skills and light a fire in her bedroom, but she wasn't cold anymore. Instead, she tumbled into bed and replayed Tom's kiss over and over until she fell asleep.

CHAPTER TWENTY

The date had been perfect, but that hadn't stopped the doubts washing over Flo once she was alone. She'd tossed and turned most of the night, dreaming of her mother. Flo had dreamed of her tenth birthday party. She'd been so sure her mother would turn up to it. Iris had helped her make a special invitation with glitter and banana-smelling gel pens. They'd walked hand-in-hand to the postbox and kissed the envelope before posting it. At ten years old, Flo hadn't understood why her mother had missed the party. Instead, a crushing sadness and sense of rejection had hit her, and she'd spent her party crying.

Flo woke on Sunday morning feeling as though a dark cloud was hovering above her. Doubts were creeping in over her budding relationship with Tom, and she didn't know if she was strong enough to ignore them. But there was no time to linger on it. The day would be busy, and she needed to compartmentalise those feelings.

A steady stream of customers poured in all day. Emma offered to help, but it was her mother's birthday, so Flo shooed her away and promised she would cope fine. It suited Flo to be alone and without anybody questioning her about last night. By lunchtime, the queue was out of the door, and Flo had sold out of Victoria sponge.

"Do you need a hand?" asked Tom, pushing past the crowd.

Flo's stomach somersaulted at the sight of him, but she was too busy to turn down the help. "Would you mind?" Flo said, in between making coffees and jotting down someone's order.

"What do you want me to do?" Tom washed his hands and put on a frilly apron.

"Can you take orders? If you can't figure out the till, write them down and tell people to pay before they leave." That was the way Iris had done it in her cafe, but she'd been very trusting.

Between them, they juggled the crowd. People were disappointed to discover the infamous Victoria sponge was out of stock, but Tom charmed them, and Flo promised to bake one this afternoon if she had time, so they could pop back before closing. They made a great team.

When the crowds abated, Flo made Tom a coffee and some lunch before she slipped into the kitchen to bake.

"I think you need to employ some help," Tom said. He was hovering between the counter and the kitchen.

"I do. I'm just worried that once the initial interest wears off, I won't generate enough turnover to pay someone." Flo whisked the batter until it was smooth.

"There's enough of a demand for you to be okay. The pub is always busy, no matter the season."

"I'll think about it soon. My best friend, Daisy, arrives tomorrow, so she'll be around to lend a hand if we get crazy busy." Flo poured the mixture into greased cake tins and slid them into the oven.

"Dibs on the first slice," Tom called before leaving to serve a customer.

Flo joined Tom behind the counter while the sponges baked. Without the distraction of customers and baking, she felt the prickle of nerves flaring.

"Hello." He nudged her with his shoulder.

"Hi." Flo turned her head, feeling shy.

"This wasn't quite the second date I had planned."

Flo swallowed a gulp. How were they already talking about a second date? "What did you have planned?" she asked, trying to mask the way her voice shook.

"I was going to ask you to the fireworks display next weekend."

A rush of emotion flooded Flo. He had thought of their second date. "I would have loved to, but Daisy and Poppy will still be here. You're welcome to come with us?" Did it still count as a second date if she invited other people?

"I don't want to intrude."

"You wouldn't be."

They shared a smile, which was interrupted by a customer approaching the till to pay.

"I should go." Tom glanced at the door but made no move to leave. "I promised my brother I'd help him organise one of the barns this afternoon."

"That's okay. I need to bake and then get ready for my guests." Although Flo was sad to see him go, the excitement of Daisy and Poppy arriving tomorrow took the edge off.

"I wish I could kiss you goodbye." Tom stepped closer. "I'll pop by in the morning before you open."

"See you soon." Their gazes lingered before Tom reluctantly left, squeezing her hand on the way out.

When Tom was there, he was like a wall between her and her worries, but as soon as he left, they all came crashing back.

The afternoon was busy as Flo juggled baking and another influx of customers, who she assumed had ventured out for a sweet treat after their Sunday dinner. It was a relief when Flo finally closed. She had a routine for cleaning and tidying at the end of the day, so she whizzed through it. Once done, she baked some more cakes, including a chocolate fudge cake, which she knew both Tom and Poppy would love.

When everything in the tea shop was ready for

the following day, she went upstairs to prepare for her guests. Flo switched the oven on for dinner and changed the sheets in her bedroom. She'd give her bed to Daisy and Poppy while she tried out her new sofa bed. With the fire blazing and the radio playing, she enjoyed pottering around her flat. Flo had bought some children's books and toys for Poppy, which she'd put in the tea shop once the little girl left. The place was feeling much more like home. She'd scoured local selling sites and picked up a secondhand lamp, a beautiful oak coffee table with a matching bookshelf, and a lovely rug. The living room felt warm and welcoming, especially now that Flo could light a fire. A few nights ago, Flo had unpacked Iris's books onto the shelf, and it felt like a piece of her grandmother was with her.

Once Flo had eaten, she picked up the phone to call Emma. She'd had multiple missed calls and texts, so she knew she couldn't put it off any longer.

"Hello," Emma answered on the second ring.

"Hi. I'm sorry it's late. I've only just sat down." Flo sank into the sofa and pulled a throw around her shoulders.

"Don't worry about that. Now I'm sitting comfortably, and I want to hear every juicy detail from your date." There hadn't been time to chat when Emma had popped in earlier in the day.

Flo sighed and squeezed her eyes shut. "It was perfect," she said and told her how comfortable she felt in the car with Tom and then about the restaurant he'd taken her to. "It was beautiful and so romantic. Oh, and the food was amazing. I've never tasted anything so good in my life." Flo's mouth watered at the memory.

"Okay, but what about the man?" Emma pushed for more details.

Flo threw the blanket off and paced the room. She still hadn't decided how much to tell Emma since she hardly knew the woman. It didn't seem appropriate to offload her childhood trauma, so she kept it light.

"He was as romantic and perfect as the setting," Flo whispered. She stopped by the window and stared out, reliving the moment Tom had walked her down the path and come inside.

Emma sighed wistfully into the phone. "You need to teach me how to find a man like Tom."

"Make an utter fool of yourself while moving your entire life halfway across the country," joked Flo.

"Hmm. Maybe I'll try a few dating apps first. Anyway, thank you for calling and updating me, but I need to go as we're about to head to the pub for Mum's birthday drinks. I'll speak to you soon. Let me know immediately if anything more happens with Tom."

Flo laughed and said her goodbyes. She threw her phone onto the sofa but didn't move. From what she'd told Emma, it sounded like the perfect date. Flo knew she should be feeling over the moon, yet her emotions were weighing her down.

CHAPTER TWENTY-ONE

Flo carefully picked out her outfit, wanting to look her best for Daisy's arrival. After much deliberation, Flo chose the dusky pink tea dress with a small bow at the waist. Poppy would love the colour and the swishy skirt. It was perhaps a little too nice for a day working in the tea shop, but Flo had people to impress. She pinned her hair back and applied a light covering of makeup, which would no doubt be smudged across her face by the time Daisy arrived.

It was still dark outside when Flo flicked on the lights in the tea shop and put an apron on over her dress. On her doorstep was a delivery of fresh butter, milk, and cream. The farm delivered dairy products the old-fashioned way. Flo put the butter by the preheating stove to soften before she put the other bits away. She retrieved the pre-baked sponges from the fridge and set about getting the ingredients for each of their fillings. To begin, Flo mixed the buttercream for the chocolate fudge cake. She combined the softened butter, icing sugar, and some rich dark cocoa powder. Once it had all come together, she added fresh whole milk until the consistency was spreadable. Flo sandwiched the sponges together with the chocolate buttercream and then spread it around the outside. The recipe had made two huge sponges, and the icing only just covered them. Even at seven in the morning, it looked delectable. Flo put the cake in the chilled counter with a fresh bowl of strawberries beside it.

As Flo wiped down, there was a light tap on the door. A wide smile involuntarily spread across her face as she spotted Tom on the other side.

"Good morning," she said, opening the door to let him in.

"Morning." He surprised her with a quick peck on the lips. "Coffee?" he asked as Flo stared after him.

"Yes. Of course. I'll make them."

"I can do it. I've watched you enough times." He washed his hands and took out his chunky mug and her delicate teacup and saucer. "Soya milk and caramel syrup?" He quirked an eyebrow.

Flo gasped. She thought she'd been good at hiding her usual coffee order.

Tom chuckled. "I've known since day one, London."

"Do you know how many black coffees I've had because I didn't want to admit my coffee order? And now you're telling me you knew all along." She shook her head.

He laughed and made their drinks with surprising efficiency for his first time using the machine.

"How many times have you watched me do that?" Flo asked.

"How many coffees have you made me?" he shot back with a cheeky glimmer in his eyes.

"I've made a chocolate fudge cake, but it's probably too early in the day for a slice."

"Can I take some for my lunch?"

"Of course. I'll make us a bacon sandwich." Flo switched on the grill and fetched the leftover bread from yesterday. "Katie hasn't been yet, but it's still good."

With ease, they worked together behind the counter to make breakfast and coffee. Somehow, this had become their morning routine.

They settled at their usual table by the window as the sun slowly rose outside the tea shop.

"Does this count as our second date?" asked Tom.

Flo slowed her chewing to give her more time to respond. "I don't know?" It came out as a question.

"If it were, then I could kiss you goodbye again."

"It doesn't have to be a date for you to kiss me goodbye," she whispered. Each time he mentioned a second date, she felt the pressure growing. Despite her resolve to ditch her three-date rule, they were growing ever closer to the magic number.

"That's good to know." He beamed before taking another bite of his sandwich.

Flo looked down at the food on her plate, but her insides were too stirred up to eat. Instead, she sipped her coffee and glanced at Tom over her teacup.

"Stop staring, you're making me feel awkward," complained Tom.

"Sorry." Flo blushed. She hadn't realised he could see her looking.

"What time is your friend getting here?"

"Early afternoon, hopefully. She's going to leave once the morning rush hour has passed. It's the first time she's driven this far with her little girl, so she's nervous."

Tom nodded. "I'll be around, so if they get lost or anything, give me a call."

"Thank you." Flo appreciated how much he cared, not only about her but also about her friend.

"I need to go. My brother's off today, so I'm overseeing the milking." He grimaced.

"I'll cut you a slice of cake to get you through the day." Flo disappeared out back and cut a generous slice.

She put it in a Tupperware box and handed it to Tom, who immediately put it down on the table.

"Come here," he whispered and wrapped his arms around her waist.

Taken by surprise, Flo steadied herself by resting her hands on his chest. She could feel his taut muscles. Her eyes flickered up to meet his before she glanced to his soft lips. As their lips met, Flo's eyelids fluttered closed, and she wound her arms around his neck to hold him closer. A weightlessness overcame

Flo as she lost herself in the kiss. Tom's hands kneaded her waist, and she inched her fingers into his hair.

There was a knock on the door. It was Katie with the morning bread delivery.

"I'll go," muttered Tom. He opened the door and held it for Katie as she bustled in with the day's bread order.

Flo knew her cheeks were flushed, and her lips were swollen. The lights inside the tea shop were all switched on, so it was more than likely Katie had witnessed their kiss.

"Morning." Katie's voice was bright and cheery as she carried the delicious-smelling warm bread over to the counter.

"Morning." Flo shook herself and went to help.

"I'll be off. Thanks for the cake," Tom said and strolled to the door.

"Bye," Flo called, but didn't look his way.

"It's been ages since I had any cake." Katie wiggled her eyebrows.

Flo feigned ignorance. "I have chocolate fudge if you want a slice?"

"I'd rather a six-foot-tall farmer who kisses like that, but I guess chocolate cake is a good second."

Flo did her best to keep the conversation flowing without bringing up the kiss again. She mentioned Daisy arriving today with Poppy and asked for any recommendations for children in the area. It worked, and by the time Katie left with a coffee and a slice of cake, Flo had endless suggestions for things to do with Poppy.

The morning passed in a daze. Flo juggled serving, preparing food, and baking extra cakes, as yet again she'd misjudged how much she'd sell. Daisy had texted to say they were an hour away, and Flo could barely contain her excitement. Her head still felt fuzzy from Tom's kiss that morning, and she wondered when she'd see him again.

Flo checked her phone. There was a text from Tom.

Best chocolate cake ever. P.S. Can't stop thinking about you xx

A swarm of butterflies filled Flo's stomach, and she grinned. Flo sent back a message to say she couldn't stop thinking about him either and suggested he join her, Daisy, and Poppy at the pub for dinner tomorrow night. Flo had decided it didn't count as a date if Daisy and Poppy were there. Tom's reply was almost instant as he offered to pick them up on his way.

"I hope you look like that when I message you," Daisy said, and Flo jumped, dropping her phone.

"You're here," Flo cried and ran around the counter to pull Daisy and Poppy into her arms.

"Aunty Florrie, you're crushing me," Poppy complained from under Flo's arm.

"Sorry." Flo let go and stepped back so she could look at them properly. Daisy looked tired, and her eyes were a little swollen, but beyond that, they both looked good. "It's so good to see you," Flo added.

"I wanted to leave Friday night when Mummy finished work, but she said we had to wait until today." Poppy tapped her foot on the ground, and Flo bit back a laugh.

Daisy nervously glanced at Flo. "Poppy, why don't you see what cakes Aunty Florrie has and decide which one you'd like a slice of?" Daisy pointed Poppy towards the counter.

"I thought she was at her dad's this weekend?" Flo whispered once Poppy was out of earshot.

"He let her down again. Then he sent a text saying he couldn't do this anymore and didn't want anything more to do with either of us."

Flo's heart broke as she saw Daisy's eyes flood with tears.

"How am I going to tell her?" Daisy's voice quivered.

"It's okay. I'm here." Flo pulled her best friend into a hug. "We'll both support her through this, and I'll help you, okay?"

Daisy gave Flo a watery smile. "Come on, we'd better catch up with Poppy before she goes behind the counter and serves herself."

As Flo had expected, Poppy opted for a slice of chocolate fudge cake. She peered through the glass dome of the cake stand to see which slice was the biggest and then pointed to it.

"Can I have a hot chocolate?" asked Poppy as she carefully held a plate.

Flo looked to Daisy, who shook her head. "I've run

out, but I should have some tomorrow. Perhaps you can have one in the morning when we open?"

Poppy nodded and wandered off to a table with her cake.

"Thanks for that. She'll never sleep tonight if we give her cake and hot chocolate."

Flo caught Daisy's gaze wandering to the cakes. "Do you want something?" she asked.

Daisy chewed her bottom lip. "Could I have a slice of chocolate cake, too, please?"

Flo settled Daisy and Poppy with cake and a pot of tea. Although there was still baking to do for the following day, she joined them at the table.

"How do you avoid eating everything before you open for the day?" Daisy asked around a mouthful of cake.

"You become a bit immune to cake after a while."

Poppy's little mouth dropped open at the idea of not wanting cake.

Flo asked them all about their journey. She wanted to talk to Daisy and find out more about Poppy's father, but she knew now wasn't the time. Closing time was nearing, so Flo suggested the girls head up to the flat and unpack while she finished downstairs.

As Flo went through her closing chores, her phone buzzed with a text from Tom.

Missing you. Have a lovely time with your friend xx

A soppy smile was plastered across Flo's face as she flicked off the lights and went upstairs.

CHAPTER TWENTY-TWO

"Is that all you have in?" Daisy asked, horrified at the sight of Flo's fridge.

"I have an online shop coming tomorrow." Flo had tried to get one at the weekend, but there were no slots.

"What shall we have for dinner?"

Flo peered over Daisy's shoulder. "There are eggs and cream," she offered.

"Two eggs between three of us." Daisy raised her brow. "How can you run a tea shop when your fridge looks like this?"

A laugh escaped Flo, and Daisy glared. Flo held up her hands. "Relax. I'm not that much of an awful host. I've got some bits in the freezer."

"Sorry, it's been a stressful few days." Daisy sighed and leaned her hip against the counter.

"What happened?" Flo pulled out a baking tray

and spread some oven chips on it, then she retrieved a pie from the freezer and put it all in the oven.

Daisy turned to check that Poppy was still engrossed in the toys Flo had for her. A children's cartoon played on the television, which would hopefully drown out their conversation.

"Sam was supposed to pick her up Friday evening. She was so excited to see him, and he'd promised to take her out for dinner. We packed her bag, and I did my best not to show how upset I was. It was getting late, and Poppy was hungry, so I called Sam, but there was no answer. I tried to convince Poppy she should have dinner, but she insisted her dad was taking her out. Eventually, I got her to have a snack. She sat at the window watching, and every time a car drove past, she pressed her little face to the glass." Daisy paused and Flo handed her a tissue. "It got dark, and I kept calling Sam, but he didn't answer. After a while, I think Poppy realised he wasn't going to turn up, so I took her out for a late dinner. We got so many dirty looks from people. Then we went to the supermarket, bought lots of sweets, and I let her choose a film when we got home. Every time a car drove past, she still glanced out the window."

"Did you hear from him?" Flo filled a glass of wine for Daisy and handed it to her. "I'm not drinking. I've got to be up early," she said.

Daisy took a sip before she answered. "He called at lunchtime the next day to say sorry. Apparently, it had been date night, and he'd forgotten. His girlfriend kicked up a fuss, and he'd taken her out."

Flo clenched her fists. "He's a waste of space, Dais. Poppy is better off without him."

"I told him he wouldn't be seeing her again until he could commit to being a father. Do you know what he said? Okay. He said okay." Daisy was crying now as she topped up her glass.

"Dais, listen to me. I know I don't talk about my mother often, and it's because it hurts too much, but I'm better off without her. She couldn't be the mother I needed, and my life was better without her in it. Poppy will be okay." Flo hugged her friend.

When she let go, Flo sent Daisy to the bathroom to wash her face and have a moment to gather herself. While she was gone, Flo checked on Poppy, who was playing. She joined the young girl, helping her to build the marble run. Poppy was so kind and gentle, and Flo's heart broke for her. Everything she had said to Daisy had been true, but there would always be a hole in Poppy's life. She might not realise it while she was young, but as she grew, it would become more apparent, and she would question what she did to make her father not want her. Flo knew exactly how she would feel because she had once been that little girl, wondering if her mother would turn up for her birthday. Every year, she was disappointed and brokenhearted, while Iris did everything she could to make up for it.

"Dinner's ready," called Daisy. She'd washed her face and changed into her pyjamas.

While Daisy dished up, Flo set up a fire in the

living room, making sure the guard was in front in case Poppy got too close. They ate dinner on their laps and watched television. Poppy was allowed to choose their film, and she chose a 2000s romantic comedy, much to Flo and Daisy's delight. They cuddled up on the small sofa with the fire flickering in the background. Poppy fell asleep halfway through the film with her head resting against Flo's arm.

"I don't think I'm ever going to be able to move my arm again," Flo whispered as the end credits played.

"I'll carry her to bed, and then I want to hear all about your date." Daisy scooped Poppy into her arms.

"Fine. I'll make us some drinks."

Flo heated a saucepan of milk on the hob. When little bubbles formed on the surface, she poured in heaped spoonfuls of hot chocolate powder. With a whisk, Flo mixed until the hot chocolate was a thick, smooth consistency. She poured it into two big mugs and filled the tops with freshly whipped cream.

"That looks amazing. Is it local Cornish cream?" Daisy asked. She sipped from her drink and ended up with a creamy moustache. "That's the best hot chocolate I've ever had."

"All the dairy products are from the local farm."

"Oh!" squeaked Daisy, before clasping a hand across her mouth. They froze, waiting to see if her outburst had woken Poppy. After a few seconds, Daisy deemed it safe to continue. "Is that the same farm that the hot farmer works at?"

"It's his family's farm," Flo primly answered, and ushered Daisy back to the sofa.

"Tell me about your date." Daisy pulled her knees up to her chest and balanced the mug on top of them. Things had been so busy that Flo hadn't had time to tell Daisy about it.

Flo recounted her evening with Tom. Daisy sighed wistfully every now and then.

"I can't believe you asked him in to 'light your fire'." Daisy laughed so hard she had to put her mug down.

Flo hid her face behind her hands and groaned. "I knew I shouldn't have told you."

"No, I love this. It's been years since I last went on a date, so I need to live vicariously through you."

Flo recounted Tom's kiss before he left, and the kiss from that morning. She already ached to see him again.

"He's coming to dinner at the pub tomorrow evening. Is that okay? I can cancel if you want me to."

"Florrie, of course it's okay. I can't wait to meet him and give him the whole 'I'll hurt you if you break my best friend's heart' talk."

Flo wanted to laugh, but she couldn't muster the emotion. "What if he does break my heart?" Her voice quivered. "What if he decides he doesn't want me anymore?"

Daisy wrapped her arms around Flo and held her. "Are you scared of him breaking your heart?" she asked.

Flo took a deep breath, sat back, and wiped her eyes. "I'm scared of anyone breaking my heart. My entire life has been one of people leaving me either by choice or by death. I don't know if I can invite someone new into my heart, knowing that one day they'll leave me."

Daisy rubbed Flo's arm. "Is this about your parents? I know you've always struggled with their rejection and your feelings of abandonment. You've never had a serious boyfriend, have you? I think the longest you've ever dated someone was six months, and that was when you were nineteen."

Flo nodded. The lump in her throat made it difficult to speak, but Daisy had already pieced everything together.

"Why are you in such a state now, though? You've been on dates before. Tell me how you feel, Florrie. Make me understand."

Flo sucked in a shaky breath. "I'm terrified that I won't be enough, Dais. I wasn't enough for my father to stick around, or for my mother to stay and look after me. My immediate default is to think people will leave, and because of that, I struggle to control my emotions. I'm not enough, Dais. There's something wrong with me, and people leave."

Daisy reached out and squeezed her hand, but didn't interrupt.

"A part of me is screaming to run full power into this relationship with Tom, but I know that would be the wrong thing to do. I'd become clingy and constantly need his reassurance, which inevitably he wouldn't be able to handle, and we'd break up." Flo scrubbed a hand across her face. She knew how that scenario would play out because it was how it had been with her first boyfriend. "The other half of me wants to run away, to end things before they go any further. I can't fear him abandoning me if there is no us."

Tears brimmed in Daisy's eyes, and she pulled her best friend into a hug. "You are enough, Flo. Don't you ever think otherwise."

"I like him, Dais. I've found myself imagining a future with him, and it's terrifying. At any moment, it feels as though he'll wake up and realise I'm not who he thinks I am. He'll see my weaknesses or whatever drove my mother away, and I'll never see him again. Risking my heart for a few months in the past has always been easy because I've never seen a future with them. I'm trying hard to be brave and to put my feelings to one side, but the more time I spend with him, the more I like him, and it's becoming increasingly difficult. Every part of me is screaming to run and to self-sabotage." As the words tumbled out, Flo felt like a weight had been lifted from her shoulders. All these emotions had been swirling around inside her, and she hadn't realised how deep they'd gone.

"I know you hate it when I bring her up, but do you think it might help if you spoke to your mum?" Daisy chewed her lip and played with the edge of the blanket.

Flo shook her head. "You know I've tried before, and it doesn't end well. She has no interest in me and has no desire to listen to me and give me the answers I need."

"I'm sorry, Florrie."

"I wish Iris were still here."

"Me too."

They sat in silence in the dwindling light of the fire, both with tears slowly running down their faces.

It was dark when Daisy finally spoke. "Florrie, how do I stop Poppy from feeling like this?"

"I don't think you can, Dais, but she has you, and you're the most amazing mother ever. We'll support her through anything that crops up, okay? I'll be here for you both," promised Flo.

"You're so far away now."

"There's always space for you here. Whenever you want to visit, you can."

"You might live to regret that." Daisy laughed.

"We should go to bed. It won't be long until Poppy wakes up asking for hot chocolate, and I need to open the tea shop."

They shared a final hug before Daisy helped Flo pull out the sofa bed. It took a few attempts.

"Goodnight, Dais."

"Night, Florrie."

CHAPTER TWENTY-THREE

Nobody wanted to get up on Tuesday morning, but Flo had to open the tea shop, so she built a fire for Daisy and Poppy and left them in bed. Her heart hurt, wishing she could stay with them, but she had to put her business first.

Flo was behind as she turned on the ovens and pulled out her baking ingredients. Katie arrived with the bread before she'd even turned the coffee machine on. "No worries," Katie said. "I can't hang around. See you tomorrow."

With the radio humming gently in the background, Flo went about her usual routine, with the noticeable absence of Tom. He texted to say he wouldn't pop by but looked forward to seeing her for dinner that evening. Flo was nervous but excited for Daisy to meet him. After last night's heart-to-heart, she needed to hear her friend's opinion before she risked her heart any further.

When Flo heard footsteps upstairs, she set about making hot chocolates. It was almost opening time when Daisy and Poppy wandered into the tea shop.

"Aunty Florrie," Poppy squealed and threw herself into Flo's open arms.

"Good morning. Did you sleep well?" Flo asked, but it was to no avail. Poppy's attention had already wandered to the mugs of hot chocolate on the side.

"Is that for me?" Poppy's eyes were wide.

"There's one for you and one for Mummy."

Daisy put a hand on Poppy's shoulder to calm her excited jiggling. "Yum. Come on, let's get you sat down, then I'll make you some toast." Daisy took the mugs to the table closest to the counter. "I tried to make toast, but you don't have any bread upstairs."

"Sorry, I usually have breakfast in the tea shop. I'll make you both something. Bacon sandwiches?"

"Yes, please. Can we move in with Aunty Florrie?" Poppy asked. She already had a big chocolate stain around her mouth.

"Let me make breakfast. You've got enough on your plate." Daisy went to fetch an apron, but Flo shooed her away.

"Absolutely not. This is your holiday, and you deserve a break. Enjoy your breakfast and then go out for a lovely walk with Poppy. It's only half an hour to the sea. Have a cold beach walk, eat some fish and chips, and bring me back a present."

Daisy's face lit up. "Deal. We'll bring you back something nice."

"Like a puppy?" Poppy looked up from her mug.

Daisy sighed. "No, not a puppy."

Flo disappeared into the kitchen to make breakfast as she heard Poppy's next suggestion of a cat.

By the time Flo brought out three bacon sandwiches and a coffee for herself, Daisy had convinced Poppy that Flo didn't need an animal as a present.

"We'll get you something nice," promised Poppy as she took the sandwich.

"Thank you." Flo joined them. She had ten minutes until the tea shop opened, so it would be a quick breakfast.

"I'm looking forward to dinner tonight. It'll be nice to meet some of your new friends and see more of your life here," Daisy said. Her eyes held the unsaid words that she promised to talk to Tom to see if he was worthy of her best friend.

It was another busy day at the tea shop. Daisy and Poppy left shortly after breakfast and didn't return until mid-afternoon. They'd visited Padstow-on-Sea and brought her back a beautiful pair of vintage gold stud earrings from The Cornish Vintage Jewellery Shop.

"We had fish and chips, but the seagulls tried to steal them." Poppy bounced from one foot to another as she recounted their day.

"Someone tried to feed them." Daisy looked pointedly at her daughter.

"It was lunchtime, and they were hungry. Look, Mummy bought me a toy seagull." Poppy held up the cuddly toy and told Flo how she had chosen him. "Can I have some cake?" she asked, barely stopping for breath.

Flo looked to Daisy. "Not today. We're going out for dinner tonight. Come on, let's get you in the bath, then we can do your hair."

Poppy reluctantly went upstairs. As she disappeared through the door, Daisy turned back to Flo. "Save me a slice of cake for when Poppy's in bed tonight." She winked before disappearing up the stairs.

By the time Flo closed the tea shop, Daisy and Poppy were ready to leave. Poppy wore a pretty chequered dress with burgundy tights and little Dr. Martens. Daisy had recreated Poppy's outfit with a chequered pinafore over a long-sleeve black top and matching tights with her own Dr. Martens.

"You both look adorable. Stand in front of the fireplace, and I'll get a picture," instructed Flo.

"Mummy says we're going to give you a makeover," Poppy said as Daisy positioned her for the photograph.

"We thought we'd help you get ready," Daisy said.

It took an hour for Daisy and Poppy to dry and style Flo's hair. Daisy curled each piece, and with Poppy's help, she pinned the curls so they held. Although truthfully, Poppy was more of a hindrance than a help. Then they did her makeup, and more than a few times, Flo flinched as Poppy came at her with a mascara brush. Thankfully, Daisy swooped in and took it from her. Eventually, Poppy settled on Flo's lap and asked her about all the cakes she baked.

"We've chosen your outfit," Poppy told her as Daisy used some setting spray.

Flo glanced nervously at them. "I love your matching outfits, but you've not got me one, have you?"

"No, although you would look good in this." Daisy glanced at her outfit. "We got talking to the lovely lady in The Cornish Vintage Jewellery Shop, and she told us about a vintage dress shop, so we stopped by on our way home and picked up something." Daisy handed over a bag. "I wanted to say thank you for always being my biggest support. Since the day I found out I was pregnant, you've been there for me. I'll never be able to repay your help over the years, but I want you to know how much it means."

Flo sniffed and wiped the corner of her eye. She pulled out a piece of clothing wrapped in pale tissue paper. Even through the paper, Flo could see the vibrant orange of the garment. She undid it and gasped at the tangerine-coloured 60s mini dress.

"I know it's not your usual style," Daisy said.

"No, but it was Iris's. She had this dress." The Mod-style dress was short with cap sleeves and a belt around the waist.

"Do you remember when she turned up at your parents' evening wearing it?"

Flo giggled. Not a single person had concentrated

that night as hushed voices all discussed Iris's outfit.

"Go put it on," Daisy insisted.

The dress fitted Flo perfectly and ended mid-thigh. She was much shorter than Iris.

"Here are some tights." Daisy handed her some woollen black tights. "We thought you could borrow my spare Dr. Martens to dress it down."

Poppy nodded in agreement.

It was a cold evening, and Poppy was already tired from the day's excitement, so Daisy drove them to the pub.

"It looks like something from a fairytale," she remarked as they walked in.

The fire roared in the background, and the hum of conversation filled the room. Denny waved as they walked in and pulled a funny face at Poppy.

"Flo," Emma shouted across the room and beckoned them towards the empty table she was sitting at.

A few heads turned, and people greeted her as they walked by.

Flo introduced everyone and went to order some drinks. There was no sign of Tom yet, so they held off ordering food. Emma and Daisy got on immediately, and Poppy was happily colouring in with the book and crayons Daisy had brought. Flo sank into her seat and enjoyed the moment. It was a relief to see her best friend so relaxed. Daisy worked hard to give Poppy a good life and often forgot to look after herself. Flo always worried about her, but even more so now, she was so far away.

"Is that him?" Daisy hissed in her ear, and Flo jumped.

Tom had just walked through the pub door looking as handsome as ever. As Flo's eyes fell on him, he found hers and they shared a smile. Tom strolled over, and Flo spotted somebody behind him. A man similar to Tom, but perhaps a little fairer, followed him to the table.

"Good evening," he said.

"Hello."

"Is this the girl you won't shut up about?" asked the man shadowing Tom.

"Flo, this is my brother, Will."

"Lovely to meet you." Flo stood to greet the man. Flo introduced everyone at the table and patted the empty seat beside her for Tom to slip into. Will took the seat next to Daisy.

Flo turned to Tom. "You talk about me?" she asked.

"Quite often," he admitted, a soft blush rising on his cheeks.

"All good things, I hope."

"Only ever good things." He pecked her on the lips. Flo was shocked that he'd done it in front of so many people. Her lips tingled, and she longed to pull him back for more, but people were already looking.

Emma pulled out a notepad and took down everyone's food orders before she went to the bar.

"She's spent too long at the tea shop," remarked Tom.

"I know. I ought to officially offer her a job."

"Aunty Florrie runs a tea shop," Poppy said. She'd put her colouring to one side and was keen to join the conversation. "And my mummy works at a hotel as their reception."

"Receptionist, darling," Daisy corrected her. "But I'm also training to be a dental nurse." Daisy wasn't the shy type, so it struck Flo as odd when she shot a shy smile towards Will.

"We're both farmers," Tom said, pointing to himself and Will.

Poppy gasped and leaned forward. "Actual farmers? With animals?"

"Lots of animals. We have sheep, cows, pigs, horses, chickens, and a few other furry creatures," Will said.

"Would you like a tour of the farm while you're here?" offered Tom.

Poppy's head snapped to Daisy with big, round, pleading eyes. "If that's okay with Tom and Will, then we can go," said Daisy.

"Are you free tomorrow?" asked Will.

Flo raised her brow. She'd expected Tom to offer the tour, not his brother. "Did you put him up to this?" she whispered as Will and Daisy made plans for the following day.

"No, I hadn't even mentioned it to him."

Dinner was delicious, and everyone got on wonderfully. Daisy managed a few chats with Tom, and Flo did her best to listen in, despite being in the middle of a conversation with Emma. Eventually,

Poppy's eyes drooped, and they called it a night. Will carried Poppy to the car and helped Daisy strap her in.

Tom pulled Flo to one side. "Text me to let me know you're home safely."

His arms wrapped around her waist, and Flo shivered. "I will," she promised.

He kissed her before walking her to the car. Flo climbed in beside Daisy with a huge grin and flushed cheeks. She could still feel the ghost of his lips against hers.

"Goodnight," called Tom as he closed her door, careful not to slam it and wake Poppy.

They drove a few minutes down the road before either of them spoke. The dark lanes wound in front of them, and both women let out a giggle.

"Tom seems lovely," Daisy said, pulling the car over.

Flo bit the inside of her cheek. "Do you think so?" she asked, her voice small in the darkness shrouding them.

Daisy gathered her hands in hers. "I do. If you're going to risk your heart, then I think he's worth it."

"And what about Will?" Flo smirked.

"What about him?" Daisy let go of Flo's hands and put the car into drive to pull away.

"I know you like him."

Daisy didn't say anything until she parked up outside the cottage. "I like him, but I'm a bit too old for a holiday romance, especially with a four-year-old in tow. It's okay. Perhaps when Poppy goes off to university, I'll join one of those apps or however you meet people in fourteen years."

Flo laughed and clamped a hand over her mouth as she checked that Poppy was still sleeping. "Well, there's nothing stopping you from flirting with him during tomorrow's tour. I can always look after Poppy for an evening if you decide you do want a holiday fling."

CHAPTER TWENTY-FOUR

"I can't believe it's our last night," Daisy huffed as she helped Poppy pull on a pair of gloves.

"It's gone so fast," Flo agreed.

"I don't want to go home," complained Poppy.

As they all piled on layers of clothes, Daisy did her best to console Poppy and promised they could visit again over Christmas.

By the time they left, it was dark outside, and the air was smoky from the bonfire at the bottom of the village. It was the annual Bonfire Night celebration, and the village was out to celebrate. Children dressed in Halloween outfits ran around the empty streets, safe since the main road was closed. People strolled around with buckets of sweets, handing them out to the children. Poppy's pockets were filled by the time they got halfway down the road. People stopped to say hello and promised to pop by the tea shop soon. Flo reminded them she would be closed tomorrow but promised to see them Sunday morning.

"You're thriving here," Daisy said.

"That drunken offer I put in on the tea shop was the best decision I've ever made."

As they reached the bottom of the village, they went through a gate into a big field. It was one of the Evanses' fields. They were hosting the evening's events, and they certainly knew how to put on a show. Stalls surrounded the perimeter of the field, selling everything from sticky toffee apples to sparklers. Tom had offered Flo a stall, but she had declined, wanting to enjoy a night off with Daisy and Poppy before they went home. There were stalls of drinks, from hot tea to mulled wine. Sausages were being cooked on open fires, and mince pies were served with fresh, thick cream. Flo's mouth watered at the sights and smells.

"Can we have a toffee apple?" asked Poppy, gazing longingly at a display of them.

Flo chuckled as she saw Daisy pull a face.

"Do you know how many fillings get pulled out every year from toffee apples?" asked Daisy, her hands on her hips.

"Poppy doesn't have any fillings."

"No, but we do, and if Poppy has a toffee apple, she won't be able to finish it, which means I'll be forced to."

"I could always finish it for you," Will piped up and threw an arm around Daisy's shoulders.

"Absolutely not. I'll be finishing it. I love a toffee apple."

Flo watched as Daisy leaned into Will's embrace. Earlier in the week, Daisy and Poppy had toured the farm with Will. Daisy had never told Flo exactly what had happened, but she'd come home and hadn't stopped smiling until she went to sleep.

Will treated them each to a toffee apple and helped Poppy unwrap hers. Flo wandered ahead to allow them some time to talk while she browsed the stalls. There was one selling hats, which drew Flo's attention.

"They're made from our sheep's wool," Tom said, making her jump.

Flo chewed the food in her mouth before she spoke. "Don't creep up on me like that. I could have lost a tooth."

"Sorry." He held up his hands. "Do you want a hat? Your head must be cold."

Truthfully, Flo hadn't worn a hat because she hadn't wanted to mess up her hair. "It is a little cold."

Tom picked up a blue bobble hat, which matched his. "Just this, please," he said and pulled out his wallet.

"I can get it," argued Flo, delving into her pocket. Her sticky fingers slowed her down, and he'd paid before she could get her card out.

Tom took out his phone and snapped a selfie in their matching headwear. "You can treat me to some mulled cider instead." He cocked his head towards the next stall.

Flo glanced back to see Daisy laughing at something Will had said. "Come on, let's go," she said and linked her arm through Tom's.

With mulled ciders in hand and matching hats, Flo and Tom wandered around. A crowd was gathering for the raffle Claire was holding. Flo had donated a cake of the winner's choice, and she was excited to see who won. They stood at the edge, and the others joined them.

"I can't see," complained Poppy.

Tom lifted her onto his shoulders so she could watch. Flo decided not to point out the bits of toffee now clinging to his hair.

Daisy leaned in to whisper to Flo. "Do you mind if Will and I go for a quick drink?"

Flo had wanted to spend the evening with Tom, but she knew they had plenty of time to do that. This was Daisy's last chance to be single and carefree. "Of course. Call me if you can't find us."

"Will likes her," Tom said as they watched them walk off hand-in-hand.

"I've not seen her like this with a man since before she had Poppy."

The raffle started, which put an end to their conversation. Tom held her hand and rubbed circles with his thumb. The village came to life as local produce was won. Emma stood on the other side of the crowd next to a tall, darker-haired man, who she seemed to be enamoured with. Flo winked, and Emma laughed.

"What are you doing tomorrow?" asked Tom.

"The tea shop is closed, so I'm going to have a leisurely breakfast with Daisy and Poppy before they head home."

"We have our annual Halloween party tomorrow. Will you come?"

Flo chewed on her lip. She wasn't much of a partygoer.

"It's not as awful as it sounds, I promise. The first half is quite formal, as my parents host, but then Will and I move the party to one of the barns. Emma's probably already coming."

Flo looked up and saw the plea in his expression. He wanted her there. "Okay," she agreed.

"It's fancy dress."

"You could have told me that *before* I agreed to go." She swatted his arm, and Poppy giggled from her perch.

"I knew you'd say no if I told you." His eyes glowed in the light of the bonfire.

"That's sneaky."

"It worked, though." His voice dropped to a whisper. "I can't wait to see what you dress up in."

Flo blushed and glanced around to make sure nobody had heard him. "At this rate, I'll have to fashion a bin bag into something spooky. Where am I supposed to get a Halloween outfit from? It's been and gone. Who has a Halloween party this late?"

"It's the weekend closest to Halloween," protested Tom.

Flo huffed. She couldn't argue with that logic.

"Ask Emma. She comes every year, so she's

probably got her old outfits stashed away somewhere."

Flo groaned, dreading what outfits Emma would produce. She wondered how quickly she could order something to be delivered, but it was already past the cutoff point for next-day delivery.

It was then that Poppy announced she'd finished her apple and needed a wee. They pushed their way through the throngs of people over to where the toilets were set up at the edge of the field.

"Where's Mummy?" asked Poppy as Flo helped her wash her hands.

"She went to help Will with something. I'm sure she'll be back soon."

"Aunty Florrie, do we have to go home tomorrow?" Poppy put her hands on her hips, imitating Daisy's earlier stance.

"I'm afraid so. Mummy has work and you have school."

"Can we visit again soon?" Poppy's voice was small and defeatist as her little hand slid into Flo's.

"Of course. If you don't come up around Christmas, then who will help me decorate my tree?"

They joined Tom back outside, and he told them the fireworks would be starting soon. He had to help his brother and dad, so he showed them to the best viewing place and left. Daisy soon joined them. She was glowing as she picked Poppy up and spun her around.

"Did you have a nice time?" teased Flo.

"Very nice, thank you." Daisy blushed. "I feel

fifteen again, drinking cider in a field and snogging behind a tree."

Flo laughed and hugged her friend.

"The fireworks are about to start," squealed Poppy. She jumped up and down with excitement.

Poppy's joy was infectious as they huddled together to watch the silent display. The air filled with the sound of 'ooos' and 'ahh' as bright lights burst in the sky above. Greens, blues, pinks, and gold fizzled across the sky, lighting up the evening. The chilly November air was forgotten, and Flo felt the bubble of happiness inside her expand. This time last year, she'd been holed up in her dank house share with the curtains firmly pulled as she listened to the sound of fireworks banging outside. It was a time of year that she and Iris had always loved, but it had felt empty without her grandmother. Now, with friends around her and a future to look forward to, Flo felt she could enjoy the night again.

Tom and Will returned with handfuls of sparklers. They handed them around and carefully lit each one. Flecks of fire sparked as they all swirled them around in a race to spell their names before the light disappeared.

"It's not fair," groaned Poppy. "You all have short names. Mummy, why did you give me such a long name?"

Laughter erupted, and everyone offered to write one letter of Poppy's name so it would be lit up in one go.

As the sparklers extinguished and they put the

leftover sticks into a bucket filled with sand, Flo managed to steal a quiet moment with Tom. "Thank you for a lovely evening," she whispered against his lips.

Tom wrapped his arms around her waist and kissed her. A few catcalls sounded from around them, but Flo didn't care. She didn't want to sneak around with Tom any more. It was clear they both liked each other, and she thought she could be ready to risk her heart for him.

CHAPTER TWENTY-FIVE

"I'm going to miss you both," Flo said, tightening her hold on Poppy.

"I'll miss you, Aunty Florrie." Poppy threw her arms around Flo's neck and nestled her head against her shoulder.

"We'll come back around Christmas," promised Daisy.

Flo helped them to the car with all their bags and gave Poppy a last hug goodbye once she was strapped into her seat.

"Let me know when you're home safely," Flo said, hugging Daisy.

"Of course, and I want all the gossip from tonight's party." Daisy hugged her tighter. "Remember, you are enough."

"I'll call you tomorrow. I still want to hear about you and Will." Flo had been eager to hear about

Daisy's time with Will, but it was late by the time they'd got home, and with the long journey ahead, Flo hadn't wanted to keep her up.

Flo waved until the car rounded the corner and then went back inside. She'd grown so used to having company and the tea shop heaving with customers that she didn't know what to do with herself. Flo had texted Tom asking if she should bring a cake to the party. He'd replied with laughing emojis and said no, it wasn't that kind of party. That had only caused Flo's nerves to grow. She busied herself cleaning the tea shop and then the flat. Last night, she'd spoken to Emma, and they'd agreed Emma would come round after lunch to get ready.

Emma arrived with a suitcase of clothes and makeup, much to Flo's horror.

"I wanted to give you options." Emma shrugged and carried the case upstairs. "Although I have already chosen your outfit."

Flo swallowed. "Do you want a drink?" she asked, needing something to distract herself.

"Coffee, please. Ooo, do you have some cucumber?"

Flo frowned. "Yes? Did you want a slice on the side?"

"No, silly. It's for our face masks."

Flo nodded as if it were the most obvious thing in the world.

"Who was that I saw you with last night?" Flo asked.

"That's Josh. He works up at the farm." It was an unusually short answer from a usually chatty Emma.

"He's quite good-looking."

"Mmm," Emma said, looking studiously at the makeup bag in her hands. "He's offered to give us a lift tonight."

"Both of us?"

Emma nodded.

"I can drive myself there, and you can go with him." Flo didn't feel like being a third wheel.

"No, then you can't drink. It's fine, honestly. He said his sister might be joining us, too."

"Okay," Flo reluctantly agreed. It was only a short drive to the farm, and she could always find someone else to bring her home. Or perhaps Tom would ask her to stay. Her heart rate picked up at the thought, and she sipped her coffee before Emma could notice the way her expression had changed.

Emma had packed brightening face masks, softening foot masks, and conditioning hair masks. It had been years since Flo had experienced an afternoon of so much pampering. Emma had refused to show her the outfits until her makeup was done.

"You're really good at this," Flo said as she examined the black manicure Emma had given her. She'd left a bottle of remover so Flo could take it off first thing tomorrow morning.

"I've been training, and I want to make the leap and do it as my job," Emma said as she opened a huge pallet of eyeshadow and instructed Flo to close her eyes. "The income isn't reliable enough, and the hours at the shop don't allow me enough time to branch out."

Flo's eyes shot open, and Emma smudged eyeshadow across her forehead. "Sorry, but I've had a great idea. I need some help at the tea shop, but I can't take someone on full-time until I know how steady the income is. You could pick up hours around your appointments. I'd be flexible."

Emma had sat down. "Would you?" Her eyes lit up.

"Of course. We could make it work, I'm sure."

"I'd love that."

"Pop by on Monday and we'll talk it through properly."

Emma wiped the smudge and went back to applying Flo's eyeshadow.

"Come into the bathroom so I can spray this on your hair," Emma said. Flo dubiously eyed the aerosol can. It was temporary hair dye.

"It will wash out, right?"

"Of course. Keep your eyes closed. I don't want you to see the final look until your hair's done."

After what seemed like hours of spraying and inhaling toxic fumes, Emma announced she was finished. "Have a look in the mirror while I go get your outfit."

Flo nervously tiptoed over to the bathroom mirror. A soft gasp escaped her as she looked at her reflection. Her face was pale, with bright red, plump lips, and dark, smoky eyes, framed with long false lashes. "Wow," she whispered and peered closer. The makeup made her icy blue eyes stand out. Her hair had turned from its usual chestnut brown to a deep black, which suited the look. This was so far out of her comfort zone, but she wasn't freaking out like Flo from a few months ago would have. Her time in Cornwall had already changed her.

"You look amazing." Emma poked her head around the bathroom door. "I've laid your costume out on your bed."

Flo nodded and went to look. She was already outside her comfort zone. What difference would a Halloween costume make?

The dress was black velvet, floor-length, fitted, with long sleeves. Flo pulled it on and marvelled at how well it fitted. The neckline was low, but not so low that it left nothing to the imagination. With a pair of her own heels on, Flo stood in front of her full-length mirror. She hardly recognised herself under the figure-hugging dress, towering heels, and long black hair cascading around her shoulders.

"I knew Morticia Adams would suit you!" Emma exclaimed as she came out of the bathroom in her costume.

"You've done amazingly, thank you. And look at you. You look stunning." Emma had dressed as Cruella de Vil with a similar floor-length dress, but hers had a huge split up the leg to mid-thigh. Over the dress, Emma wore a white fur coat and had donned a wig with the infamous half-back, half-white hair.

Josh collected them at seven. He was dressed as Beetlejuice, with a striped black and white suit and a questionable wig. His sister hadn't joined him, so Flo slipped into the back of the car alone.

Flo watched out the windows and tuned out Emma and Josh as they drove to the farm. Her eyes widened at the sight. Spotlights were trained on the house, lighting it up. Cobwebs covered the doors and windows, which glistened in the light. Fake skeletons and coffins were scattered around the front garden. As they got closer, Flo spotted thousands of fake spiders planted in the ivy, which wound around the front of the house.

A valet collected the car and parked it. Flo was speechless as she took everything in. There was no doubt about it. She'd never been to a party like this. A walkway with candles on either side led to the front door. Flo followed Emma and Josh into the house. In the hallway was a piano, playing spooky tunes with no pianist. The room was filled with people in fancy dress.

Tom was at her side almost immediately. "I've been keeping an eye out for you," he whispered and wrapped an arm around her waist. "You look amazing."

"Thank you." Flo took in his outfit. He was dressed smartly in a black tuxedo and looked the perfect host. As Flo looked him over him, she spotted the fangs protruding from his mouth and the 'blood' soaked tissue in his suit pocket. "You look pretty good yourself, Count Dracula."

"I'd promise not to bite you tonight, but you look rather delectable." His lips brushed her ear as he spoke. "I have to do some networking. Will you stay with me? I promise we'll have fun later."

Flo kept to Tom's side as he greeted people and introduced her. His eyes were warm, and he looked proud as they spoke to his friends and family. Smartly dressed waiters carried around trays of vol-au-vents. Flo took one each time they passed and marvelled at the flavours.

The night slowly transitioned into more of a party. The older guests left, and the younger crowd relocated to the barn where a DJ was waiting.

"Have fun," Claire called as she saw them sneaking out.

Music thundered through the small area, and bodies crushed together. Flo caught Emma's eye and waved before she was swept up in the crowd. Tom handed her a plastic flute of champagne and pulled her onto the dance floor. The floor shook with the bass of the music, and the lyrics mingled with people singing along. Despite being a cold November night, the barn was hot and humid. Flo soon realised that dancing while holding a drink was a skill she was yet to master, but Tom didn't seem to mind when champagne sloshed over him. His hand was firm against her waist as he leaned in to press his lips to her neck. Flo tilted her head to the side as his soft kisses peppered her skin, and he pulled her body against his.

"Shall we go back to my place?" he said, barely audible over the pounding music.

Flo squeezed his hand and nodded. He pulled them through the throng of people, and along the way, Flo discarded her empty glass. Tom guided them across the courtyard and through a front door. Flo was paying very little attention to her surroundings as Tom's hand roamed across her back and sent bolts of electricity through her. They stumbled into his home, stealing chaste kisses as Tom led her to his bedroom.

CHAPTER TWENTY-SIX

Flo woke with a headache and a dry mouth. She reached for the glass of water she always left on her bedside table. Instead of a glass, her hands grasped hair. Flo jumped and pulled the duvet around herself as she forced her sleepy eyes to focus. Bright light assaulted her pupils, and she blinked until she could make out her surroundings. She wasn't at home.

"Good morning," Tom grumbled from beside her.

"Where are we?" she groaned.

"In my bed." He threw an arm over his face to block out the light.

"Why are we in your bed?"

"Don't you remember?"

Flo racked her brains. She remembered dancing with Tom and kissing him. Then what had happened? Oh, yes. They'd stumbled their way back to Tom's. Then he'd kissed her some more and carried her up to his bedroom. The memories all flooded back, and a coy smile replaced Flo's confusion.

"It was a rather nice night, wasn't it?" She blushed.

"It was very nice." He dropped his arm to look at her.

As Flo pieced together the world around her, she moved her attention to Tom's home. She was in a spacious bedroom in the upstairs of a converted barn. The exposed beams on the vaulted ceiling were beautiful and matched the flooring. Tom's bed was black, as was all the furniture scattered around the room.

"Can I ask why your hair has turned my white sheets black?" asked Tom. His voice was still sleepy, and his hair stuck out in all directions.

Flo groaned and turned to see black hair dye across both pillows and the duvet.

"I'm sorry. I'll wash them for you, or replace them if need be."

He shook his head. "These sheets aren't going anywhere. They're my souvenir from last night." He winked.

Flo's head pounded. Her hair was half brown and half black, and she didn't want to consider what a state her face was in with last night's costume makeup smeared across it.

"Why aren't you disgustingly hungover?" she groaned, glaring at Tom until she realised it only made her head hurt more.

"Some of us drank our pint of water last night, whilst others sang to their glass of water." He looked pointedly at the full glass on her side of the bed.

Flo flopped back onto the pillows and groaned. "I'm never drinking again," she declared.

Tom propped himself up on his arms to lean over her, his bare chest brushing hers. His soft lips pressed against hers, and Flo felt the world spin as she handed herself over to his kiss.

"Wait." She put her hands on his chest and pushed him back. "What time is it?"

Tom groaned and rolled over to check his phone. "It's half seven. Why are we awake this early after a party?"

Flo cursed and sprang out of bed. She threw on her dress from last night and tried to locate the rest of her belongings.

"As much as I'm enjoying this little show," Tom said from the bed. "What on earth are you doing?"

"I should be opening the tea shop in half an hour!"

The playfulness on Tom's face morphed into one of disappointment. "You're open today?"

"Yes. I thought it would be a good idea since most of the village was at the party last night. They'll be in search of coffee and carbs today."

"You make a very good point there. The only problem is that you were also at the party."

"I know," cried Flo. "What am I going to do?"

"Relax. I'll drive you home and help you. Between us, I'm sure we can serve a hungover crowd."

"We are the hungover crowd!" Flo gathered his

clothes from the floor and threw them at him.

"Is it fancy dress in the tea shop today?" he teased.

"Tom!"

He laughed and held up his hands. "Okay. Let me get some clothes. Can I shower at yours?"

It was a mad rush to get home to open on time. Nothing was ready, and Flo still had last night's makeup smudged across her face.

"You shower," Tom instructed. "At least I don't have half black, half brown hair and a fake eyelash stuck to my cheek."

Flo peeled off the lash. "How long has that been there?"

"Since you woke up." Tom chuckled, and Flo fought the urge to flick it at him. "Go on, get in the shower, and I'll switch everything on. I can make people coffee while they wait."

It was the fastest shower of Flo's life. She was sure there were still streaks of black dye through her hair, but it would have to wait until tonight. With her hair slicked back into a tight bun, Flo threw on clothes, grabbed some painkillers, and ran downstairs to find a handful of customers already sitting at tables. As promised, Tom had plied them with cups of coffee, but they had all ordered food.

"You've got this," Tom said and handed her a cup.

"Thank you." She took the coffee into the kitchen and set about making breakfast.

As rashers of bacon sweated on the grill, Flo opened the window and gulped in a deep breath of fresh air. She made the breakfast orders, putting a couple aside for her and Tom. Once everyone was fed, Flo took a tentative bite.

Somehow, they made it through the day with only a few mishaps. Flo hadn't baked on Saturday, which meant they ran out of cake before the lunchtime rush. Tom had to step in and make sandwiches while Flo baked. He wasn't terrible at it, but a handful were sent back. Tom blamed it on being in a high-pressure environment. When they closed for the evening, they collapsed into the nearest chairs and caught their breath.

"Nobody should ever have to go through that with a hangover," Flo muttered. She'd spent most of the day breathing through her mouth as the smells of the food made her stomach roil.

"Nope, but we got through it." His foot lightly tapped hers under the table.

"Thank you for helping." Flo realised how natural it felt to accept Tom's help these days. She was beginning to think of him as a permanent fixture in her life, and rather than the usual ball of nerves that the thought would have stirred up, this time, it made her smile. "Do you have plans tonight?" she asked.

He groaned. "I do. My mother always insists on hosting dinner the day after the party. Some family and friends stay over, so they'll be there." He paused and nudged her foot again. "Would you like to come?"

The last thing she wanted to do was dress up for dinner with Tom's family and friends, but she didn't want to let him down. She drummed her fingers on the tabletop as she thought about everything she had to do for tomorrow.

"You don't have to," Tom said, watching her.

"I'd love to spend more time with you, but I feel dead on my feet already. I'm behind with baking for the week, and we're open again tomorrow."

"It's fine, honestly. If I didn't have to go, then I wouldn't. I'd much rather stay here with you."

Flo sighed at the idea. "What about Monday night? Come over for dinner, and we can sit in front of the fire?"

"That sounds perfect." He stood and pulled her up with him. "I'll miss you," he whispered against her lips.

By the time Tom left, the sun was setting. Flo made her fifth coffee of the day and turned on the radio, her head finally feeling able to withstand the noise. The tea shop had been busy, but not as busy as a usual Sunday, so Flo had leftover bread, with which she made a bread pudding. It would be perfect tomorrow, with a dollop of warm custard and a cup of tea. With the bread pudding in the oven and the gentle scent of nutmeg and cinnamon filling the room, Flo made a sticky toffee loaf cake, a couple of Victoria sponges, and a chocolate fudge cake. Once they were all cooled and put away, she went upstairs and ran herself a bath with a splash of lavender bubble bath.

The warm water eased her aching joints, and she tipped her head back and closed her eyes, allowing the delicious memories of last night to flood back. Despite the alcohol fog, she could clearly remember how Tom had swept her into his arms. With the door shut and locked behind them, he'd pressed her against it and kissed her until the world spun. Then he'd led her upstairs to his bedroom, where they shed their costumes and fell into bed. A niggle of worry gnawed away at Flo as she realised how much she'd opened her heart to him. She was falling for him, and it was too late to do anything to protect herself. Her life was unrecognisable from this time last year, but she couldn't be happier. It terrified her that so much had changed. One wrong move and she could plunge headfirst into heartbreak, but she had to be brave because maybe Tom was different.

After a dinner of soup, Flo changed into her pyjamas and climbed into bed with a hot chocolate and her grandmother's diary. She hadn't had time to read while Daisy and Poppy were there, so she still didn't know what had happened when Iris's parents arrived.

19th August 1963,

I don't know where to begin. So much has happened since Mum and Dad arrived. I could burst with happiness. At first, they were shocked and alarmed when they received my letter telling them I was engaged to one of the local men. That's my secret, by the way. After dinner at the pub, S walked me home, and we stopped by the village green. He took my hand and knelt down on one knee. He didn't have a ring, but he said he loved me and he wanted a future with me. Obviously, I said yes. Anyway, back to Mum and Dad. In hindsight, I should have telephoned them. But that's why they drove here - they were worried about me. Mum's friend had also written to her to say I'd been seen hanging around with one of the local boys. Thankfully, the letter arrived the same day as mine. I thought they'd pack my bag and take me straight home, but we all sat down with a cup of tea, and I told them about S. They wanted to meet him.

I had work yesterday, so I promised Mum and Dad I'd arrange dinner with S and his parents. Mrs J let me use the telephone at the cafe, and I spoke to S, who promised me they'd meet us at the pub. It was a busy day, and Mrs J kept me running back and forth between the kitchen and the counter. I think she was trying to keep my mind busy. Mum and Dad came in at lunchtime and were impressed by the cakes I'd baked.

Mrs J let me leave early, so I had time to go home and get ready. I wore my bright orange dress with the belt. Mum always rolls her eyes at it and says I look like a Mod. Mum and Dad are staying at the same B&B, so we walked to the pub together. Mum kept trying to rearrange my hair, but I shook her off.

It went well. Everyone got on wonderfully, and the night

ended with a toast to mine and S's future together. I'm so happy I could burst. I've just seen the time. I'm going to be late for work, so I'll tell you more later.

There was a smudge on the page between entries, which looked like icing sugar. Flo smiled as she ran her finger over it. She could imagine her grandmother rushing off to work, glowing with happiness. No doubt anyone who had crossed paths with her that day would have walked away smiling. Iris's cheerfulness was always infectious. It warmed Flo's heart to know her grandmother had been so happy here, but she wondered what had happened. Had Iris had her heart broken, or had she broken S's heart? There was so much to uncover. Below the smudge was the rest of the entry for 19th August, so Flo sipped her hot chocolate and immersed herself in Iris's life.

19th August 1963, continued...

I was late for work, so I spent all day scrambling to catch up. It was the hottest day of the year, and there was an endless stream of customers wafting through the cafe's doors. S and I had planned to have a picnic tonight, but with my parents still here, we've rearranged. He stopped by the cafe this afternoon for a slice of cake, but we were so busy I barely had time to speak. Mum wanted to discuss wedding plans, so we couldn't see each other this evening.

Wedding planning with Mum turned out to be quite fun. She'd been out today and picked up lots of magazines for us to look through. Dad wasn't the slightest bit interested, so he went to the pub. Mum and I spent a few hours cutting out pictures we liked and putting them together. We made lots of important decisions. I wanted an autumn wedding, but Mum has convinced me to wait until next summer. She says there's so much to organise that autumn would be too soon. We've agreed that I'll get married here in Cornwall at the village church. Then we looked at wedding dresses. They're all so beautiful. I don't know how I'm supposed to pick just one. Mum said not to worry, we can try a few on in London. So far, my favourite ones are white with lace. Then we looked at cakes. Obviously, we'll ask Mrs J to make the cake. I'd love her chocolate cake, but Mum said it had to be fruitcake with marzipan icing. I said that was okay as long as I could have pink roses in the church. We've made all these plans, but I need to see what S wants. Perhaps he won't like the idea of pink roses.

Anyway, it's dark now, and I really should go. Mum and Dad are heading home soon, and I don't have very long left until I join them. I don't know how I'll leave S. My heart already hurts just thinking about it, but he's promised to visit in September, so we won't be apart for too long.

Flo closed the diary and fetched a photo album from her bookshelf. She flicked through the pictures of her grandparents' wedding day. They had married at the local registry office, and Iris had worn a short ivory dress. She looked beautiful with her hair swept back into an up-do. Grandpa Eddie's arm was wrapped around her waist, and they beamed at the camera. Clasped in Iris's hands was a bunch of purple hyacinths. The pictures followed the day as they went back to Iris's parents for the reception, where they cut a towering Victoria sponge. There was a picture of Iris and Eddie cutting the cake and laughing as the cream and jam oozed out of the sides and dripped everywhere. Flo squinted at the picture. Their smiles looked genuine. There was one of Iris looking up at Eddie, and it calmed Flo's nerves to see the love in her eyes. A gentleness was reflected in Eddie's gaze. Whatever had happened, Iris had found happiness with Flo's grandfather.

CHAPTER TWENTY-SEVEN

Flo untangled her limbs from Tom's and rolled over to turn the alarm off. It was dark outside, and Tom grunted his disapproval.

"You need to get to the farm." Flo nudged him.

"I don't want to." He pulled her to him and tucked her head beneath his chin.

"We'll both be late if you don't let me go," warned Flo.

"Fine."

Flo watched from the bed as Tom pulled his clothes on. It had been a couple of weeks since the Halloween party, and he'd stayed over most nights since.

"Is Emma opening the tea shop tomorrow?" asked Tom.

"Yeah. It's her first time opening." After their conversation, Flo and Emma had devised a plan to balance both of their fledgling businesses. The pressure had been taken off Flo, and she had a few hours off a week. Meanwhile, Emma had the opportunity to start her own beauty business. The village had come out in full support, and Emma was booked up until after Christmas.

"Why don't you stay at mine tonight? My mum invited us to dinner."

"I'd like that," she said. Flo slid out of bed and wrapped her arms around Tom's neck. "See you at lunchtime?"

"Of course." He pecked her on the lips and left before they were late.

It was mid-November, and Flo was embracing the Christmas spirit. She took her grandmother's recipe book from the shelf and opened it to the steamed pudding. In the margin was Iris's handwriting, with additional instructions. Flo sifted flour into a bowl and added a pinch of salt, nutmeg, and cinnamon. Then, she added brown sugar before rubbing in the butter. Flo juiced and zested an orange and tipped it in along with an egg. She whisked it all together before pouring the mixture into individual pudding basins and leaving them to steam for a couple of hours. The kitchen smelled wonderful, and Flo switched the radio station to one playing Christmas songs.

Emma arrived shortly after, and there was a lull in customers between the breakfast and lunch rush.

"How are things going with Tom?" asked Emma.

She'd made them each gingerbread hot chocolates, and they were sitting behind the counter as a handful of walkers enjoyed a pot of tea and a scone.

Flo sighed. Last week, she'd confided in Emma about her abandonment fears. "It's good. I'm trying to be very mindful of my reactions and actions." Truthfully, it was a little exhausting having to think of the possible ramifications of anything she did or said, but so far, it was working, and she was successfully keeping her worries away.

"Good. I'm always here if you need anything," Emma reminded her.

The conversation was cut short when the door swung open and another walking group came in. Rain dripped off their coats, and their muddy boots squelched beneath them.

"I'll fetch the mop," Emma said.

The day passed with mixed reactions to Flo embracing the Christmas spirit. Some people loved it, while others thought it was too early. But they all enjoyed the steamed pudding. Flo had made a big one to take to dinner tonight. As she closed the tea shop and went through her routine, nerves flared in her stomach. She'd never been to dinner with a boyfriend's parents before, usually because she didn't allow a relationship to get that serious.

Tom had stopped by for lunch mid-afternoon, and Flo had eaten a quick lunch with him. He'd promised that dinner would be fine and his parents would love her. Since she'd already met Claire, Flo supposed the odds were in her favour. Tom insisted on picking her up. At 6 o'clock, he beeped from the end of her pathway, and she went to meet him with an overnight bag packed.

"Are you excited for your sleepover?" he asked and took the bag from her.

"Very." Flo hadn't been back to Tom's since the night of the Halloween party. He'd asked her over and suggested he cook dinner, but something always cropped up.

"Is that the pudding?" He eyed the bowl in her hands.

"Yes, and no, you can't try some now. Come on, or else we'll be late, and I don't want to make a bad impression." She reached up on her tiptoes and pecked him on the lips, stepping away before his arms could wrap around her.

The changing seasons were evident on the drive to the farm. All the vibrant, crispy leaves had fallen off the trees and blown away. Hedges were bare, and barren branches creaked above. Although Flo loved Christmas, she couldn't wait for the first shoots of spring and for the hedges and trees to blossom again.

Claire opened the door before they'd even parked the car.

"Hello," she called.

"Thank you for inviting me. I brought a pudding for later." Flo awkwardly held up the bowl.

"You didn't have to bring anything, but thank you." Claire took the pudding and pulled Flo into a one-armed hug, instantly making her feel at ease.

"Shall I bring this straight over to mine?" Tom called, holding up her overnight bag.

Flo blushed, and Claire rolled her eyes. "You do what you want. Flo is coming in with me," she told him and gestured for Flo to go indoors. "I'm sorry. Both my sons lack tact."

"It's okay. Is Will joining us for dinner?" Flo had spoken to Daisy in the week, who said she was still in contact with Will.

"Hmm. We'll see." Claire's lips pursed. "He has… company."

"Oh," squeaked Flo. She schooled her face to remain neutral, but inside, she was seething. How dare Will string her best friend along like that?

"Yes. I think it might be time we convert one of the barns for him." Claire led Flo through to the kitchen, which was warm and filled with the delicious scent of dinner cooking. "It's cottage pie. I hope that's okay?"

Flo's stomach rumbled. She lived on tea shop food for breakfast, lunch, and dinner. A home-cooked meal made her mouth water. "It's perfect, thank you."

Claire instructed Flo to sit at the table and poured her some fresh lemonade. Flo offered to help with dinner, but Claire wouldn't hear of her lifting a finger. They chatted about the tea shop as Claire stirred gravy on the hob. There was something instantly calming about being in the kitchen with Claire. The house felt homely, and Flo felt her earlier nerves ebb away.

"Sorry," Tom said, crashing through the back door. "I bumped into Dad, and he needed a hand with moving some feed. He's going to shower, then he'll be in. I need to wash my hands." Tom held his muddy hands out in front of him.

"Actually, could you show me where the bathroom is? Then I can turn the tap on for you," Flo said.

The house felt like a rabbit warren as Tom led her to a bathroom on the second floor. "It's not the closest one," he explained. "This is the family bathroom, so it doesn't matter so much when I wash my muddy hands. The downstairs one is used by B&B guests in the morning."

Tom waited while Flo used the bathroom.

"The house is lovely," Flo said as she joined him in the hallway.

"Here, have a look at these photographs." Tom led her down the hall, where family photos lined each side. He pointed out a handful of him and Will as children playing on the farm.

"This place is filled with happiness," Flo said, at the same time a woman's giggle echoed from a room off the hallway. Will emerged from the bedroom, and a giddy blonde followed him.

Flo's jaw dropped at the sight. "What on earth are you doing here?" she cried.

Daisy froze before laughing so much she doubled over. "This is the worst walk of shame I've ever had to do," she said once she'd regained her composure.

"I don't understand what's going on, and I'm not sure if I want to," Flo said. She stepped back to lean into Tom.

"Well, when a man and a woman..." began Will, but he was interrupted by Daisy, who elbowed him in the ribs.

"My parents are looking after Poppy for a few days, so I got the train down."

There were so many things Flo wanted to ask, but now wasn't the time. She walked over and slid her arm through Daisy's. "Are you happy?" she asked.

Will had joined Tom, and they were making their way downstairs.

"Very." Her smile lit up her face, and pure joy poured from her expression.

"Good." Flo squeezed her hand. "Shall we have a very awkward dinner?"

They looked at each other and laughed. "This wasn't something I ever thought we'd be doing," Daisy said as she allowed Flo to lead her downstairs.

"Will, I didn't realise you'd be eating with us," Claire said as they walked into the kitchen.

Tom's father had joined them and was sitting, sipping a beer, watching the events unfold. As he spotted Flo, he got up to greet her. "Lovely to meet you, Flo. I'm Arthur. I've heard a lot about you." He hugged her, and Flo instantly felt at ease.

"Lovely to meet you, too," she said. Arthur looked a lot like Tom, just a little older. He had a kind face and lines around his eyes from years of laughter.

"I'd love to say we've heard lots about you, but

I'm afraid we haven't. I'm Arthur," he introduced himself to Daisy, and Flo bit back a laugh.

Daisy's cheeks turned pink. "Lovely to meet you. I'm Daisy, a friend of Flo's, and, um, a friend of Will's."

There was a moment of silence before everyone burst into laughter. "A friend, hey?" Arthur chuckled.

"Well, it's nice to see both our boys happy," Claire interjected before everyone got carried away. "Sit down, I'm sure we can make dinner go around."

Dinner was a loud affair, with Tom and Will leading the conversation. It was a bit of a shock for Flo. Dinnertimes with Iris had been a quiet and somewhat formal occasion. They always sat in the dining room. A jug of water with lime or lemon would be set in the centre, and they'd get out their beautiful cutlery, which Iris had received as a wedding present. As they sat and talked over dinner, it was their precious time of the day when there were no outside distractions and they could catch up. When Flo would visit Daisy's, it was a similar affair. Daisy was an only child. Whereas here at the Evans kitchen table, conversation flowed loudly as dinner was set in the middle of the table, and everyone was left to dish up their own. Flo didn't dislike it. It didn't matter that she and Daisy were outsiders; they were instantly pulled into the family and treated the same as anyone else.

"Flo's made a pudding," Claire announced as she cleared the empty plates. Flo and Daisy had offered to help, but she wouldn't have it, saying that Tom and Will were more than capable of doing the washing up.

"I'm looking forward to this. Everyone I've spoken to over the last few weeks has told me how good your cakes are," Arthur said.

"I hope they live up to their reputation."

"They do," Will called from the sink where he was washing, and Tom was drying.

"Flo's cakes have always been amazing. She takes after her grandmother," Daisy said.

"I think she learned how to bake here. In the tea shop, actually."

Arthur glanced at his wife, but she had her back to him. "Did she really? What a small word."

"This smells delicious, Flo. How shall I reheat it?" Claire asked.

Flo gave Claire directions, and Arthur went to the fridge to make sure there was fresh cream.

The Christmas pudding went down a treat. For the first time that evening, a silence settled across the table. The sound of spoons scraping bowls echoed throughout the room.

Will and Daisy disappeared once the pudding was finished. Flo had mouthed 'call me' to Daisy on her way out.

"Don't feel like you need to stay and keep us company," Claire said. "Help yourself to anything you might need. I'm not sure how equipped Tom is for overnight guests."

"Mother," warned Tom.

"I'm just saying if your towels are a bit grubby, I have plenty in the airing cupboard. You know where everything is, so help yourself."

"On that note, I think we'll be off." Tom took Flo's hand, pulling her up.

"It was lovely to have dinner with you," Flo said and meant it. For the first time in a very long while, she felt like part of a family.

It was bitterly cold outside as they crossed the courtyard to Tom's barn. When Flo had last been there, she'd been in such a hurry that she hadn't taken the time to explore his home.

"Welcome," he said, opening the door and allowing her to walk ahead.

"Thank you." Flo stepped straight into the living area and realised the entire downstairs was open plan. Last time, she'd run down the stairs and straight out the front door. There was a spacious kitchen towards the back with doors, which opened out onto a terrace with a view of the fields. A large corner sofa was pushed against the nearest wall, with a projector above it. A glass coffee table sat on the rug with a few coffee table books on farming. Flo suspected Claire had designed the space.

"What do you think?" he asked, busying himself with setting a fire in the log burner.

"It's very modern, but I like it."

"Do you want a drink? I don't have any caramel syrup, but I did get some soya milk, so I can make you a coffee?"

Flo smiled at how thoughtful he was. "I'd love a coffee, please."

They settled on the sofa with their drinks and spoke about everything and nothing all at once. Flo shared memories of Christmas with Iris. It had always been a quiet affair with just the two of them. In contrast, Tom shared his memories of busy Christmas days with cousins coming to stay and the farm still operating. It sounded like utter chaos, but with a big, loving family at the heart of it.

Neither of them mentioned Will and Daisy, and Flo was grateful for it. She only hoped her best friend could find happiness.

CHAPTER TWENTY-EIGHT

The days were growing shorter, and the weather colder. Inside the tea shop, the windows steamed up as customers sipped hot drinks and ate sugary treats. Flo had only been open for an hour, but she was already on her third coffee. Tom hadn't slept over last night as they'd had a late delivery of feed at the farm, and the order was wrong. The time apart had given her the space for her doubts to arise. With a rare night alone, Flo unpacked her final box from London. She had tucked it away in the corner of her living room, and Flo had been trying to ignore it. The box was filled with old photo albums, and she'd been putting off delving into them, knowing it would dredge up a plethora of emotions.

There were albums that spanned the entirety of Iris's life. Flo flicked through some of Iris's childhood until she reached 1963. She was disappointed to find only a handful of pictures from the year and none from the summer. The next album she picked up was filled with photos of Flo's mother, from a baby to her teens. A heaviness wrapped around Flo's heart as she watched her mother grow up. In every picture, she beamed at the camera, her eyes a replica of Flo's. After taking a deep breath, Flo opened the album from her childhood. The first picture was of her as a tiny baby in the hospital, in her mother's arms. Flo swallowed against the lump in her throat. She trailed a finger over the picture.

"What happened?" she whispered. Iris had always excused her daughter's behaviour as being free-spirited, but deep down, Flo had always thought she was the reason her mother ran away. As a child, she felt unlovable. Over the years, as Flo matured, she'd learned the fault didn't lie at her feet, but those childhood emotions were a shadow on her soul. She could never completely shake the feeling that she was the reason her mother had left. Although she was doing her best to ignore her worries, as her feelings for Tom grew, she knew her fears were growing behind the wall she'd put up.

A customer walked in, and Flo relaxed her shoulders, grateful for the distraction to avoid the usual tide of anxiety that washed over her when her mind wandered down that route.

A little while later, Claire popped in. She wasn't her usual perky self as she ordered a coffee and a few slices of cake to take away. "It's utter chaos at the farm," she said, leaning against the counter.

"Tom mentioned when he called last night. Has it been resolved?"

Claire shook her head. "We're trying to send all the animal feed back, and we're waiting for a new delivery."

"I'm sorry," Flo said as she handed over a takeaway coffee.

"Thank you. Anyway, enough about the farm. I came here for another reason. It's very last minute, I know, but I'm trying to put together a small Christmas market. This year is a trial, and if it goes well, we'll expand next year. I thought we could host it in our events barn and showcase local products. Which leads me to the reason for my visit. Would you like a stall?"

"I'd love one." Flo had more than enough custom at the tea shop, but she couldn't afford to let sales fall now she had employed Emma, and a Christmas market sounded like a great way to top up her income should customers drop off in the new year.

"Brilliant. I'll text you the details once I'm more organised."

"Sounds great." Flo boxed up the slices of cake.

"Thanks, Flo. I've got a few more stops, then I'm taking the cake back to the boys. Tom asked me to say he'd see you later."

During the quieter moments, Flo began making lists for the market. She could make individual puddings for people to buy and eat on Christmas Day, and she could put together baking kits of pre-weighed ingredients for people to make at home. There were so many options that her thoughts were whirring at a hundred miles an hour. It was what she needed to stop her mind from wandering to Tom and her growing feelings towards him.

"Morning," called Emma as she walked in for her lunchtime shift.

"You look very happy with yourself," commented Flo.

"I had a date last night." Emma shook off her coat, scarf, and gloves and hung them up.

"Tell me more." Flo put down her pen and tucked the notepad underneath the counter.

"Josh took me to Port Isaac for dinner at the pub there. The Fisherman's Rest. Have you heard of it?"

"Yes, that's where I went with Tom." Flo smiled as she remembered their first date.

"It's beautiful, and the food is amazing."

The timer went off, and Flo went to fetch a cake from the oven. "What about Josh?" she asked as Emma lingered in the doorway, keeping an eye out for any new customers.

"He was lovely company. Picked me up and dropped me off." Emma blushed. "He kissed me goodnight."

"I think you've found a good one there."

"Me too."

"You deserve it." Flo put the sponges under a net while they cooled. She'd ice them once the lunchtime rush was over.

Lunchtime always brought with it a surge of

customers. Teachers from the village school would pop by on their lunch break; tired mums needing a break from the house treated themselves to a sandwich made by someone else; and even a few tourists still dropped in despite it being out of season. Flo and Emma were a good team, and orders went out to happy customers. Once the rush had died down, Flo made them sandwiches, and they ate at the counter.

"No Tom today?" asked Emma.

"There's been a problem at the farm."

"How are you feeling?"

Flo picked at her sandwich. "I don't know. When I'm with him, it's so easy to get swept up in his company. My feelings for him are growing, but when I'm alone and acknowledge it, it terrifies me."

"He's a good one." Emma gave her a sad smile.

"I know." Flo sighed. "But I worry I'm not good enough for him and he'll wake up one day and realise it."

"Have you spoken to him?"

Flo shrugged. She didn't want to bring it up because if she did, then she'd have to confess how she felt about him, and she wasn't ready for that.

"Talk to him, Flo." Emma patted her shoulder before taking their plates through to the back to wash up.

The rest of the day went smoothly. Once the after-school rush of customers left, Flo sent Emma home early.

"I'll pop on an audiobook and clean the place. You get off and get ready to meet Josh for a drink," Flo said. Josh had texted Emma about an hour ago, asking if she wanted to meet him at the pub.

"Are you sure?"

Flo nodded, not trusting her voice.

Alone, Flo set about cleaning and tidying the tea shop. Although she tried to quieten her mind with an audiobook, little voices still managed to creep through. *What if Tom was looking for excuses to avoid seeing her? Had she said something wrong the last time they were together?*

On some level, Flo knew her worries were silly, yet she couldn't stop her mind from overthinking everything. She needed Tom around to stop the doubts creeping in, but she knew she couldn't expect him to always be there. Flo tried to focus her attention on getting the tea shop ready for tomorrow's influx of customers.

Once she'd finished, Flo checked her phone to see a message from Tom. He was running late and told her to have dinner without him. Flo's heart rate picked up at the idea of another night alone. Another night of having to confront her feelings rather than use him as a shield. She trudged upstairs and turned the oven on, operating on autopilot as she reheated a jacket potato from lunchtime. They had planned to have a fancy meal of steak and homemade chips, but Flo couldn't face cooking for herself.

She ate her jacket potato with cheese and beans and flicked through the television channels as she tried to find something that wasn't a quiz show. Eventually, she gave up and turned it off. The silence was deafening. Flo fetched Iris's diary and decided to lose herself in another entry. It was dark outside, so she switched on the lamps, and with the glow of the fire, the room felt cosy.

20th August 1963,

I'm going home in four days. Can you believe how fast it has gone? Mum and Dad left this morning. I waved them off on my way to work. Mum tried to convince me to go home with them, saying we could start wedding planning, but I refused. As excited as I am to go dress shopping, I'd rather have a few more days with S. There'll be plenty of time to plan when we're apart.

Today was my last day working at the cafe. S is taking me away tomorrow for a night at the seaside. I didn't tell Mum and Dad, and have been on tenterhooks in case Mrs J said something in front of them. Thankfully, they didn't visit the cafe often during their time here.

After work, S met me, and we walked to the stream. He set his jacket down for me to sit on and pulled out an apple. He'd grown it on the farm and wanted me to have it. He's so sweet. We watched the water trickle by and talked about the wedding and our future. It breaks my heart to know I have to go home, and we can't just be together. S joked about eloping, but my parents would never forgive me. We've agreed that some time apart will be nothing when we have the rest of our lives together.

It hurts, though. I don't know how I'll return to life in London. I'm not the same girl I was when I left, but I'll be expected to slip back into the same role until I'm married. There's so much to think about, but I'm going to ignore it all and focus on our trip to the seaside. I'm so excited. I should go to sleep now. S is picking me up bright and early to make the most of our time.

Flo felt a pang of emptiness as she put the diary down on her coffee table. She wanted to make a pot of tea and sit down with Iris and ask her about the mysterious S. Something in the entry had stuck with Flo and made her heart hammer in her chest. Iris had mentioned S growing something at the farm. Was it possible he had worked at the farm? Perhaps he still lived around here. If he did, then Flo could get the answers she craved and learn more about her grandmother's first love.

"Hello?" called Tom from downstairs. He'd let himself in with the spare key Flo had given him.

"I'm upstairs," Flo said and blinked a few times as her eyes adjusted to the world again.

"Sorry, I'm late. It's been a hectic few days." He emerged from the stairway, and something about his warm, friendly face pushed Flo's emotions off the edge of their precipice. Silent tears poured from her eyes, and without saying a word, Tom covered the distance between them and wrapped her in his arms.

"What's wrong?" he asked as he smoothed her hair down.

Flo fought to suck in a breath deep enough to stop the sob building in her chest. "I'm fine," she protested.

Tom tilted her head up to look into her eyes. "You're not fine."

"I'm feeling a bit overwhelmed." She shrugged, trying to downplay it. Flo was realising she had a habit of doing that. She swallowed and readied herself to be honest with him. "Come and sit down," she said, taking him by the hand to the sofa.

They sat facing each other, and Flo swiped at a stray tear trickling down her cheek. This was it. She had to tell him how she felt and tell him about her fears. "I've been reading my grandmother's diary, and it's made me realise how much I miss her." The words left her mouth before she could comprehend what she was doing. At the last minute, she'd run away, unable to open herself up to him and share her worries.

Flo felt awful as he gathered her in his arms and comforted her. Why couldn't she have been honest with him? But to tell him how she felt would be to reveal the most vulnerable side of her. What if he agreed with her and said she wasn't good enough?

CHAPTER TWENTY-NINE

Flo looked at her list again and furrowed her brow. She was sure something was missing. "Victoria sponge, Christmas pudding, brownies, scones, and cookies," she muttered. The cakes were stacked in the corner to take to the farm for today's Christmas market. Claire had hired a coffee machine and asked Flo to man it on her stall, which meant that *The Cornish Vintage Tea Shop* was moving up to the farm for the day. Emma stood nearby, waiting for Flo's permission to begin loading the car. "I'm sure we're forgetting something," muttered Flo. Tom had already collected a few boxes, pointing out that everything wouldn't fit in her tiny car. Flo had sent him with the baking kits, chocolate-coated honeycomb, and gingerbread men.

"Mince pies!" Flo clapped as she finally figured it out. "That was close." She couldn't run a Christmas cake stall without mince pies.

"Does that mean we're finally ready?" asked Emma.

"I think so." Flo nibbled at her lip.

"Flo, you've done everything you could in two weeks. Come on, let's get this in the car and drive up to the farm."

They loaded the cakes carefully onto the back seat of the car, and Emma held the Victoria sponges. The last two weeks had been a whirlwind of planning. Flo had thrown herself into it, spending hours perfecting the mince filling for her pies. The first batch had turned out perfectly, but she'd been determined to improve them. Tom and Emma had watched her with worried eyes, knowing she was focusing on the market as a distraction, but neither knew her well enough to know why.

Claire had done a wonderful job pulling the market together in such a short space of time. The events barn was filled with stalls from local businesses in the village and a handful from further afield.

"Flo, you're here." Claire pulled her into a quick hug. "Thank you so much for your recommendations for vintage clothes and jewellery. It's a shame Mabel couldn't make it. You're over there." Claire pointed to an empty stall between Rosie and Belle.

"Perfect. Thank you."

Tom had dropped off the first load of goodies but was nowhere to be seen. "Let's get the lace tablecloths on, and then we'll unload the car," instructed Flo.

They set the cakes and sweet treats out on the table, and Flo decorated around them. She sprinkled icing sugar over the brownies to look like a dusting of fallen snow. Between the dishes, Flo scattered Christmas snowflake confetti. The barn was coming to life with a live band playing festive tunes, multi-coloured fairy lights had been strewn around, bringing a sense of nostalgia to the setting, and a Father Christmas sat in the far corner ready to greet children. Flo knew it was Arthur in the suit and brought him a mince pie and coffee once she'd set up.

All day, the market was busy with a mix of customers from locals she recognised, to people who had travelled a couple of hours. Claire had done well to market the event, and everyone left with a smile on their face and a Christmas trinket in their hands.

"Are you having fun?" Tom asked, and Flo jumped at his sudden appearance. She hadn't seen him all day, as he'd been busy running things behind the scenes.

"It's lovely to see everyone. Although your mother has put me in a dangerous spot. I've already spotted three dresses and six pairs of earrings I want to buy."

Tom chuckled and helped himself to a coffee from the machine. Flo put a mince pie on a napkin. "Where's Emma?" he asked.

"Josh popped by, so I told her to take a break and

wander around with him."

"I'll keep you company then," he said.

It was quiet in the barn at the moment, as most people had wandered outside for a very chilly dog competition. "Are you feeling better now the stress of today has eased?" he asked before biting into the mince pie.

Flo tore the edge of a napkin. She wasn't feeling better. If anything, she felt worse. Christmas was always a difficult time for her. It was a reminder of the family she didn't have, and losing Iris had only made it worse. With the distraction of the market gone, she was left to focus on her emotions again. Flo put the napkin down and smiled. "Sorry, have I been that obsessed with the market?" She blinked and watched as his face softened and his worries ebbed away. Flo's stomach churned at how easy it was to fool him into thinking she was fine. After a lifetime of suppressing her emotions, she'd become an expert at it.

"Good, because it's time for us to get into the Christmas spirit. I thought we could go Christmas tree shopping next weekend?" His face lit up with excitement.

"I'd like that. I've never had a real tree before."

"There's a great place nearby. I'll bring the truck since I thought we could get one for the tea shop and one for your flat." He popped the last of his mince pie into his mouth.

"That sounds great. Thank you." Flo battled with her feelings as a warmth filled her. However much she didn't want to fall for him, she already was, and it terrified her. Her desire to self-sabotage the relationship was becoming harder to ignore.

"I look forward to it. I should help my mum. We've set up an area for children to pet sheep." He rolled his eyes. "I'll be back to help you clear up once the market's finished." With a quick peck on the lips, he disappeared outside.

The next hour passed slowly as Flo felt the walls of the barn closing in. She fought to get control of her emotions to stop them from spiralling. So many doubts and worries filled her head that she didn't know how to ignore them. She needed to talk to Tom, but couldn't with so many people around them.

"What do you think of this?" Rosie interrupted her internal crisis.

It took a moment for Flo to focus on the dress in Rosie's hands. She held a black velvet A-line tea dress with pearls around the square neck. It was beautiful. "Wow," Flo whispered and wiped her hands on her apron before she stepped closer.

"Isn't it gorgeous? I think it would look stunning on you." Rosie gave her a cheeky smile.

"I couldn't," she whispered, reaching out to touch the dress but pulling back before her fingertips could brush the fabric. "I'd never wear it."

"It would be perfect for Christmas Day, or a New Year's Eve party."

Flo scoffed. "It's a little over the top for Christmas Day traipsing around alone in my flat." She held back a laugh at the thought of her sitting on the sofa in the gorgeous dress, scoffing a box of liqueur chocolates while endless Christmas films played in the background.

"Won't you be spending the day here with Tom?" Rosie's eyes flickered in the direction of the big house.

Flo passed the hem of her apron through her fingers. "I don't know. I hadn't thought about it." All of Flo's festive thoughts had been directed towards the market and the tea shop's menu. She'd not spared a second to consider what the big day might look like for herself.

"You wore the last dress, didn't you?"

She had. The dress Flo had been reluctant to purchase was the one she'd worn on her first date with Tom. Just the memories of that night brought a smile to her face. Flo had texted Rosie a picture of her wearing the dress, so she couldn't deny it. "Okay, I'll take it," she said. The market had been successful, so she could afford to treat herself. Although she was already eyeing some pearl earrings on Belle's stall that would go wonderfully with the outfit.

Flo didn't know whether she was coming or going. A huge part of her wanted to run from Tom and protect her heart against the inevitable pain. Meanwhile, the other part of her was buying a dress in the hope he'd invite her to spend Christmas with him and his family. She puffed out a breath as her card was accepted, and the transaction went through. "Next year, I'm asking for a stall far away from you two."

By the end of the day, Flo had bought the earrings. Emma had talked her into it when she returned to the stall. She was buoyed by her hour with Josh and had encouraged Flo to splurge and treat herself. Easily swayed, Flo had waltzed over to Belle's stall and had almost thrown her card at the woman.

"I can't believe how quickly today has gone," complained Emma as she helped Flo clean up. The last customers had left, and the band had stopped playing. There wasn't much for them to do since all of Flo's cakes and sweet treats had been bought.

"It was good. Perhaps we should keep an eye out for others during the year. It might help to top up the income during the slower months. We could also get some flyers printed for your beauty business."

"I'd love that. Thank you." Emma stacked the takeaway cups and carefully put them into a plastic box to take back.

Flo folded the tablecloths and shook them into a nearby bin. "You get off home," she told Emma. "There's not much to do, and Tom will be here soon."

"Thanks, Flo. I'll see you Monday morning."

Flo wrapped tissue paper around her cake stands and packed them into boxes to go in the boot of her car. It was much easier now that they weren't laden down with baked goods. There was no sign of Tom, so Flo carried the boxes to her boot and stacked them. For the first time, she regretted choosing such a tiny car. With some difficulty, she made everything fit.

"Flo," called Tom, jogging over. "You should have waited for me."

"I can do it myself." She squared her shoulders as she slammed her boot and turned to him.

He held up his hands. "Sorry, I just wanted to help."

Flo swiped a hand across her face. "I know. I'm a bit touchy at the moment."

"Are you okay?" He stepped towards her.

With a deep breath, Flo spoke. "No," she said.

Tom's expression shifted as she looked at him with pain in her eyes.

"Tom," Arthur called from the barn.

"In a minute, Dad," Tom said, his eyes not leaving Flo's.

"The Christmas set has collapsed. I can't lift it on my own," Arthur said, his tone urgent.

Tom sighed. "Coming," he called. "Don't go anywhere." He squeezed Flo's hand and went to help his dad.

Flo's shoulders sagged in relief as she watched him walk away. Once he was out of sight, she slipped into the driver's seat and drove home. She'd tried to talk to him, but fate had other plans.

CHAPTER THIRTY

A week passed, and Flo hadn't found the courage to speak to Tom. After the Christmas market, he'd met her back at the cottage and hadn't brought up the conversation. He turned up with a hamper of Christmas goodies from the farm and told her it was from his mother as a 'thank you' for being part of their first festive market. With the fire lit, they ate their way through the crackers, biscuits, cheeses, and chutneys. In the time it had taken Flo to drive to her cottage, she'd built a wall between herself and her worries. It was so easy to pretend they didn't exist when she was in the moment with Tom.

"Are you ready?" Tom called up the stairs.

Flo pulled on her hat. "Coming," she called back. They were going Christmas tree shopping. Emma was covering the tea shop until closing time.

On the way to the Christmas tree farm, Flo turned the radio station to a festive one and hummed along to the tunes. The farm was busy, but they got the last parking space. Fairy lights wrapped around the entrance gate, music played from speakers, and people wandered around, clasping hot chocolates piled high with fresh cream. With two trees to buy, Flo and Tom went straight to the Christmas Tree Walk, where trees were already cut and on display for customers to choose from. Going into it, Flo thought the task would be easy, but she was soon proven wrong. Just when they thought they'd found the perfect tree, they realised it was too small, or the side had a bald patch. Flo wrapped her coat tighter as an icy wind blew through the trees.

"I think we just have to make a decision and stick with it," she said, glancing longingly at a woman who walked by with a hot drink.

Eventually, they settled on two. One was bushy but shorter than Flo would have liked, and the other was perfect if you angled it the right way and couldn't see the missing branches at the back. Tom loaded them into his pickup truck while Flo ordered hot chocolates. She got Tom a plain one with whipped cream and a flake, while she ordered herself the same, but with gingerbread syrup.

Emma had closed and cleaned the tea shop before she went home, so there was nothing for Flo to do. They carried one tree upstairs to her flat and cleared a corner in the tea shop for the other. During the week, Flo had ordered some lights. Underneath her bed was a box of Christmas decorations that had belonged to her grandmother. Rather than keep them upstairs to herself, she had decided to decorate the tea shop's tree with them. It was what Iris would have wanted. Flo dashed upstairs to get them while Tom wrapped the lights around the tree.

"What are these?" Tom asked as she set the box on a table and took out decorations individually wrapped in tissue paper.

"These belonged to my grandmother," Flo said as she carefully lifted out a garish plastic Father Christmas.

"That's, um, lovely." Tom cleared his throat.

Flo bit back a laugh. "They're vintage."

"I prefer a vintage malt," he muttered.

They carefully unpacked the decorations, and Flo hung them on the tree. There was no pattern in how she placed them. Iris had always insisted on making Christmas fun, and doing the tree was no different. There were no rules and no emphasis on the perfect tree. Iris always said a tree should reflect the fun you had decorating it.

Tom sat back and allowed Flo to decorate.

"Are you okay?" she asked, noting the line in the middle of his forehead.

"This is very different to how things are done at home."

"How's it done at home?" Flo reached on her tiptoes to place a particularly gaudy reindeer on one of the top branches.

"My mother does it. We have a silver tree, a gold tree, and a red tree. Then the big tree in our hallway is decorated by a team of professionals who also deck the halls, so to speak. We have fresh garlands up the bannisters, on the fireplaces, and around doorways."

"I'm sure it looks amazing, but Christmas should come from the heart." Flo stepped back to admire her work. The tree was an explosion of the eighties and nineties, but it reminded her of all those happy years with Iris, just the two of them, as they opened presents early in the morning before opening the cafe and cooking Christmas dinner for those who had nowhere else to go.

"It's awful but brilliant at the same time," Tom said, coming to stand beside her.

"Thank you." Flo stepped back until she brushed his chest. He wrapped his arms around her and rested his chin on the top of her head.

"Can I help you decorate the one in your flat?" he asked. His voice was quiet and small, as though he expected her to reject him.

"Of course." Flo turned in his arms to look at him. "I'll even let you put the star on the top." She reached up on her tiptoes to kiss him.

On their way up to the flat, Flo picked up a handful of gingerbread men and some spices. While Tom dressed the tree in pretty white lights, Flo emptied a bottle of red wine into a pan on the hob and a glug of brandy. She then added segments of fresh oranges, sticks of cinnamon, whole cloves, star anise, and a squeeze of maple syrup. The scent of mulled wine filled the air, and once Tom finished with the lights, he made a fire.

"This is romantic," Tom said as she put two

glasses down.

"It is," she agreed and took a large gulp from her glass, wincing as it burned her mouth.

They decorated the tree with the new decorations Flo had ordered online. She'd bought a pack of red and gold baubles, but she'd also ordered some novelty ones to represent her life. There was a pastel cupcake, a fluffy sheep, and two gold flowers; one in the shape of a daisy, the other a poppy. Flo wanted to add to her collection each year to one day recreate Iris's mishmash of baubles.

"These are beautiful," Tom said.

"The sheep represents you."

He smiled and went back to putting a decoration on the tree.

Once the tree was finished, they ate a quick dinner before Flo topped up their glasses and Tom chose a festive film. In the glow of the fire and the twinkling tree lights, they cuddled on the sofa.

Tom's fingers traced lazy patterns on Flo's leg as her head rested on his shoulder. In moments like this, she could push away all her worries and enjoy being with him. The outside world and heartbreak couldn't touch them inside their bubble.

"Flo," Tom said and paused the film. He turned to her, his eyes shining in the warm glow of the room. "I love you." He leaned forward and pecked her on the lips.

Unsure how to react, Flo froze. Tom didn't notice as he kissed her quickly and turned back to the film. Her mouth opened and closed, but she didn't say anything. Couldn't say anything.

Their romantic bubble now felt suffocating as Flo delved into her feelings. Did she love him? She didn't know, but what she knew for sure was that she wasn't ready to bare her emotions to him.

The film finished, and Flo couldn't recall whether it was a romance or a thriller. With few words said between them, they switched off the lights and went to bed. Tom didn't utter those three words again, and Flo was grateful.

She tossed and turned, watching shadows cross the room from the tree outside her bedroom window. The curtain was open a crack, letting the moonlight flood through. Flo felt restless as her mind whirled. After a long time of lying there and listening to the heavy rise and fall of Tom's chest, she slid from the bed, grabbed her grandmother's diary, and went to the living room.

Flo took the blanket from the back of the sofa and wrapped it around her shoulders. With just the tree lights switched on, she opened the diary to read the next entry.

27th August 1963,

My life is a mess.

It's only been a week since I last wrote in my diary, but it seems like years have passed. Everything has changed. I've changed. My heart is broken, and I don't think I'll ever be happy again.

Oh, it all went so wrong. My last days in Cornwall were like a dream. We walked along the beach, ate ice cream, sat underneath the stars, talked for hours, and kissed lots. It was perfect, and I felt I would burst with happiness. It was like a peek into our future, and I thought we both walked away eager for our life together to begin.

Going back to London broke my heart, but S promised he'd visit soon. He said I'd hardly have time to miss him since I'd be so busy with wedding planning. Why did he say that when he didn't mean it? I wish he'd just broken my heart then and there. Instead, he produced a ring from his pocket. We were on the station platform, and he got down on one knee with a beautiful sapphire ring. He said he couldn't let me go home without a ring on my finger. I spent the whole journey home staring at the beautiful round cut sapphire with a halo of diamonds.

When I got home, everything was normal for a couple of days. I meant to update you, but life was so busy. All my friends and family popped in, wanting to hear about my wedding plans. Everything was so perfect. Until yesterday, when the post came. Oh, I'm going to cry just thinking about it. I can't tell you. I'll put the letter below this entry. It'll forever be the moment that shattered my heart.

Iris,

I hope you're well.

Thank you for calling to let me know you returned home

safely.

I have news, and I'm sorry for the heartache it will cause you. I've met somebody else. She's the daughter of one of the local farmers, and I already love her.

Iris, you were perfect in every way, but our lives are too different. I don't think you'd ever be truly happy here on the farm.

There'll always be a place for you in my heart, but I'm afraid my heart is no longer yours.

Do what you wish with the ring.

Best wishes,

Simon Evans

I'd been so excited to receive the letter from him. I was going to reply and send him some pictures of wedding cakes. Mum heard me crying and came to see if I was okay. She read the letter and hugged me. I must have cried for hours. When I finally ran out of tears, my eyes were puffy and my head hurt. Mum made me a cup of tea, and I gave her the ring, asking her to return it to him.

I don't think I'll ever be happy again.

Flo closed the diary and let it fall to the floor. Her poor grandmother had her heart broken. She'd planned her entire future with S. Iris was planning their wedding and preparing to move across the country for him, but as soon as she'd returned home, he'd moved on with someone else. Flo wished more than anything she could hug her grandmother. She picked up the diary again to see if there was another entry, but there wasn't. It looked as though Iris hadn't written in her 1963 diary again. Flo scanned the page until her gaze fell on something familiar. The name. Simon Evans. He was related to Tom.

The room was spinning, and Flo's chest tightened. Her breath came in short gulps as she gripped the side of the chair. Why had she taken the risk and let Tom in? Flo needed to know more about what had happened between Iris and Simon, but there was only one person she could ask. Flo waited until her breathing was steady and pulled out her phone.

"Hello?" Victoria answered on the third ring. "Who is it?"

Flo ignored the fact that her mother *still* hadn't saved her phone number. "It's Florence," she said, her voice small.

"Why on earth are you calling me at two in the morning?" Victoria grumbled.

"I need to ask you some things about Iris."

"This is getting ridiculous. I know you loved your grandmother, but she's gone, and you need to come to terms with that. You can't keep calling me."

Flo pulled the blanket tighter around her shoulders. Two phone calls in a year, and Victoria thought she was calling all the time. She pushed those thoughts aside. "What do you know about Iris's time in Cornwall?"

There was a pause, and Flo could hear the rustling

of bedsheets. "I don't know anything," Victoria said, her voice barely above a whisper.

"Did she ever mention a man named Simon or S?" Flo asked, feeling the chance of answers slip away.

"No." There was a muffled noise on the other end of the line.

"Mummy?" a child's voice called, and Flo's stomach tightened.

"Go back to bed, sweetie. I'll be there in a moment," Victoria said. Her voice sounded far away from the phone, but Flo could still make out the words. A cold chill ran down her spine, and she hung up before Victoria could say anything. The phone slid from her hands and onto the floor as she stared at the Christmas tree, looking right through it.

It was her. It had been her all along. The conversation hadn't told her anything more about her grandmother, but it had confirmed to Flo that she was the reason her mother never loved her.

CHAPTER THIRTY-ONE

With heavy eyes, Flo weighed out the ingredients for a chocolate Swiss roll. On the side, a batch of scones, a Victoria sponge, and a chocolate sponge were cooling. Her grandmother's recipe book lay open. She'd been baking for hours, but nothing had taken her mind off her worries. As the birds began to sing, she knew she needed something more to distract her wayward thoughts. Iris had always said a Swiss roll was one of the hardest things to make because you put all your love and effort into the sponge, but it could all be for nothing if it cracks while you roll it. More than anything, Flo wanted a hug from her grandmother, but since she couldn't, she settled for reading her words in the book.

"Flo?" Tom's sleepy voice was barely audible over the hum of the ovens. He stood at the doorway to the kitchen in his pyjama bottoms and nothing else.

A breath caught in Flo's throat, but she shook it off and tipped sugar into the mixing bowl. "Sorry, did I wake you?" she asked.

"No. My alarm went off, and you weren't beside me in bed." He padded across the floor with bare feet.

"I couldn't sleep, so I thought I'd get ahead of myself." She shrugged and kept stirring.

Tom looked towards the cooling sponges. "What's going on?"

"I bake when I can't sleep." It was true. On the night of her A-level exam results, Flo had baked a three-tier coffee and walnut cake. Iris had put candles in it to celebrate after she'd got straight As.

"But why can't you sleep?" Tom absentmindedly took a scone and picked at it.

"There's butter and jam." Flo cocked her head towards the fridge.

"Flo?" he asked, moving towards her, but she stepped out of his reach.

"I'm struggling, Tom. I spoke to my mother last night and discovered she has a new family." Flo's shoulders shook, but she refused to cry. Despite the hours spent baking, Flo was still struggling to decipher her feelings.

"Do you want to talk about it?"

"No, but thank you."

Tom nodded and buttered the scone. In silence, he watched as she poured the cake batter into a greased tray.

"You'll be late if you don't leave soon," Flo pointed out.

Tom glanced at the clock. "You're right. I'll see you later?" It came out as a question rather than the jaunty goodbye it usually was.

"See you later," Flo said. She took her mixing bowl and utensils to the sink to wash them by hand. Tom's footsteps retreated, and she could hear him moving around upstairs as he readied himself to leave for work.

Flo timed it so she slipped upstairs and into the shower before he could say goodbye. As she washed the flour from her hair, he shouted 'bye' through the closed bathroom door. Once she was sure he'd left, Flo turned the faucet off and wrapped herself in a big fluffy towel. She wandered into the bedroom, sat on the edge of the bed and cried as the last twelve hours caught up with her. For years, she'd dreamed of someone telling her they loved her, but the reality had only hurt her already injured heart. She'd pushed away all her doubts and worries, hoping it would make them disappear, but instead, they'd returned with a vengeance. Flo unplugged her phone from by the bed and dialled Daisy's number.

"Hello?" Daisy answered on the second ring, her voice frantic with worry.

"Sorry, Dais. I forgot how early it was."

Flo could hear the rustle of Daisy's duvet as she sat up. "What's wrong?"

"Everything." Flo told Daisy about Iris's diary and how the mysterious S was related to Tom and Will. Then she told her how Tom had said he loved her. And finally, she told her about Victoria's new family. "It's me, Dais. I'm not enough, and soon Tom will realise that and he'll break my heart like his grandfather broke Iris's."

"Everything's going to be okay," Daisy said soothingly. "Do you think it's time you spoke to someone about this? You've been through a lot, Florrie. There's trauma dating back to your childhood. Losing Iris and meeting Tom have brought those feelings to the surface. Love is always a risk, but what you've been through has made you think it's a risk not worth taking." Daisy paused for breath. "It's worth it, Florrie. I promise you it is. And you are enough. I don't know what I'd do without you, and Poppy loves her Aunty Florrie, she hasn't stopped talking about visiting again."

Flo took a deep breath. "I don't know what to do, Dais. I want to run from everything."

"Don't make any rash decisions, okay? Talk to Tom and tell him how you feel and what's been happening. Find a therapist that you can talk to. It's not long until Poppy and I visit, so wait until then before you decide whether you can risk your heart."

Flo made a non-committal grunt.

"Promise me," Daisy said, her tone harsher this time.

"I promise," Flo said. Her fingers were firmly crossed behind her back.

"Good. Call me whenever you need to talk. I don't mind what time of day it is. I'll see you soon, okay?"

"Okay. Love you, Dais."

"Love you, Florrie."

Flo put the phone down and found herself wondering why it was so easy to say those words to Daisy, but when Tom had said them last night, it had turned her blood to ice.

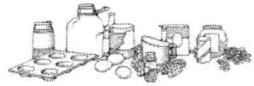

The day passed painfully slowly. Emma wasn't in, and despite a steady stream of customers, Flo kept on top of it with little effort. During the lull, she baked until she ran out of ingredients. Everyone commented on how lovely the tree looked, and questions were asked about some of the ornaments. Flo took great pride in telling the stories behind them and sharing pieces of Iris's life with the village. It was a small reprieve from the heaviness that had settled in her chest.

By the time the tea shop closed, lack of sleep had caught up with Flo. She made a coffee and cleaned. Tom hadn't popped in, and Flo hadn't checked her phone to see if she'd heard from him.

As Flo put away the cleaning products, there was a knock on the door. Tom stood there holding a paper bag.

"I got us a takeaway from the pub," he said, gesturing to the bag.

"Thanks." Flo's stomach rolled. She hadn't been able to eat all day.

"Come on. Why don't you have a quick shower while I dish up?" Tom suggested.

Despite the food being ready, Flo took her time in the shower. She knew Tom would want to talk, and deep down, Flo knew it was the right thing to do. The time for excuses had passed.

Tom had put the food on plates in the oven to keep warm. As Flo emerged, he set out a couple of trays.

"Shall we sit at the table?" suggested Flo. She'd recently bought a small fold-up wooden table, which was pushed into the corner.

"Sounds good. These plates will be hot." Tom pulled the table out and fetched the two chairs.

It was strangely formal to be sitting opposite each other, eating dinner. They usually ate on their laps in front of the television.

"How are you?" asked Tom as he watched Flo push the food around her plate.

"I don't know where to begin." Flo put down her cutlery.

"Okay. Well, let's work back from this morning. Tell me the real reason you couldn't sleep."

"There were a few things. The first was my grandmother's diary. She spent two weeks in this village in 1963 and kept a diary of her time here. I've been dipping in and out of it since I moved. She worked here, and she fell in love." Flo let out a shaky breath. "Last night, I read her final entry for 1963. She had her heart broken by the person she thought she was going to spend the rest of her life with."

"I'm sorry, Flo." Tom reached across the table to take Flo's hand, but she pulled back.

"That's not all. The man who broke her heart was called Simon Evans." Flo watched the recognition in Tom's eyes. "Who is he?"

"Simon was my grandfather. He was my mother's father. When my parents married, my father took the Evans surname to keep the farm."

Flo drummed her fingers on the tabletop as she mulled over the new information. S was Tom's grandfather. "He really hurt Iris," she mumbled. She'd hoped he'd deny knowing a Simon in the family. Maybe it had been a complete coincidence. But here he was, confirming it wasn't. Did Tom take after his maternal grandfather?

Tom squeezed her hand and waited for her to continue.

"I called my mum to see if she knew anything about it." Flo hadn't told Tom much about her mother, only that she hadn't been a part of her life. "It didn't go well, and I heard a child in the background calling her mummy." The pain washed over Flo again. Her throat hurt as she resisted the urge to cry.

"Flo," Tom whispered. He reached for her, but Flo pulled back.

"You said you loved me," she whispered. "But you can't, Tom. Don't you see it? I'm impossible to love. You might believe you're in love with me, but sooner or later, you'll see me for who I am and realise how wrong you were." Flo bit the inside of her cheek to stop her emotions from spilling out.

"Flo," Tom's voice broke as he spoke her name.

"I do know you, and I know you're not unlovable. You're amazing. I love how strong and confident you are. You're fearless. Look at how you packed up your life and moved across the country. The first time I met you, I was angry and in a terrible mood, but you didn't back down because you cared for the animal you were trying to help. The more I get to know you, the more I love you, Flo."

"Don't." Tears poured down Flo's cheeks.

"I love you, and I will always love you."

"You can't make promises like that."

"I can."

"No, you can't." Flo knew nobody could make promises like that. She'd experienced heartbreak from a tiny baby and had grown up knowing it was intrinsic to people. As a child, Flo had learned not to put her hope or love into anyone other than Iris, but even the time had come for Iris to leave and break her heart. Flo was beyond broken and didn't have the strength to keep fighting.

"I'd like you to leave, please," she said.

"Flo." Tom's voice cracked.

"I'll bag up the few things you have here and ask Emma to drop them around to you later in the week." Her words were cold and detached.

"I love you, Flo. I'm not giving up on us." His eyes were hollow, and his mouth taut. With a nod, he stood and grabbed his coat from the hook by the door. Flo couldn't bring herself to watch him walk away. She turned her head and held her breath until she heard the tea shop's door close. Her body crumpled, and she slumped to the floor. Huge sobs racked Flo's body, and as hard as she tried, she couldn't stop them. She'd done exactly what Daisy had warned her against doing, and it hurt like nothing she'd experienced before. She'd pushed him away before he could break her heart, and he'd walked away.

The room grew darker, and the food on the table went cold as Flo hugged her knees and cried for all the losses in her life. Despite it all, this one hurt the most.

CHAPTER THIRTY-TWO

In the days after, Flo went through the motions. When Emma had seen her the following day with red, swollen eyes, she'd begged her to tell her what was wrong, but all Flo could say was that she and Tom were over.

"Is Tom popping in today?" Emma asked as she ran two shots through the machine before they opened. She'd asked the question every day that week, and each time, Flo shook her head.

"He won't be coming in again, Emma," Flo said, her voice void of emotion. Despite Tom's promise of not giving up, she hadn't heard or seen him all week.

Emma handed her a cup of coffee. "I don't understand what happened. It was going so well."

"I don't want to talk about it," Flo muttered for what felt like the hundredth time and disappeared into the kitchen. Missed calls from Daisy were piling up on her phone, but Flo couldn't bring herself to answer. Flo knew she'd entered a self-sabotage mode, but she couldn't stop. The more she retreated into her own company, the more she wanted to push people away. Her fear of heartbreak and rejection felt so strong that it was easier to keep everyone at arm's length.

Every night that week, once the tea shop closed, Flo had baked for hours. The cake stands were overflowing, and there were only so many free cookies she could give away with orders. But still, she baked because it was the only thing that silenced her thoughts.

That evening, once everyone had gone home, Flo embarked on a quintessential English bake. An apple crumble with homemade custard. She washed and peeled the apples before cutting them into segments. On the hob, Flo added the apples, brown sugar, the zest of a lemon, and a sprinkle of cinnamon. As the mixture bubbled and the sugar melted, Flo weighed out her ingredients for the crumble topping. Once the apple mixture was off the heat and left to cool, Flo added the cubed butter and flour to her bowl and, with her fingertips, rubbed them together. Once it resembled breadcrumbs, she added sugar and then poured it over the apples.

The kitchen filled with the sweet scent of caramelised apples and the warmth of cinnamon. While the crumble baked, Flo made the accompanying custard. Flo had gone through all the eggs she'd had delivered from the farm, and with another delivery not due until tomorrow morning, she'd popped into the village and bought some from the shop. She whisked the custard until it was smooth and thick, then set it aside while she retrieved the crumble from the oven.

Flo glanced at the cooling dishes and considered running upstairs for a shower while she waited, but her plans were scuppered when there was a knock at her front door. Nerves bubbled in the pit of her stomach, and she tiptoed to the doorway to peer through. Flo's heart leapt into her throat as she made out Daisy and Poppy standing on the other side.

"What on earth are you doing here?" asked Flo, unlocking the door and ushering them in from the cold.

"If you'd answered any of my phone calls, you would know," Daisy glared. "Are you okay?" she asked, her voice soft.

"I'm in shock." Flo knelt to hug a tired-looking Poppy.

"That's not what I meant, and you know it," grumbled Daisy.

"How was your journey?" Flo asked Poppy as she helped her shrug off her winter coat.

"I slept for most of it." Poppy yawned and clutched her teddy bear.

"It was good. We left straight after Poppy finished school," Daisy said, taking Poppy's coat and hanging it up with her own.

"So, what are you doing here?"

"We're moving here," announced Poppy.

Flo's jaw slackened, and her mouth fell open. "You're moving here?"

Daisy nodded. "Like I said, if you'd have answered your phone, you'd know!"

They sat at one of the tables, Flo too shocked to suggest they go upstairs. "Start from the beginning."

"I've finished my dental nurse training. Passed with flying colours, actually."

"Congratulations." Flo squeezed Daisy's hand. She'd always known her friend would.

"Anyway, Will's been helping me look for a job nearby, and one came up."

"And just like that, you're moving here?" Flo quirked an eyebrow.

"Well, it wasn't just like that. There's a cottage on the farm's estate that Claire has offered to rent to me. She said I could have it at half price for the first six months while I find my feet. I couldn't say no to that, could I?"

Flo had to agree. "No, you couldn't, but are you sure about moving here?" She glanced at Poppy, who was distracted by a game on her tablet. "It's a long way to move for a man."

Daisy scoffed. "I'm not moving here for a man. Although it is a nice bonus. I'm moving here for myself and Poppy, but I'd be lying if I said having you around the corner isn't a huge pull. You know how life back home has been lately and the stress of a certain someone's father." Daisy glanced towards her daughter. "When we last visited, we had so much fun, and it showed me that there's more to life. Look at all the countryside and beaches on our doorstep. In the summer, I can take Poppy down to the beach after school. We can hunt for shells and eat chips with sandy hands." Daisy paused. "This is the future I want for myself and Poppy. The fact that you're around the corner makes it even better. And, yes, I'd be lying if I said I wasn't excited to see where things with Will lead."

"Well, if you're happy, then so am I. I can't believe you're going to be living down the road." Flo hugged Daisy, and for the first time all week, her smile was genuine.

"Now, your turn. What's going on?" Daisy stepped back so she could read Flo's expression.

"I'll tell you later. Let's not ruin this happy moment."

"Aunty Florrie, you said I could help you decorate your Christmas tree?" Poppy eyed the already decorated Christmas tree in the tea shop.

"Of course." Flo had to think quickly or else she'd be outsmarted by a four-year-old. "I didn't mean this one. I thought you could decorate the one upstairs. Look, I've made crumble. Why don't you have some? You must be starving after that journey." Flo disappeared to plate up crumble and custard before Poppy could ask any more questions. She put the bowls down in front of them. "I'll be back in a minute," she said and raced upstairs to take the decorations off the tree.

By the time Flo returned, the bowls were emptied, and Poppy was asking for seconds.

"Would you like to decorate the tree before bed?" Flo suggested. She could see Poppy's mood was shifting as Daisy told her she'd had enough for one evening.

"Yes, please." Poppy bounced up from her seat, the pleas for more crumble forgotten.

Daisy shot her a grateful smile. "I'll get our bags from the car and meet you up there," she said.

Flo organised Poppy with the baubles and showed her how to slide them onto the lower hanging branches. Since Poppy could only reach the bottom half of the tree, that was all they decorated.

"You dropped a decoration," Daisy said. She'd collected their bags from the car and put them in the bedroom. They didn't have much with them since the removal van was arriving tomorrow.

"It's a sheep," squealed Poppy, and Flo felt her stomach lurch. The blood drained from her face as she turned to see the sheep bauble dangling from Daisy's finger.

"Where shall we put it?" asked Daisy, oblivious to Flo's reaction.

"Right there." Poppy pointed to the front, right where there were no other ornaments. There would be no missing the shaggy white sheep.

"It looks wonderful," Daisy said, scooping Poppy into her arms and twirling her around.

Flo bit back the sob rising in her chest as she watched the precious moment. This was a happy time for her best friend, but Flo couldn't find the energy to push away the sadness clouding her heart to join them. Instead, she left them to their celebrations and went to shower.

When Flo emerged with wet hair and smelling of mint and bergamot body wash, Daisy was sitting on the sofa with two mugs of hot chocolate, but there was no sign of Poppy.

"She's gone to bed," Daisy said. "It's been a long day."

"Sorry, I should have asked if she wanted a bath before I jumped in the shower." Flo sat at the opposite end of the sofa and pulled her knees up to her chest.

"You ended it with him, didn't you?" Daisy asked, getting straight to the point.

Flo nodded, unable to find her voice.

Daisy didn't utter another word. Instead, she pulled Flo into her embrace and held her.

"Are you ready to talk?" Daisy asked. She handed Flo some tissues.

Flo blew her nose and took a deep breath. "I think so." She scraped her wet hair into a bun and told Daisy what happened the night she told Tom it was over. "The emotions overwhelmed me, and I lashed out." She sniffed, and Daisy passed her another tissue.

"It's what you do, Flo. You push people away when you get scared or if you're worried they'll hurt you. I've watched you do it our entire lives."

"I know, but I can't stop myself. There comes a point where I feel myself becoming comfortable with someone, and I push back. It's not just relationships but friendships, too. You and Iris are the only ones I've ever allowed close to me. I'm close to Emma, but I still keep her at arm's length."

"I've not left you, have I? Not everyone will break your heart, Flo. You have to trust people and give them a chance."

Flo sucked in a shaky breath as she mulled over Daisy's words. She was right, she'd never let her down. Despite everything Daisy had been through, she'd always been there for Flo. When Iris died, Poppy wasn't sleeping, and even though Daisy was tired to the bone, she stayed up for hours, talking on the phone and reminiscing. "You're the best friend anyone could ever ask for," Flo said.

"So are you, Flo. Our friendship has lasted because we've both been there for each other. Do you remember when I had Poppy, and I was terrified at the thought of leaving the hospital? I watched all those women waddle out with their partners carrying the baby, and I was dreading having to do it on my own. You stayed until they discharged me, and you carried Poppy out. I'll never forget that, Flo. Those first few nights you stayed meant the world to me. I don't know how else I would have got through them and found my feet." Daisy placed the box of tissues between them. "What I'm trying to say, very badly, is that relationships take work on both sides. Our friendship wouldn't have survived all these years if we hadn't put the work in. Your mother didn't put the work in on her side, but that's not your fault, Flo. Not everyone will reject you because your mother was a selfish idiot."

Flo nodded. Her tears were drying up, and Daisy's words were settling in her heart.

"You have to give people the chance to show they're in it for the long haul. Tom seemed utterly besotted with you, and if he's anything like his brother, he's a good egg."

Flo's voice shook as she spoke. "It's too late, Dais. I've ruined things between us."

"I doubt he's moved on already. There's still hope, Florrie."

"What do I do?"

"Forget about Tom for now. First thing tomorrow, we're going to find you a therapist. Then you can talk to Tom and explain everything."

"What if he meets someone else?"

"Then he was just another life lesson. Your person will be out there, but first, you need to heal."

CHAPTER THIRTY-THREE

Daisy moved into her cottage the following day. Flo didn't help since she was busy in the tea shop, and she suspected Tom would be around. Daisy had promised her she'd be fine. Flo packed them off with sandwiches, cakes, and a flask of tea to sustain them.

Emma arrived a little later that morning since she had a client first thing.

"I've just heard that Daisy and Poppy are moving here," Emma said as she was almost blown through the door by the wind. News travelled fast around their little village.

"I only found out last night when they turned up on my doorstep." Flo set a pot of tea and teacups down at one of the tables and followed Emma back to the counter.

"You look happier today," she remarked.

"Thank you." Flo had woken up feeling a little

lighter. Things with Tom were still unknown, but she'd found some numbers for therapists, and she was going to call them during her mid-morning break.

"Have you heard the news?" Emma said, pausing by the coffee machine, which was unusual for her. Usually, Emma prioritised coffee over everything.

"What news?"

"Tom is leaving the village."

Flo fought to steady the tray in her hands. With a thump, she put it down on the counter and took a moment to steady herself. "Leaving?" she asked.

"He's going to Australia. Something to do with a farm initiative for young children."

"Right." Flo nodded slowly. "I need to check on a cake." She ran into the kitchen and closed the door behind her. Tom was leaving. All he'd said about not giving up on her was a lie. Flo raked a hand through her hair. The tiny kernel of hope in the pit of her stomach was crushed. Flo knew she had to be brave and accept that Tom was one of life's lessons. She dug the scrap of paper from her apron pocket and dialled the number for the first therapist on the list.

That evening, Daisy texted to say everyone had gone home and invited her around to see her new home.

"It's lovely," Flo said once Daisy had finished giving her a tour. The cottage was small, but newly decorated and cosy. It was perfect for the two of them. Poppy was thrilled with her new bedroom and had already unpacked her toys. The living room had an open fireplace with a roaring fire.

After Flo read her five bedtime stories, Poppy finally fell asleep. Daisy made a pot of tea, and Flo took out the cake she'd brought around. It was a lemon drizzle, Daisy's favourite. They sat on the beautiful L-shaped sofa. Flo suspected Claire had purchased the furniture specifically with Daisy in mind.

"Tom was a huge help today," Daisy said, pouring their tea.

Flo didn't want to speak about Tom. She'd have to tell Daisy about him moving soon, but now didn't seem like the right time. "I phoned around some therapists this morning, and I have an appointment next week."

"I'm so proud of you, Florrie."

"I've half a mind to send the invoice to my mother. Do you know how expensive private therapy is?"

"It's an investment in your future."

"Perhaps."

Daisy handed her a cup and saucer. "I thought I might throw a little moving-in party. What do you think?"

"That'll be nice. We'll go for dinner at the pub soon, so you can properly introduce yourself to the locals."

"Actually," Daisy trailed off, and a blush rose on her cheeks. "Will's taking me out to dinner tomorrow night. Claire offered to babysit."

Flo felt something akin to jealousy in the pit of

her stomach, but she immediately doused it. There was no place for envy in her relationship with Daisy. "I'm so happy for you. If you ever want a sleepover with Will, I can have Poppy."

Daisy's blush deepened. "I think I preferred it when we were discussing your problems."

Flo choked back a laugh. "Can we have an evening where we don't talk about past trauma, families, or boyfriends?"

"Of course. What shall we talk about?"

They sat in silence for a few minutes.

"Let's put a film on," suggested Daisy.

When Flo left the cottage, she glanced around before she jogged to her car. She could see the farmhouse from Daisy's front door, and Flo was terrified of bumping into Tom.

"Flo, is that you?" a voice called from the road.

Frozen to the spot, Flo turned to see Claire walking up the driveway. "Hi," she said, internally groaning. Flo hadn't thought to look down the driveway.

"What do you think of the cottage?" asked Claire, stopping by Flo's car. Her cheeks were red from the cold air, but she was bundled up in a coat and scarf.

"It's lovely. Thank you so much for helping Daisy and Poppy."

Claire waved a hand to brush aside the compliment. "It's the least I could do. At least one of my sons is happy."

Flo cringed beneath Claire's gaze. "I didn't mean to hurt him."

"I know. I've been meaning to talk to you. Do you have a spare half an hour?" She tilted her head towards the house, and Flo's stomach plummeted. "He's not there," Claire assured her.

Flo couldn't think of a good reason to say no. "Okay. Get in the car. I'll drive us up to the house to save me the walk back later." Flo was dreading the conversation ahead, but Claire was her main supplier, so she had to maintain some level of communication.

The drive was short, and Claire filled the time telling Flo about the village meeting she'd just attended and invited her to the next one in the new year.

"Come in." Claire led her around to the kitchen door. Inside was dark, but warm from the aga. "They've gone to the pub," Claire answered the question in Flo's eyes. "It's their routine whenever I go to a village meeting. Rather than cook, they treat themselves to dinner and a few beers. They won't be back for at least another hour."

Claire flicked on the lights and switched on the kettle. "I'll take my coat off, and I want to fetch something. Why don't you make a pot of tea?"

It felt strange to be pottering around Claire's kitchen without her there. Despite Claire's assurance that Tom wouldn't be back for a while, Flo's heart lurched at every noise. She prepared a pot of tea and got out a couple of cups while she waited for Claire to return.

Flo took a seat close to the aga and slipped off her coat, even though she wanted to keep it on so she could make a quick escape if necessary.

"Here we go," Claire said as she returned with a wooden box under her arm. She set it on the table and took the seat beside Flo. "Tom told me about your grandmother," she explained as she poured the tea.

Flo's brow knitted. "He told you about her relationship with Simon?"

"Yes. Simon was my father." Claire rested her hands on top of the box. "And I think you deserve to know the truth."

Flo was left speechless as Claire opened the box to reveal a stack of letters and a handful of photographs. Claire handed her one. "This is the only photograph in colour," explained Claire.

With shaking hands, Flo lifted the photo to look at it properly. Iris beamed back at her, wearing her orange dress that Daisy had gifted Flo a replica of. Beside Iris was a young man whose arm was wrapped around her waist. They both stood in front of the pub and smiled at the camera. Flo swallowed against a lump in her throat. She remembered Iris's diary. It was the evening Iris and Simon's parents had met each other.

"You have your grandmother's eyes," Claire said, shattering the silence which had settled around them.

"Thank you," sniffed Flo.

"Am I right in thinking you believed Simon had broken Iris's heart?"

Flo nodded. "There's a letter from him in my grandmother's diary. Shortly after she returned to London, he ended things with her and said he'd met someone else."

Claire frowned. "Here, read this." She handed Flo a tatty piece of paper, which had been read many times over the years.

Simon,

I hope you're well.

I can't believe it's only been a few days since I called you, telling you I'd arrived back in London.

I have news, and I'm sorry for the heartache it will cause you. I've met somebody else. He's the son of someone my father works with. Coming home and seeing him again made me realise how much I love him.

Simon, our lives are very different. I don't think I'd ever be happy on the farm.

I have returned the ring with this letter.

Best wishes,

Iris

The paper slipped from Flo's hands and floated down to the table. "Simon thought she had broken his heart?" she asked.

"Yes. The ring was returned. See, it's here in the box." Claire pulled out a velvet ring box and showed Flo the sapphire and diamond ring nestled in the box.

"Claire, this letter is almost identical to the one Iris received." Flo thought back to the diary entry. Something Iris had said played on her mind. Then it hit her. "Iris said in her diary that she'd given the ring to her mother to send it back to Simon. This letter must have been written by Iris's mother. Her parents split them up."

Claire pursed her lips. "It looks that way. My father thought she'd moved on."

"He spoke of her?"

"Occasionally. My parents were very happy together, but they weren't each other's great loves. When they met, my mother was a young widow, and my father's heart still belonged to Iris. They loved each other and enjoyed each other's company, but I'm not sure they were ever in love. My father turned his back on the farm. I didn't grow up here. I was born in Devon, and my uncle ran the farm. He had no children and had trained Arthur to take over. Our marriage wasn't planned, but as soon as I met Arthur, I knew he was my person."

Flo didn't know what to say. The letter Iris had received said Simon had met the daughter of another farmer. He'd feared life on the farm wasn't for her. Yet, he walked away from the farm. They'd been deceived. A deep sadness washed over her, and she wished Iris were still alive to know Simon had loved her. He'd run away from the village after the heartbreak and hadn't returned.

"He doesn't leave until the new year, Flo. There's still time to stop him." Claire folded the letter and put it back in the box.

Flo didn't need to ask who she was talking about. She pressed her lips into a line.

Not waiting for her response, Claire carried on. "There are more letters in here. You're welcome to pop over and read them another time. You'd best be getting off now. The boys will be back soon."

Flo nodded and rose. She put her coat on, barely recognising the movements.

"Take care, Flo." Claire pulled her into a quick hug before seeing her out.

Inside her car, Flo turned up the heating and slowly drove home. She passed a car, and with a jolt, she realised it was Tom driving. Pushing back any feelings of attraction or longing, she focused on the dark road ahead.

Once home, Flo locked the doors behind her and went straight to bed. Wrapped in the duvet, she allowed her mind to wander over the evening's revelations. Simon hadn't broken Iris's heart. He had thought she'd broken his. Poor Iris had suffered thinking he'd met somebody new, but really, her parents had split them up. Was that why they'd always come here on holiday? Had Iris always hoped she'd bump into him again? And then there was the other train of thought, which Flo's mind kept wandering back to. If Simon hadn't broken Iris's heart, then her fear of Tom taking after him was unfounded. But that didn't change her. Flo was still the problem.

CHAPTER THIRTY-FOUR

Flo's shoulders softened as she walked out of the therapist's room, and her aching muscles relaxed for the first time in days. Her swollen eyes told the tale of the session, but Flo walked out feeling buoyed by the experience. The therapist had assured her that together, they could work on her fear of abandonment and had promised that her coping mechanisms were not unusual. There was comfort in knowing there was some normality in her reactions.

"Would you like to book another appointment?" asked the receptionist.

"Yes, please." Flo fumbled for her phone to check the tea shop's rota.

"Would this time next week suit you?"

Emma was working that shift, so Flo booked her next appointment and walked out with a spring in her step. Once back in her car, she looked at the messages she'd missed over the last hour. There were a few from Daisy, mostly pictures of Poppy on the farm. They'd moved into the cottage almost a week ago, and they'd settled in well. Poppy was starting at the local school after Christmas, with a handful of drop-ins before they broke up, so everybody could get to know each other.

The final message from Daisy was an invitation to dinner tonight. She was throwing a small housewarming party. The emotions dredged up from today's session lifted from Flo's heart at the thought of a fun night with her best friend. That was until she read the last part of the message. Daisy had invited Tom. They still hadn't spoken, and as far as Flo was aware, he was still planning on jetting off to the other side of the world in the new year. Her heart constricted at the thought, but she used the technique the therapist had taught her. Flo reminded herself that nothing would happen if the worst happened and Tom left. She was strong enough to get through it, and her entire life wouldn't implode because of his absence. Although it helped her mind from wandering, it didn't stop the heavy feeling in her chest.

"Why did you invite him?" Flo asked when Daisy answered.

"Flo, hi. Poppy, you stay here with Tom and Will. I'll just take this conversation outside." There was a pause, and Flo could hear Daisy's footsteps. "Sorry, I was in the barn with them."

"Why did you invite him?" repeated Flo.

"He's been great this week and has shown Poppy around the farm. He even taught her to ride a horse this morning."

"Dais!" groaned Flo.

"Sorry. I thought you wanted to talk to Tom? This could be a good opportunity. You have no excuses now that you know professional heartbreaker doesn't run in his family. It's your one chance before he leaves."

Flo nibbled her lip as she watched an elderly couple cross the road. Their arms were linked as they slowly walked together, smiling at something one of them had said. "Too soon, Dais."

"I thought you were going to message him?" asked Daisy.

"I was going to, but I never got around to it." Flo had spent the last few evenings staring at her phone. She'd typed numerous texts to Tom and then swiftly deleted them before she could hit send.

"Do it now, then it won't be so awkward tonight."

"I'm not coming tonight."

Daisy sighed, and Flo could picture her pinching the bridge of her nose. "Yes, you are. I'll see you at seven. You don't have to bring anything."

"Not even a cake?"

"Poppy's making a cake."

"Oh, you are good." Flo ground her teeth. "You know I can't say no now. Poppy will be excited for me to try her cake."

"She's been talking about it all morning." Daisy's

tone was smug.

"You're being demoted from best friend."

"Don't forget to send that text. Love you." Daisy hung up before Flo could respond.

Muttering under her breath, Flo turned on her car and drove to Padstow-on-Sea. Once there, she went straight to the Little Cafe by the Sea and ordered herself a maple soya latte. At a table by the window, she took out her phone. Her fingers hovered over the keys as she sifted through her thoughts, wondering what to say. It wouldn't be some big declaration telling him not to leave, but she wanted him to know he was on her mind.

"Here's your latte." The waitress set down her drink, and Flo thanked her.

Stalling for a few more minutes, Flo sipped the drink and closed her eyes to savour the flavour. Emma was looking after the tea shop and had told Flo not to rush back, so with a rare few hours to herself, Flo decided to make the most of it. She needed some time to decompress after her therapy session. However, worrying about what to say to Tom wasn't helping.

After numerous deleted messages, Flo finally cobbled together something she didn't hate.

Hi, sorry it's been a while. There's so much to say, but it's difficult to put it in a message. I've just finished my first therapy session, and I feel really good about it. I'm sorry I took my worries out on you and hurt you. Perhaps we can talk soon? X

Flo had settled for a single kiss at the end. Before she could overthink it any further, she hit send and put her phone screen down on the table. It buzzed a few times while she finished her drink, but she refused to look. Besides, it was unlikely Tom would respond that quickly. She watched as people milled around the harbour, most of them doing their Christmas shopping. Clara from The Cornish Vintage Bookshop passed, pushing a trolley of boxes, which Flo assumed contained more books. She chuckled and waved when Clara spotted her. Perhaps she'd pop by the bookshop and pick up something for Poppy.

Flo's cup was empty, and she'd reached her limit on people watching, so she checked her phone and was surprised to see a message from Tom. She'd been so sure he would be too busy to reply.

It's good to hear from you. I'd really like it if we could talk. I'm looking forward to seeing you at Daisy's party tonight xx

Flo left the cafe with a spring in her step. After the upset of the last couple of weeks, she felt she was finally taking control of her life again.

The harbour was busy with people looking for last-minute gifts for loved ones. Flo crossed to the other side, where The Cornish Vintage Jewellery Shop was. Belle wasn't working today; she was away celebrating her recent engagement to local builder Nick. They'd gone to France to visit her father before they returned and spent Christmas with Nick's family. Belle had shared the news in the *Vintage Girls* group chat, and although Flo hardly knew the woman, she was happy for her.

There were so many pieces of beautiful, sparkling jewellery, and each one caught Flo's eye. She bought a vintage, square-cut aquamarine ring for Daisy's Christmas present and a similar child-size blue topaz ring for Poppy.

Next, Flo visited The Cornish Vintage Bookshop. Clara was busy restocking shelves, but she helped Flo pick out a book for Poppy.

"Do you have time for a coffee?" asked Clara, gesturing to the coffee nook.

Flo glanced at the time. "I'd love to, but I need to get back to the tea shop. Emma's got plans this afternoon."

"Another time," said Clara as she slipped the book into a paper bag with the shop's pink logo on it.

With her gifts bought, Flo made her way back to the car. Seagulls squawked, and the air smelled of fish and chips. Flo's stomach rumbled, but she'd have to wait until she got home for lunch.

It was a slow afternoon. With Christmas approaching, they'd seen a drop in customers, with people using their spare time and money on present shopping. The local school had hired Emma to do their makeup for their nativity, so she'd left as soon as Flo got back.

"Say hello to Poppy for me," Flo called. Daisy and Poppy were going to the nativity for Poppy to meet her teachers and classmates.

As Flo baked and served, she felt lighter. A handful of customers commented how lovely it was to see her with a smile on her face again. It was only as she emerged from the fog that she realised what a state she had been in. Her therapist had reminded her that she'd been through a lot, and there'd been some big changes in her life recently, so she should be kind to herself. Although she was trying, Flo couldn't shake the feeling of guilt as she realised what she'd put those close to her through, but she was determined to put it right, and tonight would be the perfect opportunity.

CHAPTER THIRTY-FIVE

Once the tea shop closed, Flo rushed through her evening routine. The cakes were well-stocked, so she didn't have to bake for the following day. Instead, she ran upstairs, got out her fancier toiletries, and showered. Flo dressed in a burgundy turtleneck with a short black skirt, tights, and ankle boots. Her hair fell down her back in its natural waves, and she applied some makeup, keeping an eye on the time. It was the first time she would see Tom in a couple of weeks, and she wanted to make an effort.

Poppy answered the door, wearing an emerald dress and with a matching bow in her hair.

"Do you like it?" she asked and twirled for Flo.

"You look beautiful." Over the last week, Poppy had blossomed in her new surroundings. Her fascination with the farm grew each day, and when she and Daisy popped in for a biscuit mid-afternoon, she always had lots to tell Flo.

"I'm in the kitchen," called Daisy.

Flo followed Poppy through. The cottage was warm, and the fire in the living room was blazing. Daisy stirred something on the hob while Will poured wine into glasses. Music played throughout the cottage. The songs switched from calm jazz to upbeat children's tunes.

"Not for me, thank you," Flo said. She'd only just fought her way through an emotional obstacle. She didn't need alcohol to skewer her newfound clarity.

"Tom should be here soon," Will said, not quite catching Flo's eye.

"Are you setting us up?" Flo said, careful to keep the edge out of her voice.

"Maybe." Daisy giggled, and Will wrapped an arm around her waist. It was lovely to see her best friend so happy, but Flo felt a twinge of jealousy.

"I'm going to take Poppy into the living room while you two finish cooking." Flo led the little girl from the room. "What shall we play with?" asked Flo.

"Let's bake." Poppy pointed to the wooden mixing bowl and spoon.

"What are we baking?"

For the next twenty minutes, Flo and Poppy made imaginary butterfly cakes. They were the first cakes Flo had ever baked with Poppy. She was only two when they made them in Daisy's tiny kitchen, but Poppy was sure she remembered it. Flo had brought some gold glitter spray, and they'd smothered the cupcakes in it.

"They look delicious," Will said as he walked in, closely followed by Daisy.

"Thank you." Poppy smiled proudly down at the empty plate.

"Dinner's ready." Daisy checked her watch. "Tom should have been here a while ago."

Flo's stomach was doing somersaults. Any second, Tom would knock at the door, and she'd be face to face with him. Daisy would no doubt usher everyone into another room so they could talk. Flo knew she'd have to be brave and open up. It might be too late for them, but she wasn't willing to give up without one final try.

Will took a seat and sipped his drink. "He's probably been held up at the farm. It happens quite a lot. There's my phone. It'll be him." Will answered, and Flo watched as his expression changed from jovial to horrified.

"What's wrong?" whispered Daisy.

Will looked up but didn't say anything. "Okay. I'll meet you there," he said and hung up. His hands shook as he pushed the phone back into his pocket. "There's been an accident at the farm. Tom's been rushed to the hospital."

Flo felt all the air leave her body. She was glad she was already sitting down, or else her legs would have given way beneath her.

Will grabbed a set of keys from the side and cursed. "I've had too much to drink to drive."

"I've not had anything. I'll drive." Flo knew it was her speaking, but she didn't know how. She stood and picked up her keys.

"Are you sure?" asked Daisy.

Flo shook herself. She'd always been good in emergencies, just because it was Tom lying in the hospital bed shouldn't change that. "Yes. Come on."

"Call me when you know how he is," Daisy shouted after them as she hugged a worried Poppy.

It was dark outside, and Flo gripped the wheel as she navigated the country lanes. Will had plugged his phone in and got up the directions to the hospital.

"How bad is it?" Flo finally found the courage to ask the question that had been playing on her mind.

It took a moment for Will to reply. "Do you remember the mix-up we had with the feed? Well, they never collected the wrong order like they said they would. The new one came today and, because we didn't have the space, we've had to store it in one of the older barns. Tom stayed late to finish stacking the bags." Will paused and took a deep breath. "One of the bags got pushed back too far, and the barn crumbled around them. Tom was the only one who didn't get out. His legs got trapped whilst all the debris fell around him."

Flo gasped. She fought against the emotions to concentrate on the road ahead. As she drove those last few miles, there was only one thing Flo knew for sure. She loved Tom. It was a cruel twist of fate for her to realise her feelings for him while his life hung in the balance. She had to get to him and tell him she loved him.

They left the car in the first free parking space. It was parked half on the line and at an angle, but Flo didn't care. They jogged to the hospital entrance, where a kind-looking woman at the reception pointed them towards Resus.

"Why's he in resuscitation?" gasped Flo as she struggled to keep up with Will's long strides.

"I don't know," Will's voice was small. He slowed for Flo to catch up and grasped her hand as they walked the last few corridors. They rounded a corner to the waiting room, where Claire and Arthur sat. Claire jumped up and pulled them both into a hug.

"How is he?" asked Flo, her voice muffled as she was pressed against Claire's shoulder.

"They're prepping him for surgery." Claire let them go and dragged a hand across her face.

"Why are they operating?" Flo asked when she found her voice again.

"He's shattered the bones in both legs." The words hung in the air long after Claire uttered them.

A nurse walked through a door. "Would anyone like to see Tom before he goes into surgery?"

"You go, Flo. We've already seen him." Claire squeezed her hand.

Flo nodded, unable to speak around the lump in her throat.

In the far corner of the overly bright room, Tom lay on a hospital bed. Flo's stomach heaved at the sight of his legs. She kept her gaze focused on his face. His head was covered in bloody gashes where debris must have hit him. A nurse stood by his bedside, stitching up a deep cut in his left arm. Careful not to knock any tubes or wires, Flo went to his side. "Hey, you," she whispered. His eyes flickered to hers, and for the briefest of seconds, Flo could see the pain.

"Flo," his voice was weak, but his lips pulled into a small smile.

"You know, you could have said no to Daisy. This is quite extreme to get out of dinner," she joked, stifling a sob that was building inside her chest. She had to be strong for him.

Tom chuckled but winced, and his body tensed in pain.

"Don't hurt yourself." Flo gently took his hand in hers, careful not to squeeze. "We were going to talk, weren't we? I don't want to wait to talk. I need to tell you now. I love you, Tom." He went to speak, but Flo pressed a finger to his lips. "Let me finish. I love you, and I've been an absolute idiot. I was so scared of being hurt and losing you that I thought pushing you away would be easier, but I was wrong. I thought heartbreak was the worst thing that could happen to me, but it's not. The worst thing that could happen would be a life without you. I'll miss you when you go to Australia, but I'll wait for you. If you'll still have me." Flo held her breath as she waited for Tom's reply. She'd laid her heart on the line and had no control over the outcome.

He smiled, and the cut on his lip split, blood trickling down onto his chin. "I love you, too."

A nurse wandered over and dabbed at the blood. "We're ready to take Mr Evans for his surgery now."

"Will you be here when I wake up?" Tom asked, his eyes fearful as the nurse undid the brakes on his bed.

"I'm not going anywhere, I promise you. I love you." With one last glance at his face, she stepped back to allow the nurses to wheel him away.

The waiting room was silent as Flo wandered back out. "They've taken him down," she said and sat in the empty seat beside Claire.

The same nurse from earlier poked her head around the door. "He'll be a while. If you want to wait in the canteen, someone will come and fetch you when he's out."

They made their way to the hospital cafe and ordered cups of tea. The drinks sat untouched, growing cold. All Flo could think of was Tom lying on a table in an operating theatre whilst she sat watching a skin grow on her untouched cup of tea.

Eventually, the little hatch serving tea and coffee closed for the night, but the seating area stayed open. Claire tried to convince Will to go home and get some rest, but he refused to leave in case there was any news. They sat in silence, occasionally making small talk, or Will and Arthur would say how much they wished it had been them who had been crushed. It was the longest night of Flo's life. She was almost grateful for the first signs of the sun rising outside. Surely that meant Tom would be out of surgery soon. Unable to bear the crushing silence in the closed canteen, they walked back to the trauma unit, ready for when the doctor came to give them an update on Tom's progress.

Flo watched as families came and went. The emotions of everyone surrounding her were tangible. Everyone was buzzing around frantically, trying to find their loved ones, whilst nurses and doctors went about their business. It felt like time had stopped inside this frenzied bubble. After what seemed like forever, the doctor from the trauma unit approached and informed them that Tom was out of surgery and it had gone as well as could be expected. Flo's legs gave out beneath her, and she dropped into the plastic chair with a thump.

CHAPTER THIRTY-SIX

"Are you sure you'll be okay?" Flo asked, juggling a backpack, an overnight bag, and her handbag.

"We'll be fine," promised Emma.

"Send our love to Tom," called Daisy, gently pushing her out of the door.

Flo felt she could do the drive to the hospital with her eyes closed. She'd been back and forth for the last week, but Tom had been on such strong pain medications that he'd slept for most of her visits. However, they were weaning him off, and Claire had texted earlier to say he seemed more alert today. Emma and Daisy had been looking after the tea shop so Flo could come and go. She didn't know how she would have managed without them.

"Hey, you," Flo said, beaming as she walked into the hospital room to see Tom sitting up in bed. "Is that tea?"

Tom huffed. "I've already had three coffees. The nurses won't serve me anymore, so I've had to resort to tea."

"They know what's best for you." Flo put her bags down and went to peck Tom on the cheek. He was obviously feeling better today as he turned his head and captured her lips with his.

"It's good to see you," he said and gestured for Flo to pull a chair closer.

"How are you?"

"Better. The last few days feel a bit like a dream. I'm not sure what's real and what my mind's made up." He frowned.

"What do you think could be made up?"

"You told me you loved me." He met her gaze, and Flo could see the uncertainty in his expression. Her heart clenched, and she reached out to hold his hand.

"Tom, I love you. That part was real."

He breathed out a sigh of relief. "What happened, Flo?"

"I lost control of my emotions and my fears," she said, scuffing her shoe along the floor. "I still have a lot of fear and pain from my mother's abandonment, and it felt easier to run away from you, from us, than confront the pain." Flo sucked in a shaky breath. She'd known this conversation was coming, but that didn't make it any easier. "I ran away, Tom, but I was a fool because it still hurt. I'm so sorry for hurting you."

Tom's eyes roamed over her, and Flo held his gaze. "Why didn't you tell me how you were feeling?"

Tom turned her hand over and trailed his finger across her palm.

"It's something I've always been ashamed of." Flo dropped his gaze. "I can't commit to anyone because I'm terrified of them leaving me. Over the years, I've convinced myself that I'm not enough for anyone, and they'll eventually realise it and leave me. At least that's what my therapist tells me I do." It had felt as though someone had poured a bucket of icy water over her when the therapist had summarised Flo's feelings in a matter of minutes. It seemed Flo wasn't as unique as she had once thought. In fact, she was completely average, and her abandonment fears reflected the textbooks piled high in the corner of the room. The therapist had lent Flo one to help her understand her feelings.

"You'll always be enough for me, Flo." Tom intertwined their fingers and squeezed her hand.

"How can you know that?"

"Because I've been a mess without you. I even booked a flight to the other side of the world."

"I heard about that." Flo's mouth was dry, and she glanced up to find him already staring. "Are you still going?"

Tom patted the edge of the bed, and Flo moved to lie beside him. It was difficult, and she had to be very careful not to disturb his legs.

"I'm not going anywhere," he whispered and pressed his lips to the top of her head as she cuddled into his side. "Honestly, I don't know if I ever would have got on that plane. At the time, it seemed like a good idea to run away from the village and from you, but I soon realised that I'd only be on the other side of the world with the same thoughts and feelings."

"It's taken me a lifetime to realise you can't run from your emotions."

They lapsed into silence, the gentle hum of the hospital machines filling the air.

Flo eventually spoke. "Can you forgive me?" she asked, needing to know the answer.

"There's nothing to forgive. Just promise me you'll communicate better? If you're feeling overwhelmed or scared, then let me know. I might not be able to help, but I can hold you and tell you how much I love you. I'll even list everything I love about you if you need me to, but we'll need a few spare hours."

A bubble of happiness burst in Flo's chest. "I love you," she said and tilted her head up to kiss him.

"Flo?"

"Yeah?"

"I'm scared." Tom's voice sounded unusually small. "What if I can never walk again? How will I help on the farm? Will you still want to be with me?"

"I promise to always be by your side, Tom. You're more than the farm. If you can't physically help, you can still run the business side. I know you'd miss the work, but there are options. Let's not worry about that yet. The doctors say there's a good chance you'll make a full recovery. We have to be patient, and you mustn't push yourself before you're ready."

"I know, but I can't completely ignore the possibility."

"We'll deal with it together, okay?"

Tom nodded. "Did you bring me any cake?"

Flo laughed. "Of course, but I didn't bake it. Emma and Daisy have been looking after the tea shop. They've been following Iris's recipes, so it should taste the same."

Tom took a bite of chocolate brownie and chewed.

"What's the verdict?"

"It's good. If I'd never tasted your baking, I'd think it was amazing." He took another bite. "It's not as light as yours."

"I'll bake you a batch for tomorrow."

CHAPTER THIRTY-SEVEN

Tom was discharged on Christmas Eve. After a lot of fuss, it was decided it would be best if he returned to his own home. He'd be in a wheelchair for the next couple of months and would need a lot of care. The hospital had arranged his transfer home, and Flo waited eagerly to hear the crunch of tyres on the gravel.

"He'll be here soon," Daisy said and squeezed her hand.

"Do you think Tom will let me ride on his chair?" asked Poppy.

"I'm going first," Will teased her.

"Here he comes," shouted Poppy.

Flo bounced from foot to foot as the ambulance stopped, and the driver undid the ramp. Slowly, Tom was wheeled down.

"Merry Christmas," Claire said and hugged him.

"You're a Christmas miracle," joked Will. Despite his words, he hugged his brother.

Tom's eyes sought Flo, and she walked to his side, clasping his hand in hers. He squeezed, and she felt another broken piece of her heart mend itself back together.

"We're having Christmas Eve dinner in a couple of hours, once Daisy's parents arrive. Why don't you go and get settled? Let us know if you need anything," Claire said before she ushered everyone inside the house.

"Back to yours?" asked Flo.

Tom dropped her hand from his grip. "I might need some help," he said, refusing to meet her gaze as he gestured to the gravel beneath his wheels.

The barn had been transformed. A ramp had been installed so he could easily cross the threshold. Inside, the living room was now a bedroom, with the sofa having been pushed up against the far wall. Flo knew Tom would hate the setup. He didn't want any fuss. However, he needed everything on one level, as he couldn't go upstairs.

"Are you okay?" asked Flo as Tom stilled his chair and looked around.

"I'll have to be."

"It won't be like this forever," Flo reminded him.

The next few months would be difficult while Tom's bones healed, and he would need to learn to walk again. He would have physio appointments both at the hospital and at home. There was a long road ahead, but Flo had promised she'd be by his side through it all. They both had their healing to do, but nothing would come between them again.

"You don't have to do this, Flo," said Tom, his voice just above a whisper.

Flo knelt so she was at his eye level. "I want to do this. I love you, Tom."

"I love you, too." He took her hands in his and pulled her onto his lap.

"When I came here, I found it difficult to accept your help, but eventually, I realised I needed it. You're going to have to do the same, Tom. It's not coming from a place of pity but from love." She kissed his forehead. "We'll muddle through the next couple of months. I'm sure there are things you can do in the office to help your mum, and perhaps some days you can keep me company in the tea shop?" He couldn't get up the stairs to Flo's flat, so she'd be staying at the barn.

"That would be nice. It's going to be difficult to go from being busy every day to nothing," he admitted.

"We'll keep you busy," promised Flo.

They ventured back into the house an hour later. There was a beautiful, towering Christmas tree in the hallway, which had been decorated by professionals. Not a bow was out of place. In the living room, the tree was rather less polished. During the week, Claire had allowed Will and Poppy to decorate it. Flo had watched Claire cringe as each bauble was hung, but to her credit, she had left it as it was and hadn't moved anything. While Tom was in the hospital, Claire insisted that Flo spend her free time with the family. They'd got through it together and had all grown closer.

"We don't have a tree," Tom said.

"Next year. Besides, we decorated the one at mine." Flo didn't tell him that Poppy had redecorated it.

"I like the sound of that." He smiled as she pushed him into the room.

Claire fussed around to make sure Tom had everything he could possibly need to hand. Flo sat beside him with her hand clasping Tom's in his lap. Daisy's parents had arrived, and Poppy was telling them all about the farm. Over the years, Daisy's parents had become family, so it was nice to spend Christmas with them, too.

Dinner was a lively affair. They ate in the formal dining room. There was a huge table, which they gathered around. Tom was at the head, so he had enough space for his chair. In the corner was a third Christmas tree. It was another that was professionally decorated, but it was a little less polished, with a handful of handmade decorations strung from the branches. As Flo peered closer at them, she realised they were handmade by children.

"I made the cow," whispered Tom as he caught her looking.

Flo chuckled as she took in the misshapen cow, which was sporting six legs and a rather curly tail.

"I was three," added Tom.

They'd had caterers in to prepare the meal. Claire said there would be enough cooking tomorrow, so they all deserved a treat. Still, Flo had made the dessert. She'd baked a selection of chocolate fudge cake, steamed treacle pudding, and a mountain of mince pies. The tea shop had been busy that morning, but both Emma and Daisy had helped, so she'd had plenty of time to bake.

Huge smiles were on Claire and Arthur's faces as they celebrated Christmas Eve with their sons and their partners. Despite the challenging few weeks, Flo felt lucky to be by Tom's side. There was still a long way to go, but they loved each other, and Flo had come to learn that was all that mattered.

After they'd eaten, they retired to the living room, but Tom was exhausted. Will and Arthur helped him to the barn and into bed while Flo said goodnight to everyone. By the time she made it to the barn, Tom was already snuggled under the blankets with the television playing a festive film. As quickly as she could, Flo changed into her pyjamas and joined him. His arm wrapped around her, and she nestled into his side.

"This is nice," he said, his breath skimming the top of her head.

"It is." She closed her eyes and leaned her head against his chest.

"I'm sorry I haven't got you a Christmas present. It was a little difficult from a hospital bed."

"You don't have to get me anything."

"Next year," he promised.

Flo smiled sleepily. They spoke about next year

a lot, and it no longer scared her. The idea of a future with Tom filled her with excitement, rather than the fear it once elicited. They were committed to each other, and Flo's worries of heartbreak and abandonment were slowly slinking away with each therapy appointment she attended and with Tom's reassurances.

"Merry Christmas, Tom," she whispered, almost asleep.

"Merry Christmas, Flo."

EPILOGUE

"Morning," Tom's soft voice pulled Flo from her slumber.

Flo prised open her eyes to see him hovering over her with a coffee in hand. He was already dressed for work in his green overalls. "Morning," she said, her voice groggy as she pulled herself into a sitting position.

"I'm running late," he said and handed her the cup. "I'll see you tonight. Don't forget I have a surprise for you." He pecked her on the lips and left before Flo could pull him back for another kiss.

The flat was silent as Flo enjoyed a few extra minutes in bed and sipped her coffee. They split their time between her flat and Tom's barn. Since the tea shop was open today, and Flo was opening, they'd stayed the night at the flat. Flo glanced at the time. She ought to get up. The sun was already rising with the promise of a beautiful summer day.

She padded down the stairs with her empty

cup. Each morning, Tom made her coffee from the machine downstairs, and he always used a pretty china cup and saucer. He had a surprise planned for them that afternoon. Flo didn't know what it was, and she'd promised she wouldn't think about it too much, in case she ruined it. With her promise in mind, she set about preparing for the day and baking some fresh cakes. Iris's book lay open on the counter, with a glass cake stand dome on top of it to stop any spillages from damaging the pages. It had been one of Daisy's ideas.

The lunch rush was over by the time Flo's mind wandered back to the surprise, and she was edging ever closer to closing time. She wondered what to wear. Tom had told her to dress casually, and it was a swelteringly hot day.

As Flo made pots of Earl Grey tea and sliced Victoria sponges, she mentally flicked through the clothes in her wardrobe. Eventually, she settled on an A-line gingham dress she'd recently purchased from The Cornish Vintage Dress Shop during a trip there with Daisy and Poppy last weekend. They were going abroad soon with Will, and Daisy wanted to treat herself to some new outfits. Flo had been determined not to buy any more clothes, but the dress was too pretty to leave behind.

Once the tea shop was closed, Flo changed and pulled her hair back into a plait. It was messy, and a few strands immediately fell out, but it was too hot to have her hair around her face. There was a beep from outside, and Flo ran to the window to see Tom outside, waiting for her. Reluctantly, he was driving her Fiat 500. While his legs had recovered, he was still strengthening the muscles, and he found the car much easier to drive. Flo didn't mind. She was glad to see him regaining his independence after a tough few months of recovery. They'd pulled together during that time, and their relationship was stronger for it.

He had the car windows wound down and wolf-whistled as she walked towards him. She couldn't stop an enormous smile from spreading across her face. He was all hers, and she couldn't be happier about that.

"Do you want me to drive?" she asked.

He gave her a look, and Flo slipped into the passenger seat.

"Where are we going?" she asked as they drove towards the farm. The hedgerows along the lanes were in full bloom, with delicate flowers in pinks, yellows, and purples. A gentle hum of insects filled the air.

"My favourite spot on the farm."

They passed Daisy's cottage, and Flo caught a glimpse of Daisy, Poppy, and Will splashing around in a paddling pool. Her friend had immediately made the village her home, and Poppy had settled into the local school. It was also lovely to have them around the corner. Once a week, they took turns hosting dinner and having a catch-up.

Flo's little car jostled over the unmade farm track

as they neared Tom's favourite spot. In the distance, Flo could make out a picnic blanket. They pulled up alongside it, and Tom went to the boot to fetch a basket. Tom was much slower than he used to be, but Flo kept to his pace.

"Take a seat," instructed Tom. He set about unpacking the picnic basket. Inside were salads, pasta salads, quiches, sandwiches, cakes, and even some pastries.

"Where is all this from?" Flo asked. Her jaw dropped. She was sure that quiche was one of hers.

"I stole a few bits from the kitchen this morning," he confessed. "Then the rest was made by my mum with my help this afternoon."

Flo laughed but didn't comment. Tom took a bottle of champagne and two flutes out. He uncorked the bottle and poured them each a glass. "To us," he said, and they clinked glasses.

As she sipped her bubbles, Flo took in her surroundings. The sea was gentle in the distance, and she could make out people swimming. They were little dots in the distance, but if you strained your ears, you could hear the pearls of laughter on the wind. The field they were sitting in was out of use this year to allow it time to regrow, so it was scattered with wildflowers delicately blowing in a welcome breeze.

"Are you okay sitting on the floor?" Flo asked, taking in Tom's stature as he half lay, half sat on the picnic blanket. He smiled lazily back at her and reassured her he was fine before stuffing a sausage roll in his mouth.

"Stop worrying so much and just enjoy our evening together." Tom reached over and smoothed the frown lines between her eyebrows. His touch was soft and reassuring.

He edged closer, wincing at the pain. Flo went to stop him, but he gave her a look that told her to stop being so overprotective. They'd learned to be there for each other, whilst allowing the other their independence. It had been a learning curve, but they'd kept communicating. Flo was still seeing her therapist, but on the whole, she felt like a different woman. She'd learned to accept that her mother was the problem. She'd deleted Victoria's number and made peace with the fact that she may never know why her mother had abandoned her. Flo now understood that it wasn't her fault.

Tom moved so his arm wrapped around her shoulders, and he pulled her against him. Despite the hot weather, it felt nice to be in Tom's embrace, watching the world pass by and having nothing to do. They didn't get enough time like this together.

"I love you," Tom whispered as he nuzzled his face against the top of her head.

"I love you, too." Flo smiled, feeling so incredibly happy and lucky. Tom shifted beside her and unwound his arm from her shoulders. She looked to him, and he gave her a nervous smile. It had been the perfect moment, as if the world had stopped turning and allowed them a few moments to revel in their love.

"Flo, I know this is quite soon since we've not even been dating a year, but I love you so incredibly much, and I know you're the person I want by my side for the rest of my life. I want you to know how committed I am to you and our relationship." He pulled something from his pocket. "Flo, I won't ever leave you."

Flo's heart hammered in her chest as she glanced at the velvet ring box in Tom's hands. He looked up, and his eyes met hers. They were full of love and anticipation.

"Will you marry me?" he asked. His words lingered in the air as he opened the box to reveal a ring inside. Tears filled Flo's eyes. It was Iris's ring. The centre stone was a rich, deep blue sapphire, which shimmered in the sunlight, and around it was a halo of sparkling colourless diamonds.

"Yes," she uttered the single word. It was all she could muster.

Tom took hold of her hand and slipped the ring onto her finger.

"Is it okay to use Iris's ring?" he asked, still holding her hand. "My mum gave it to me."

"It's perfect," she said before his lips met hers.

The Cornish Vintage Bookshop

2026

Pre-order your ebook now

THE CORNISH VINTAGE FURNITURE SHOP

Mabel shivered as another droplet of rain landed on the back of her coat. It slid below the neck and slivered along her spine. With a huff, she dropped the screwdriver. It fell to the concrete floor with a loud thud. The screws were stuck on the Art Deco dressing table she was working on, and it was what felt like the hundredth day of rain. Her workshop was damp, and even the radio couldn't drown out the sound of rain pounding on the corrugated roof. She grumbled and stood, stretching her aching joints.

"I need a holiday in the sun," she muttered as she picked up her umbrella and stepped out into the dismal day. Since a holiday was outside her budget, she decided to go into Port Isaac for a hot chocolate.

Mabel's walk down the cobbled road to the harbour was slippery. The wind blew a gale, and rain pelted down at an angle, meaning her brolly was completely useless. Below, the sea crashed ferociously. Despite being soaked, Mabel paused by the wall to look at the harbour. Wave after wave crashed against the shoreline as the wind blew the sea foam onto the beach. It was a dismal day, yet there was beauty in the ferocity of Mother Nature. Mabel continued her descent and smiled as she walked past the ice cream shop, which would be buzzing in the coming months. She couldn't wait to order a triple chocolate ice cream cone with a flake. It would melt in the midday sun, leaving a sticky trail across her hands.

By the time Mabel reached Fisherman's Brew, she was wet through to the skin. Hair was plastered to her face, and her feet squelched in her boots. She pushed open the door and sighed as warmth wrapped around her shivering body.

"Mabel, dear." Betty spotted her as she walked in. "Leave your umbrella by the door and come sit by the fire. Do you want your usual?"

"Yes, please. Thank you." With chattering teeth, Mabel peeled off the dripping coat and hung it on the stand by the door. The coat claimed to be waterproof, but it seemed that didn't extend to the Cornish rain.

The windows had steamed up, and a handful of people sat inside, warming themselves with a drink and a slice of Betty's Victoria sponge. A gentle hum of conversation wound its way around the cafe, interspersed by the hiss of a milk frother. Mabel scraped her wet hair into a plait, allowing a few wispy tendrils of blonde hair to frame her face. There was an empty table by the fire, and Mabel took the chair closest to the flames. The cafe was cosy and homely, filled with memories. On the opposite wall was a sideboard Mabel had refinished for Betty. It was a beautiful, hand-crafted piece with delicate carvings and mouldings. Mabel had painted it sage green to match the cafe's decor and added gold to highlight the Rococo mouldings. It was pretty, and in the dim light of the cafe, the gold shimmered. Mabel had stripped the top back to raw wood, knowing the piece would be heavily used. Betty displayed cutlery, napkins, and condiments on it. Everyone always complimented it, and Betty would proudly tell them about Mabel and her business.

"Here we go. A hot chocolate with cream and a flake," Betty announced. Thick hot chocolate filled a glass cup, swirls of freshly whipped double cream bobbed on top, and a milk chocolate flake balanced across the glass, slowly melting. Mabel's mouth watered at the sight.

"Thank you. I don't know what I'd do without your treats." Mabel smiled at the elderly woman who had run the cafe for as long as she could remember. In her twenty-eight years, Mabel's order hadn't changed. Once old enough to speak, she always begged her mother for one of Betty's 'melted chocolate drinks'.

"What are you working on?" Gwen called from a couple of tables over. She always sat near the counter so she could chat with Betty. Gwen was one of Port Isaac's well-known residents. She knew everyone and everything. Each morning, Gwen sauntered into the harbour, her hair perfectly coiffed into a French chignon, and her outfit would always match the season. Today, she wore black trousers, walking boots, and a cashmere grey jumper. Despite the weather, Gwen looked elegant. Not a single hair out of place, or a hint of a crease on her clothes.

"I've got a beautiful Art Deco dressing table. It's got those typical curved sides, and a huge, round mirror. I've been struggling with getting the handles off this morning. My client wants to replace them, but the screws have all rounded and are proving to be a nightmare." Mabel scooped cream onto the flake as she watched Gwen visualise the piece.

"What have they asked you to do to it?" Gwen asked, her lips pursed.

"They're keeping the burr walnut veneer drawers, but are replacing the handles as they've been damaged."

"What about the body?" Gwen drummed her fingers on the table.

Mabel scuffed her shoe on the floor as she readied herself for an argument. "The veneer is beyond saving. The client has opted to paint it instead of recovering the piece."

Gwen's face contorted. "Painted furniture," she

muttered. "It's an abomination."

"You know my process, Gwen. I ensure everything is done properly so in the future, the piece can be returned to its original form with a new veneer." Mabel rehashed the same conversation they'd had countless times.

Mabel sipped her hot chocolate and waited for Gwen's next barb. It was eleven o'clock and Mabel should have known better than to visit the cafe. Gwen would be there until the early afternoon to revel in the gossip that flew in with the lunch rush. Mabel assumed it was because Gwen was lonely.

"I met a man yesterday," Gwen announced. Mabel coughed as her drink went down the wrong hole. It had been the very last thing she'd expected to come out of Gwen's mouth. Gwen's husband passed many years ago. He had been the love of her life, and Gwen had never shown an interest in anyone else.

"Poor man," Betty muttered. She'd wandered over with a cup of tea and sat opposite Mabel.

"Not for me! He's buying the pub."

"Our pub?" asked Mabel.

"Yes. The Fisherman's Rest."

"After all these years, it still amazes me how you know everything, Gwen. You're the first to hear of anything that happens in Port Isaac, sometimes even before those involved. I wonder what this man's intentions are," Betty said.

Mabel shared a concerned glance with Betty. The Fisherman's Rest closed a year ago after the pandemic depleted the owner's finances, and it became an unviable business. Mabel had arranged a fundraiser to help, and all the locals turned out, but it hadn't been enough to save the heart of their community. Toby closed Fisherman's Rest a few weeks later and the residents of Port Isaac lost their pub. Betty had hired more staff and opened later into the evening, but it didn't fill the pub-shaped hole in the community.

"Maybe it's a good thing?" Mabel said.

"Yes. I could do without the evening trade, to be honest. I'm not getting any younger and people don't want coffee and sandwiches at that time of night," Betty agreed.

"Nothing good will come of this," Gwen muttered. By now, everyone's attention was on her.

"Who's buying it?" someone called from near the entrance. Mabel turned and spotted her brother in the doorway, his coat dripping onto the floor. His short fair hair was covered in raindrops, which dispersed as he ran a hand through it.

"Michael! Come sit with Mabel. I'll get you a coffee in a moment," Betty called him over.

Mabel waved but turned her attention back to Gwen as the cafe waited with bated breath for her answer.

"Thinks he's Port Isaac's answer to Rick Stein," Gwen said.

"What do you mean?" Mabel asked. She broke off a piece of flake and offered it to Michael, who was staring longingly at it.

He shook his head, so Mabel ate it.

"The man buying The Fisherman's Rest. He's a fancy chef from London. Waltzed in and offered the asking price." Gwen shrugged.

"He's not turning Port Isaac into a playground for his rich London friends," an angry local called.

"Here, here," came the affirmation from the rest of the cafe.

"We'll have to wait and see what happens." Gwen's eyes danced with glee as questions poured in for her to answer. "Oh, Mabel? He needs furniture for the pub, so I recommended you to him. You don't mind, do you, dear?"

Mabel's mouth opened and closed, but no words emerged.

"Thanks, Gwen," Michael said, noticing Mabel's struggles.

"I can't work for this man," Mabel whispered across the table. Betty had gone to make Michael's drink, and the rest of the cafe's attention was firmly on Gwen. "I fought to keep the pub in the community. It goes against everything I believe in to help someone turn it into a fancy place that out-prices the locals. This is just the beginning. His London friends will move in and buy property, and we'll all be left without homes."

"Mabel, stop for a moment and catch your breath. You haven't even met the man yet. For all you know, he could have connections to the area. Do you believe Gwen's gossip?"

"It sounds like she's met him." Mabel scooped a mouthful of cream.

"Don't jump to conclusions, okay? I know you're not in the position to turn down work." Michael had always been the calmer and more logical one of them. Despite being twins, they were each other's opposite. Where Michael excelled in his career as an accountant, Mabel had inherited all the creativity.

"I need a new accountant." She slurped her drink.

"Good. I can finally replace you with a client who actually pays."

"I pay. I pay you in childcare." She stuck her tongue out. Michael had two little girls whom Mabel adored and often looked after when Michael and his wife wanted an evening out.

"Your skinny, decaf latte," Betty said, screwing her nose up.

"That is offensive." Mabel's expression mirrored Betty's.

"It's Elowen's idea. We have to be role models for the girls."

"The girls aren't here," Mabel pointed out.

"I know, but it's a lifestyle change."

Mabel's shoulders shook as she held back a chuckle. Michael sounded exactly like her sister-in-law.

"Whatever," he huffed. Betty shot Mabel a wink and returned to the counter to serve a group of tourists who had wandered in.

"Do you want a sip of mine? I won't tell Elowen."

"No. She'll find out. Gwen will probably tell her." Michael glared at the contents of his mug.

"Cheer up. Milly's six and Mia is four, so you've only got another fourteen years until Mia is off to university and you can drink hot chocolates again."

Michael groaned and plonked a sugar cube into his coffee. "Don't you dare tell El."

"My lips are sealed. What are you doing out and about on a workday? I thought you'd be chained to your desk."

"I wanted to speak to you. Don't you ever answer your mobile?"

Mabel pattered her pockets, but she didn't have the phone on her. "You know I'm useless with technology."

"You give me so many sleepless nights. What if you fell and hurt yourself? You'd need to call me."

"Michael, I'm twenty-eight. I'm not a ninety-year-old living alone with ten cats."

"You do own a cat."

Mabel kicked him under the table. "Sorry, my foot slipped," she said with a sickly grin. "Why were you trying to get hold of me?"

"Do you want to come for dinner tomorrow night?"

"Is it healthy?"

"Mabel, it won't hurt you to eat a vegetable occasionally."

"I'll come if you promise Elowen won't cook a lentil shepherd's pie again. Who swaps mince for lentils? It was the most depressing thing I've ever eaten."

"It was pretty awful. I can't promise what it'll be,

but you have my word it won't be lentil shepherd's pie." Michael held his hand out and Mabel shook it. They stared sternly at one another before dissolving into a fit of giggles.

"It's like having you two in here as children," Betty commented as she squeezed past them to put another log on the fire. "Your parents are very lucky."

"They are," Gwen added from across the room. For a brief moment, her expression softened and a small smile crossed her face before she cleared her throat and turned her attention back to a table of tourists.

"Thank you, Betty," Mabel said.

"How are they?" asked Betty. She leaned her hip against the table. Betty was older than their parents, but didn't have children. Instead, she'd devoted her life to the little cafe and the community. Betty was like an aunt to Mabel and Michael.

"They're okay. Granddad came out of the hospital yesterday," Mabel said. She'd spoken to her mother last night. Granddad Thompson had been in hospital for the past two weeks after a nasty fall. Their parents had rushed to Kent and had been there ever since. During last night's phone call, Mary, Mabel's mother, announced they were putting Granddad Thompson's house up for sale and he'd be coming home with them. She didn't know how long it would take to sort everything, so they were staying for the foreseeable. Mabel's father, Martin, had called out in the background to send his love. It had been a difficult conversation, and Mabel missed them.

"Your poor mother. It'll be good to have them home," Betty said before returning to serve another customer.

"I need to go. I've got a meeting in half an hour." Michael downed his coffee, wincing as he swallowed. "See you tomorrow."

Mabel sat back in her chair and sipped the dregs of her hot chocolate. She could still hear worried locals asking Gwen questions, but she tuned them out. It was something she'd worry about another day. Buoyed by her sugar rush, Mabel paid and left the cafe, ready to spend the afternoon battling with screws.

AFTERWORD

Thank you for visiting The Cornish Vintage Tea Shop. This book holds a very special place in my heart as it's loosely based on the first book I ever wrote (although I set that one in North Wales). I enjoyed pouring my love of baking (and eating!) cake into this story.

My books are written to be an escape from reality, so I hope you enjoyed your visit to The Cornish Vintage Tea Shop. If you're not ready to return to real life, why not try another of my books?

THANK YOU

Thank you for reading! If you have time to leave a review on Amazon or Goodreads I would be incredibly grateful.

You can follow me on Amazon

Sign up to my newsletter at www.elizabethhollandauthor.com

You can also purchase signed copies on my website

Other books...

THE CORNISH VINTAGE SERIES

THE CORNISH VINTAGE DRESS SHOP

THE CORNISH VINTAGE JEWELLERY SHOP

THE CORNISH VINTAGE FURNITURE SHOP

THE CORNISH VINTAGE TEA SHOP

COMING SOON....

THE CORNISH VINTAGE BOOKSHOP

THE PEACE, JOY AND LOVE SERIES

A MERRY CHRISTMAS AT THE CASTLE

A SPRING FLING AT HOTEL MAYFAIR

Printed in Dunstable, United Kingdom